CASTLE MANOEUVRE

TILLY WALLACE

ONE

Seraphina Winyard woke with a start—as though someone had thrown a bucket of cold water over her. Gasping, she sat upright, flung her hands out with palms forward, and commanded her magic to strike out at her tormentor with a bucket of lukewarm pudding.

Except her gift did not respond.

Memories struggled through the thick honey in her mind, her thoughts muddled and confused. Lord Rowan had brewed the poison that killed her guardian, Lord Branvale. Lady Abigail Crawley had delivered it to Branvale's valet. And at last, Abigail's song and the potion had poisoned Sera, too.

Abigail, her friend, had... betrayed her.

Only now did Sera consider her surroundings. She sat on a narrow bed in a prison cell, its mattress thin and hard under her. Three walls were thick, grey stone blocks. The fourth was made of iron bars. One of the stone walls had a gap about a foot wide, as though the builder had run out of stone. The space was filled with the same iron bars that formed the front of her cell, and it allowed her a view into the next cell. Her prison contained a small table with a single chair pushed up against the wall opposite the bed. A side table stood against the stone opposite the door and beside the bed. On top of it, a pitcher and ewer. Next to those was a stack of books. A rectangular rug of a muddy brown and green covered most of the cold floor.

"The Repository of Forgotten Things," she whispered as she rose.

With one hand on the chill stone, Sera closed her eyes and searched her body for any trace of her magic. Her limbs were leaden and ordinary, but she refused to give up. When her traitorous friend had leaned close, she'd let slip one important piece of information. The spell brewed by the old mage hadn't removed Sera's magic like a physician with a scalpel, cutting out rot. Abigail had whispered that Sera's magic was in hibernation. It still dwelt inside her. Somewhere. But it slept.

All she had to do was wake it up, and she could escape.

Sera let her mind wander through every pathway of her being, searching for anything that seemed out of place. After what seemed like an eternity of scouring her entire body—and trying not to panic—at last, Sera found the tiny spark. Slumbering deep at her very core, it emitted only the faintest glow to reassure her it was still alive and unharmed. No matter how hard she tried to summon it, her magic remained curled upon itself and unable to answer her command.

Opening her eyes, sweat beaded on her forehead, and her legs wobbled from exertion. Sera staggered to the table and let her body drop into the chair, her head in her hands as she staved off a wave of despair. Minute by minute, the shaking in her limbs ceased and her breath came more easily to her lungs.

How long was I unconscious? It could have been an hour or a year.

"Elliot!" She called her footman's name. Her last memory was of him fighting off three large men in the hallway of her Soho home. Was he unharmed? And what of Vicky, her maid, and Rosie, the cook? Worry clawed through her, along with a steely resolution.

Abigail and Lord Rowan would pay for what they had done. Once she escaped the grey prison.

Sera paced to the bars and wrapped her hands around them. She tugged, not expecting them to give, but you never knew. Pressing her face to the metal, she peered in both directions. A short, wide corridor ran in front of a row of cells. One end stopped at a stone wall, the other at a closed metal door.

A series of wheezing noises from the adjoining cell drew her attention. Turning, Sera crept close to the foot of her bed and stared into the next space, between the bars they shared. Her companion occupied a room with no furnishings—was even deprived of a bed. Instead, a stone platform jutted out from one wall, a worn blanket balled up at one end. A figure curled upon itself on the hard stone, their back to Sera.

An extremely *hairy* back. That might explain why they weren't using the blanket at their feet. Nature had provided its own.

There was something about the size, shape, and volume of snoring that made Sera think the other resident was male. Although they would need to be awake and chatty for her to confirm that assumption.

"Hello, I'm Sera, your new neighbour," she called. While it was rude to wake the sleeper, they might know vital information about their prison, and she didn't want to sit around all day waiting for them to finish their nap.

Curiosity nibbled at her about the other person. From what little she knew, the Repository held dangerous supernatural inmates. The person asleep on the bench was either a mage, an aftermage, or an Unnatural. Since there were no missing mages apart from herself, they must belong to one of the latter two categories.

Just as she began to wonder if they were so soundly asleep that they hadn't heard her, the shape made a grunt and twisted their body off the bench.

Sera took a half-step backwards at the visage that stared at her. From his naked form, her fellow inmate was indeed male. His face was elongated into a snout. Jagged, protracted teeth in a prominent jaw, lips pulled back in a snarl. Long fur, in a mix of deep grey and black, covered patches of his arms and chest. When he raised his hands, they ended in thick, furry fingers with a yellow claw. His ears curved upwards, terminating in a small tuft, and jutted through a tangle of dark hair that fell to his shoulders.

The creature lunged at the bars in a fluid leap that took him from the bench to their shared wall in an instant. Grasping one bar, he stretched the other hand into Sera's cell and lashed out. Scratching, seeking, trying to catch her. All the while, his snout was pressed to the bars, and he snarled and whined.

The creature emitted an odour like an open grave when the lid had been left off the casket under a summer sun. Unwashed skin, unwashed hair, unwashed body, unwashed whatever was trapped under his yellow claws. He smelled like he was rotting away.

Instinctively, she had jumped back and out of reach, and thrown up her hands to create a shield. Panic spread through her when no magic pooled in her palms. Her hands were simply flesh, easily torn by the long claws of the creature.

Lowering her hands, and from the safety of distance, Sera examined him. He had a sharp, angular face with a defined jaw and a high forehead. But his gaze unnerved her. With slightly tilted eyes ringed by shadows, his pale grey stare seemed to penetrate her with an intensity that could peel back the layers of her soul. He was tall. As tall as Hugh, should the physician have been close by for comparison. But this person was of a wiry construction.

"I am sorry I disturbed your sleep. I am trapped, just like you," she whispered as the creature switched arms and continued to lash out at her.

The high-pitched snarling turned to a more guttural growl of frustration. After several minutes of venting his rage on the thick bars, the fellow glared at her and whined.

Reassured the bars wouldn't give way, Sera took a cautious step forward. "I cannot help you. I am sorry."

He snorted and stalked back to the bench, where once again he curled up facing the stone wall. Ignoring her entirely.

Apparently, there would be no deep conversations with her neighbour about their mutual plight and how they might escape. Which meant she was alone.

And cut off from her magic.

A wave of despair crashed over her, and she crumpled to the floor. With her back to the bars, Sera drew her knees up to her chest and wrapped her arms around them. A single sob escaped her chest at her hopeless situation. How could she have been so stupid as to trust Abigail?

With her eyes closed, Sera dissected her relationship with the other woman and the warning signs she had overlooked. What had made her continue to seek the other woman's friendship and approval? Only one word appeared in her mind. *Desperation.*

"You've been a fool, Seraphina Winyard," she whispered.

Desperate for family, for friendship, for approval,

she had ignored the tingle that always kept a distance between her and Abigail. Yet as she compared one relationship to another, she realised no such barrier had ever existed with Kitty. True friendship didn't have terms and conditions attached. And if anyone was going to impose those, it would have been the sharp-minded Kitty.

A friend supported you, celebrated your achievements, lifted you up, or smacked you on the back of the head when you needed it. Thinking of her dear friend, pragmatism swooped down like a kestrel intent on snatching a mouse from the grass.

"You are not alone," Sera murmured.

Elliot would have raised the alarm. Even now, Kitty and Hugh would be ensuring her staff were unharmed and plotting how to find her.

"Well, I always wanted to see the Repository—just not like this." Sera picked herself up and, with nothing else to do, examined her surroundings.

She peered beyond her cell. The forbidding door at one end of the corridor was dotted with metal rivets in an unusual pattern and had cast-iron hinges bigger than her hands. The doorway was large enough to allow access for a gargoyle in stone form, without their having to duck. Sera estimated there were four cells in the row. Only two seemed occupied. The wall opposite ran uninterrupted, without a single window.

She lifted the rug to examine the slates. None were loose, nor were there any trap doors. Next, she peered under the bed and found a chamber pot. The drawer in the side table contained a stash of paper and an ink set. The provided books were *Gulliver's Travels* by Jonathan Swift, *Evelina* by Frances Burney, and a book on Greek mythology. Was there a subtle message in the choice of *Evelina,* and its tale of an illegitimate young woman who learned to navigate society's treacherous waters? Putting aside the books, she rapped on every stone. Then she tugged on each bar and examined the lock holding the door closed.

Periodically, she peered through the bars of the shared wall, but no response came from her companion. Nor any noise. So he was either awake and listening, or not yet so deeply asleep that he snored.

Having finished her inspection and with nothing else to do, she picked up *Gulliver's Travels* and sat at the small square table. Flicking the pages, she couldn't concentrate enough to read, so she studied the illustrations instead. She was tracing the depiction of the enormous man pinned to the ground by hundreds of ropes when the metal door clanged.

Footsteps rang on the slate. A surge of worry mixed with excitement swirled inside her. Who could it be? Abigail with a profuse apology or Lord Ormsby to gloat?

An old man appeared on the other side of the bars, balancing two trays, one on top of the other. With thinning grey hair and a narrow frame, he squinted at her as though he had forgotten his spectacles—or had never owned any. Deep wrinkles pulled his skin down and his hands were gnarled with age and twisted by arthritis. He placed both trays on the ground and picked up the top one, which held an uncovered bowl. Removing the bowl from the tray, he slid it under the bars of her companion's cell. Then he picked up the second tray, which held a plate covered by a tin dome, a small teapot, and a saucerless cup, and approached her cell.

"Good day, Lady Winyard. I am Jerome Parr, caretaker of the Repository." He stooped and slid the tray under a gap in the bars. The short, fat teapot was the exact height to pass underneath. Then he stepped backwards to stand equidistant between the opposite wall and her bars, as though he didn't dare venture too close.

Sera eyed the tray and her stomach rumbled, making her wonder again how long she had been asleep. She held her fear and anxiety under a tight rein and straightened her spine. "There seems to be some sort of mistake with my accommodation. I asked for a room with a garden view and a fireplace."

"I am sorry, but Lord Rowan was most insistent that you be kept here. At least initially. These cells can be rather cold and dreary, unfortunately." He spread his hands wide in a gesture that resembled a shrug.

"Initially? Let me guess—if I am a good girl and do whatever he requests, my situation will improve?" She picked up the tray and deposited it on the table.

An apologetic smile flashed across Jerome's narrow face. "Yes."

"Why am I being held here against my will? I demand you release me immediately." But she knew why. Despite his advanced years, Lord Rowan could act like a petulant child. What control did he wield that so many did his bidding without question? He was retired, and no longer sat on the Mage Council.

"I cannot do that. I must follow my orders." His gaze wandered to the adjoining cell, where the inmate made slurping noises as he consumed his meal.

"I have not committed any crime. How can I be imprisoned without due process? I demand to be allowed to consult with my solicitor. Where is our English justice?" How could a person be snatched from their home and hidden away, and society turn a blind eye? Frustration and anger bubbled under her skin. At the very least, she should be allowed to consult with Mr Napier to argue for her freedom.

Jerome shuffled from foot to foot but did not answer.

Sera stalked back to the bars. "I am no criminal, Mr Parr. My only transgression, apparently, is to be a head-strong woman who refuses to be the chattel of a man. I am hardly the only such woman in society. Will we all be imprisoned here for being... troublesome?"

"I am sorry, Lady Winyard. I am following the orders of Lord Rowan." Jerome glanced at her, then dropped his gaze to the toes of his boots.

"Lord Rowan is not the Speaker of the Mage Council. What has Lord Ormsby to say about my imprisonment?" As soon as she said the words, a short hysterical laugh burst from her throat, and she slapped a hand over her mouth. The Speaker would most likely be delighted to discover that the thorn in his side had been removed and would bother him no more.

Jerome's lips thinned. "The mandate concerning your imprisonment does not come from Lord Ormsby, but from the king himself."

That knocked the argument out of her. "The king? There must be some mistake. King George loves my entertainments."

He shook his head. "The king's edict states that you pose a threat to the common people and need to be sequestered until it is decided what to do with you."

So *that* was how Lord Rowan worked. He pulled the strings of their monarch. "Write to Queen Charlotte, please. This is all a horrible mistake." The common sense of the queen would prevail.

Jerome drew himself up and inhaled, on the brink of refusing her request, no doubt, when his expression softened. "Very well. I can see no harm in that. I shall seek the advice of the queen in this matter. I am sure it will be resolved in due course, milady."

"Am I at least allowed some time outside each day?" Even prisoners could walk the perimeter of the grounds, to exercise for an hour or so each day.

Jerome remained silent.

Fear bounced around inside Sera, and she struggled to keep it under control. What if she never left this cell? Would she grow old and die without ever again feeling the sun on her face? Her eyes burned with unshed tears at the thought of never talking to Kitty again or feeling Hugh's caress. She drew a shuddering breath.

She waved an arm at the grey stone surrounding her. "How am I to know when to sleep and when to rise, if I cannot see the sun or moon?"

"You will find your own rhythm in this place, and I will provide breakfast when I am alerted that you are awake," the caretaker said. "Supper will be some twelve hours after that."

"What am I to do to pass the hours?" Now the panic began to take control of her limbs. Day after mind-numbing day trapped in the cell. Cut off from her magic and Mother Nature and with nothing to do. Insanity beckoned like a bright light on the horizon.

"I am instructed to supply you with books, paints, or needlework—"

"*Needlework?*" Sera repeated in a mortified tone. Did Lord Rowan seriously expect her to spend her life in a cell doing *needlework?* The only thing she would use embroidery scissors for would be to dig a tunnel out —or stab him in the eye.

"I shall return after you have had your supper. You must be hungry." He turned to leave.

"Mr Parr, wait! How long was I unconscious?" Without her connection to the earth or a glimpse out a window, she struggled to know how much time had elapsed since Abigail had sung her poisonous lullaby. Had it been a few hours or a day?

A sad smile flitted across Jerome's face. "Long enough to be hungry, milady."

Two

Sera didn't want the caretaker to go and leave her alone with the creature next door. Wracking her brain, she grabbed hold of the first thing she might ask to make him stay a little longer.

"My companion... what is wrong with him? He does not seem to talk." She gestured to the next cell.

The sad expression returned to Jerome's face. "I fear his mind is too far gone for him to offer any sort of companionship. I call him Lionel. I don't know if that is his actual name, but it is what I settled upon."

"What is he? He is not quite a man and not quite... a wild creature." There was something canine mixed in there, of that she was certain. He seemed far too dishevelled to have any whiff of the feline about him, and Sera assumed he was some classification of Unnatural with which she was unfamiliar. Possibly one whose natural habitat was a midden pit.

Jerome turned in the creature's direction. "Lionel is a lycanthrope."

"Lionel the lycanthrope?" Sera hoped she had misheard.

Jerome cast his eyes downward. "He came to us without a name. Initially, I called him Mr Lycanthrope, but over time, it became quite tiresome and far too formal. So, I started calling him Lionel, and he has not objected."

"But he doesn't look like any lycanthrope I have seen in books." The men who could change into wolves were gifted an incredible physique in their human form. Sera felt sorry for Lionel. And for herself, since he was the first wolf shifter of her acquaintance. That made her ponder if Walter the werewolf would have been a better name or worse.

"Poor devil is stuck between forms, except in certain circumstances. He only ever returns to his full human form in the deepest of sleep, when he completely relaxes." Jerome's gaze darted sideways, as though he was uncomfortable discussing Lionel in the lycanthrope's hearing.

The slurping noises ended, followed by a clack as the wooden bowl skidded along the ground and came to rest at Jerome's feet. The caretaker picked it up and held it in both hands. He rubbed its smooth wood with his thumbs. "When I bring his meal is one of the few moments where he will let me get close enough without snarling or trying to attack me."

How miserable Lionel must be, all alone in his cell

like that, without much human contact or under-standing of what was happening around him.

"Does he ever shift into his wolf form?" Today seemed to be the day for fascinating discoveries. Not only had Sera seen the Repository, but here was her opportunity to study a lycanthrope as well. Hugh would be jealous.

"Yes. When he's very angry, and under a full moon. But don't worry, the bars hold him." Jerome was growing more animated on the topic.

"He's not much of a conversationalist." Sera would use the paper in the drawer to record her observations for Hugh. It would give her something to do and keep her mind from dwelling on her fate. Perhaps there might even be a way to help Lionel.

A frown further wrinkled Jerome's already deeply carved forehead. "No, but he can talk. Over the years, a few words have passed between us. I think it takes rather a lot of effort for him in his current state. Or he simply might not have anything to say."

Over the years. Sera plucked questions from her mind, both to avoid thinking of such a horror and to delay the caretaker's leaving. "Is he imprisoned here because he cannot control his shift back into a man, to enable him to walk the streets of London undetected?"

Sadness filled Jerome's watery eyes. "No. He's here because he terrorised a village in Suffolk and killed three people before he was captured."

"Oh." He deserved his fate, then. Unlike herself.

"Enjoy your dinner, milady. I shall return." Jerome

nodded and retreated before she could bombard him with more questions.

Sera turned back to her tray. Lifting the tin lid revealed a hearty, if somewhat plain, stew and two slices of buttered bread. The squat teapot contained a rather ordinary tea to which someone had already added milk. What sort of monster poured milk into the teapot? That small action of disdain made it clear she was no house guest.

Her stomach ceased its complaints once she had eaten. The stew contained an unknown meat and plenty of vegetables in rich gravy. The only compliment she could bestow on the tea was that it was hot.

Sera pushed the empty tray back under the bars and wandered her confines. It took only five strides to cross from one side of the cell to the other. Back and forth she paced, her arms wrapped so tightly around her that she could feel her fingernails biting into her palms and see her knuckles turn white. As her heels connected with the stone floor, the impact sent tingles up her legs and pinged along her spine.

Even though she had eaten, a hollowness lay at her core. The magic that had once flooded every part of her with warmth and light was trapped in its own prison.

Fear tried to invade her mind. *What if I'm never able to free my gift?*

No. She refused to contemplate a future without the tiniest spark of magic. She would prevail. Somehow.

She continued to pace. There had to be a way to

break out of this place or a way to restore her magic so that she could escape. But how? No longer was she a powerful mage, but an ordinary woman of no special abilities.

Back and forth she walked, trying to make herself fatigued enough to enable sleep. How many turns before the bars would it take to wear a groove in the slate floor? When her body and mind grew numb, she retreated to the cot. Sera propped the pillow up sideways behind her and nestled into the corner. Then she tucked the woollen blanket around her legs.

Once she'd made herself as comfortable as possible, she closed her eyes and set about examining the binding that had driven her gift into hibernation. What cunning spell had Abigail and her grandfather concocted? The potion that had put her to sleep had worn off. So why did its effects continue to hold her power captive?

It reassured Sera that a spark of her magic still remained inside her. If she had searched and found only an empty void, it would have driven her into a nightmarish despair. It was one thing to choose not to use her gift, but another entirely to have it forcibly excised from her body, thus depriving her of it forever.

In her mind, she cupped the seed and blew upon it, testing for any reaction. Turning it this way and that, she slowly let Lord Rowan's casting seep into her skin. Once she understood how the old mage had imprisoned her magic, she could unravel his spell. Like her body, her gift dwelt in a prison that at first glance seemed impossible to escape. When she freed one part of herself, she would have the resources to free the remainder.

While she held tight to the determination that she would ultimately win, she was growing a little tired of having to constantly free herself from ensorcelled shackles.

When she grew mentally fatigued from the minute examination of the spell, Sera reached for *Evelina*. She wondered again if the choice of reading material was a coded message from her former friend Abigail. The tale was one of a young woman of ambitious social standing who attracts unwanted attention and is the cause of much speculation in society.

Her reading was occasionally interrupted by snarls and howls from Lionel. The thuds and rattles came from his hurling himself at the bars. While Jerome had assured her that they were strong enough to hold the mad shifter, he wasn't the one stuck next to the creature. A moment of vulnerability washed over her. No longer was she England's most powerful mage, able to defeat any assailant with a wave of the hand. She was now an ordinary woman with only her wits and what strength she possessed in her frame to defend herself.

Settling down in her bed and pulling the blanket over her shoulders, Sera spent the time before she fell asleep determining what weapons could be improvised from the contents of her cell. In the end, she decided that if Lionel broke through the iron bars, she would smash the chamberpot over his head.

When Sera woke, the tray was gone from outside her cell and a new one awaited her. The pitcher on the side table held fresh water, and the chamber pot had been emptied. After performing her ablutions, she fetched the tray. Glancing into the next cell, she found Lionel on his side facing her and watching with his pale gaze.

"Hello." Should she say good morning or good afternoon? She would ask Jerome for a clock, to mark the passage of time. Although that conjured an image of her going insane as she listened to its *tick-tock* for years and years.

Lionel blinked but didn't return the greeting.

"I never thought I would miss Elliot and his chatter," she muttered as she took her tray to the table.

Under the cover was a bowl of steaming porridge. A small jug of cream sat next to a plate holding a pat of butter. The same squat pot contained the same milky tea.

"Good morning, then." Sera ate and drank without enjoyment, her thoughts focused more on her current predicament than on the flavour of the meal.

It had been afternoon when Abigail had poisoned her tea and sung the lullaby. By Sera's reckoning, that had been only the day before.

If Lord Rowan planned to hold her for any length of time, she would insist on the addition of a wardrobe to her room and a bath. Or was she expected to become a wild, naked creature like her neighbour?

After breakfast, Sera slid the tray back under the

bars and paced. Her skin itched at being confined to a single room. Even under the strict governance of Lord Branvale, she had been allowed to prowl the garden, climb trees, and sit on the grass. How did ordinary people in ordinary prisons face each day?

She decided there must be two types of prisoners. Those who bowed their heads and retreated into their minds to shuffle through each day. And those who would try anything to escape the unrelenting boredom and the walls that held them. Deciding she was cut from the latter kind of cloth; Sera retrieved her spoon from the tray.

She settled cross-legged on the cold floor and ran her thumb over the metal spoon. She still had two hands, and if she had to, she would dig a tunnel with the modest utensil and escape that way. Although she rather hoped Kitty and Hugh would mount a rescue long before she dug a usable tunnel.

She had decided to try to chip away at the stones behind her side table, in the vain hope that it would lead her to freedom. The stone was harder than she expected, but as she pushed away chips of granite with each strike of her tiny shovel, she imagined herself a miner trying to dig for gold.

She allowed herself a smile at that thought before focusing on her task. The chips of rock felt oddly satisfying beneath her fingertips as she worked. Then again, anything was better than sitting still in this little cell.

When her fingers cramped, she tossed the spoon back on the tray and picked up a book instead.

Retreating to the bed, she tucked the blanket around her chilled legs and read. She found solace in the stories, grateful for a source of distraction from what might otherwise be an unbearable wait. Time passed until the words swam on the page and her eyes had trouble focusing.

With no way to mark the passage of the hours, Sera didn't know whether days rolled by outside or she was frozen in time. Boredom piled up in her mind, like grains of sand being pushed in under a door by a strong wind. At first, she brushed it away, but as the mound grew, it dragged at her every step.

If a plant were removed from sunlight, fresh air, and the healing touch of rain, it would fail to thrive. Then it would curl in upon itself, its leaves turning brown and withering. If not rescued in time and nurtured back to health, the plant would die.

Sera was that neglected house plant shoved in a dark, windowless cupboard. A chill invaded her bones that refused to budge and, more and more, she curled up under the blanket, trying to get warm. What wouldn't she do for a cheerful fire! At least the flames would have offered her companionship. Each time she woke, it became harder to throw off the blanket and swing her feet to the floor.

Her attempts at escape with the spoon had grown feeble, her movements sluggish as if weighed down by an invisible force. When she tried to lose herself in memories of happier times, it only served to highlight the hopelessness of her situation. A fresh wave of despair threatened to overtake her each time such thoughts crossed her mind.

Unable to distinguish night from day, worries gnawed at her. Where were her friends? Had they all abandoned her to her fate? Had Queen Charlotte written back to Jerome?

Every time Jerome slid a tray under the bars, he shook his head when she asked if there was any news.

The sand in her mind filled every space with a crushing presence until it could hold no more. Then it overflowed, pouring into her limbs. Every part of her became leaden with it. Then her tears of frustration turned the sand damp and dark. The point came when she could no longer bear the weight of it all and it dragged her under. Pulling the blanket over her head, Sera turned her face to the wall and wept.

For minutes, hours, days, she remained buried under the heaviness of her despair. Sobbing for all she would never do and the unfairness of life.

"Lady Winyard?" Jerome's voice called to her, and she ignored it.

Feet shuffled; the door clanged. Lionel let out a howl. Did that mean it was evening, and he bayed at an unseen moon?

To her fuddled mind, at least a dozen more times

Jerome stood at the bars and tried to rouse her. She remained motionless under her blanket, her breathing heavy and laboured as if restricted by invisible shackles. Let him shout. She would not be moved. What was the point? Her mind baulked at spending the rest of her days confined to this stone cell. Better to end it now than to go mad.

"Lady Winyard? I really think you should get up." Yet again, Jerome tried to lure her from under the comforting blanket.

"Go away!" she yelled and pulled the woollen cover more tightly around her.

"Very well, milady. But Lord Rowan is on his way, and I thought perhaps you'd rather he didn't see you like this."

Sera's breath caught in her throat. Her mind struggled to surface from its hibernation. "Lord Rowan?"

"Yes. He is perhaps an hour away."

Lionel snarled, as though he also knew the name.

Sera pushed the blanket down and stared at the ceiling. Finally, inch by inch, she stirred. She sat up with difficulty, her movements slow, as though she battled a strong current, her body aching from the lethargy of her despair.

There was woefully little she could do given her current circumstances. The old mage probably thought to find her exactly as she was—mired in despair and desperate for freedom. A condition that would render her malleable and agreeable to whatever he proposed.

A snort burst from her.

As if she would ever give him the satisfaction. He thought he was in control and wielding all the power, but he had much to learn about troublesome women. She might be bereft of her magic, but he hadn't stolen her intelligence.

Mentally, she dragged herself out of the mire she had created and shook herself free. She most probably looked a fright, and her cheek was stiff with the salt of her dried tears. She would need all her wits about her for the verbal duel ahead.

"I need coffee, Mr Parr. A rather potent brew, if you would be so obliging." Rubbing the heels of her palms against her eyes, Sera lowered her feet to the floor. Her body protested the movement. Muscles only now waking up needed to stretch.

For how long had she allowed fear and despair to rule her mind? A few days, perhaps?

"Of course. I shall bring you something to eat as well. There is fresh water for you to wash with, and I found a brush for your hair." He waved at the side table, then hurried away.

Sera stripped to her chemise and washed her arms, legs, and face, rubbing at her flesh with a cloth soaked in the cold water. That alone did much to revive her senses. By the time Jerome returned with the aromatic coffee and a bowl of hot porridge, she was lacing herself back into her gown. The brush did a serviceable job on her tangled hair, but only Vicky's magic touch would tame all the snarls. Then she divided it roughly into thirds and made a thick plait, knotting the end on itself to stop the braid from unravelling.

Seated at her small table, Sera picked up the teapot and poured a thick, dark brew into the cup. She took a sip and screwed up her face. It was bitter and strong and blew through her brain like a gusty blast. As horrid as it was, the coffee scoured away the last of the sand clogging her thoughts.

THREE

ONCE SERA STARTED EATING, hunger roared through her. She almost fell on the bowl with the same ravenous appetite as Lionel displayed at every meal. She used a thick slab of bread to clean the bowl of any last scrap of porridge and still her stomach grumbled for more. Hopefully, the coffee would settle it. Sera was sipping her second cup of the horrid brew when the prison door opened and footsteps rang out on the slate. More than one set of shoes approached.

She drew a long breath through her nose and imagined Hugh sitting beside her. He would place a hand on her arm and whisper caution in her ear, murmuring, "Do not let your temper control your actions." Well, without her magic, all she could do was scream, and that would probably only make Lord Rowan laugh. Digging deep, she found a bland and somewhat bored expression to paste on her face and leaned against the back of her chair as she pretended to savour her coffee.

Just as Lord Rowan strode into view.

He was followed by Jerome, who carried a chair with a seat upholstered in blue velvet. The caretaker set the chair down close to the wall and directly opposite Sera's bars before retrieving her tray. He gave her a quick nod, then retreated, hurrying back through the thick metal door as though he expected a fiery mage battle to explode behind him.

Rage flowed cold through her body, and her hands curled into fists around the coffee cup. Ordinarily, sparks would have flown over her skin as her temper flared, and she would have called on her magic to strike down the man who had cast her into this cell. But the slumbering ember could not answer, and a pang of grief bounced around the hollow its absence left.

Heated words bubbled up instead, but she discarded most of them. Hurling insults would achieve nothing, and she suspected the smug smile on the old man's face would only grow wider. Besides, words alone would never satisfy her anger. He needed to suffer.

As did his granddaughter.

The old mage shook out his cloak before sitting. He rested his forearms on the arms of the chair, one finger tracing the whorl carved into the wood as he gazed at Sera.

"I had hoped it would not come to this, Seraphina. Your actions have brought this fate upon yourself." He used a gently chiding tone as though she were a naughty grandchild who had traipsed mud across the carpet.

She recalled George, the child the mage had turned into a toad and placed in a glass terrarium to think about his transgressions. Her imprisonment could have been worse. At least she retained her human form. She could have awakened from the ensorcelled sleep to discover she had been turned into a chicken with its wings clipped, locked in a small coop.

Refusing to unleash her emotions in front of him, she set down the empty cup and folded her hands in her lap. There, unseen by Lord Rowan, she could dig her nails into her palms until she pierced the skin so that the pain would give her a different sensation to focus on. All the while, she counted to ten in her head.

Only when she felt in control of her senses—Hugh would be proud of her—did she speak. "I do hope you informed Lord Ormsby that I'll not be able to perform my prescribed tasks this week, due to being... indisposed. He does get ever so grumpy when I am away from London." It was a vain hope that the Speaker might revoke Lord Rowan's order, and demand that she be set to clearing drains once more.

She would give almost anything to clear a drain again.

Lord Rowan tented his fingers and chuckled. "Oh, he knows. Lord Ormsby seemed somewhat relieved when I advised him that you had voluntarily sequestered yourself in the country. I said you sought education in how to follow the dictates of your superiors, and how to behave like a proper lady."

If Sera had still been able to summon a fireball, she would have incinerated the old mage where he sat. Somehow, flinging the contents of her chamber pot at him wouldn't give her anywhere near the same level of satisfaction. As amusing as it might be.

There was one benefit to all the unexpected free time on her hands. She'd had ample opportunity to craft the perfect revenge for both him and his granddaughter. Abigail's downfall would see her deprived of every single thing she valued. Her standing in society. Her pristine reputation. Her chance to be a duchess.

"Like a naughty child, I am sent to my room until I am penitent. You must realise, Lord Rowan, that you cannot hold me here indefinitely. My friends will notice my absence and ask awkward questions. Mr Napier has ways to make his voice heard in Parliament if necessary. And I am a particular favourite of the queen. She will not be fooled by your tales of sending me to some sort of finishing school and will demand the truth. Along with my release." Sera uncurled her fists and wiped her palms on the wool of her gown.

"Queen Charlotte has not remarked upon your absence, nor would it interest her. She has other concerns pressing on her mind," he murmured in a manner that sent a chill washing over Sera's skin.

What had they done to the queen? Sera thought that these events had only impacted her life, but if Lord

Rowan dared touch the royal person… what else would he stoop to?

"You will be contained here, Lady Winyard, until you are no longer a danger and understand how to be subservient." He watched her from under bushy grey eyebrows.

In that case, she would never be set free.

"I was never a danger. You, and those like you, simply cannot handle a woman who knows her own mind and who refuses to be dictated to or allow some man to pull her strings." She rose and approached the bars, curling one hand around the metal. "One day, troublesome women like me will shake the world so hard you will have no choice but to listen to us. We will break our shackles like water bursting free of a dam, and men will never again control us."

"A pretty sentiment, but women will never reach the halls of power where men rule. You should be content with your families and households. Things more within the scope of your abilities." He turned his hand over and inspected his nails.

Sera had changed her mind. She would fling her chamber pot at him. Only when she turned to her little cot, she realised the porcelain bowl wouldn't fit through the bars. Blast. Instead, she carved his words into her mind. They would form the basis of her revenge against him. Envisioning it in her mind, she smiled at him.

"One day, you will be an old, powerless man. Ignored by all. Your voice silenced. Reduced to collecting dung to dry for fires or sweeping the crossroads. Your final years will be spent cold and alone." Sera's voice had a cold tone as she made each word a promise.

Lord Rowan huffed and waved an unconcerned hand at her. "You cannot touch me, just as you cannot escape this place. Where are the Fae bracelets? My men searched your house but could not find them. The spelled box I gave you to keep them safe was empty."

In what state had his men left her staff and home? Sera changed her mind about possible methods of revenge. Gathering horse dung seemed too honourable an occupation. Perhaps she would follow his example and turn him into a small toad imprisoned in a glass terrarium. Then she would gift him to the Foundling Hospital. He would never know another moment of peace for as long as he lived. His days would be spent with children tapping on the glass, tipping him on his side, and dropping things into his prison to torment him.

"You had better not have harmed my staff." The words came out like a growl and Lionel snarled in response. A memory flitted through her mind of Elliot struggling with the Crawley footmen in her narrow entrance hall.

The old mage shifted in the chair, moving his weight to one side as he crossed his legs. "Your footman will recover in time. The women offered no obstacle and huddled together in the kitchen. Where are the bracelets?"

She drew long breaths through her nose and forced

back tears. Never would she display weakness before her enemy. Instead, she wrinkled her forehead and stared up at the ceiling. "Odd. Without my magic, I find I cannot remember. Removing my gift has made me such a scatterbrained woman that I seem to have lost track of what I did with them. Or how to retrieve them."

His eyes narrowed, and his beard twitched as he clenched his jaw. "If you think to use them to negotiate for your freedom, you are too late. I will find them. No little cloaking spell of yours will keep me from them for long."

Sera thanked whatever instinct had urged her to place the bracelets in Hugh's large hands for safekeeping. She might not be able to use them to win her freedom, but the surgeon might. Pretending boredom, she turned and presented her back to the bars. "Then it seems we have nothing left to discuss. If you don't mind, I would like to get back to my book."

After a long moment of silence, her adversary spoke. "I believe we were supposed to have a conversation about the Nereus. Finally, I can fully satisfy your curiosity on that subject."

Not only was she being held against her will, but now she was going to be lectured. Sera walked to the table and poured the dregs of cooling coffee into the cup. "About that—you are too late. I already know about such a being. It is the child of two mages, who is as powerful as their parents combined."

"Ah, but you are mistaken. It is not their power combined. If you had been a man and educated in mathematics, you would know the sum is not derived from adding the two components. Nor multiplying them. The power is magnified exponentially—that of one mage raised by the factor of the other. Power such as mere mages can only dream of holding." His voice increased in volume as he spoke and betrayed his enthusiasm for the topic.

Now that was interesting. Damn. She couldn't help but be drawn into the conversation. To stop herself from appearing too eager, she dropped into the chair and sipped the syrupy coffee. The stuff really was horrible, but it had revived her tired senses. "A mage's power diminishes with each generation. Their after-mage descendants are of decreasing magical ability until the gift disappears entirely from their line after the seventh generation."

"Ah, but there is just one exception—when two mages create a child." Lord Rowan leaned forward in his chair; his eyes gleaming.

Ha! About that, he was mistaken. Sera smirked into the cup and took another mouthful. "You are misinformed. There are two exceptions. You are forgetting the pairing of a mage and an Unnatural. In such cases, the ability is perpetuated, undiminished, throughout the subsequent generations. Although Mother Nature does restrict how many are gifted in each generation to the original number conceived." Sera had met the other exception. The Crows. Three talented women descended from a mage hundreds of years ago. Despite the passage of time, they possessed the same level of power as Morag's daughters.

"What do you know of such things?" His hands turned into claws on the ends of the chair arms, and he half-rose.

She smiled and uttered one name. "Morag."

Lord Rowan snorted, and his bottom dropped back to the padded seat. "You are the one who is wrong. While that woman lived longer than expected, there are no children of hers recorded in the mage genealogy."

Was it possible that Lord Rowan didn't know about the Crows? Impossible, when he knew how the children of mages and other beings were affected by magic. He was merely bluffing to see how much she knew. She tapped a finger against the cup and looked off to a corner of her cell. "I noticed that, too. It must have taken quite a number of mages to erase the details of her children from the book. I imagine the entire Mage Council drained themselves to exhaustion to complete the task."

Glancing up, she held Lord Rowan's gaze for several seconds before he laughed. "It took me decades to uncover more than mere whispers about the existence of those creatures. How did you come by such knowledge in only a few short months?"

"Birds of a feather flock together," she murmured and lowered her eyes. This was how she would defeat him—by leaning on her women supporters. Men constantly underestimated their sex, and that would be their downfall.

He sucked in a breath and leaned forward to shake a gnarled hand at her. "Where are they? I need to study them. Is it true their power is undiminished, even though many generations have passed?"

Sera shrugged. "I don't know where the Crows choose to fly. But perhaps they disposed of the bracelets for me, somewhere far beyond your reach." Let him think she had given them to the Crows. If he had not found their nest in all his years of searching, he wouldn't now.

"Foolish girl, to give such items to bird-brained women." His hand turned into a fist, and he punched the air in a futile manner. Like an old man who had lost something he most dearly wanted to possess. A thump sounded from deep within the building as though he had hurled some invisible object against a far-off wall.

He had proven himself wrong yet again. There was nothing bird-brained about the Crows. The animal cunning of Elliot's family flowed in their veins, and they knew how to protect their own. "You are wasting your time holding me here. I will never become a demure puppet like Abigail. As long as I draw breath, I will fight to be free of this prison and your control."

The words became a vow she carved deep into her bones, to remind herself when the sands of despair tried to pour into her mind again. She would resist. She would fight. She would be free.

"I have waited decades for the opportunity to bring another Nereus into the world. You sadly underestimate me if you think your lack of co-operation will ruin my plans." He spat the words and splotches of colour appeared in his face.

A chill crept into Sera's bones. He wanted to create another Nereus, whether or not she co-operated. *Now* she understood her imprisonment.

"You think to use me as your broodmare." A broodmare who would need to be hobbled, as she would never submit. It didn't matter who she was as a person, or the things she could achieve in the world. To him, she was simply a womb and a means to an end.

"I am told Lord Tomlin is tolerable and, as you have already so vehemently stated, no one expects you to marry him. Indeed, he took a wife some months ago and, by the swell to her belly, has proven his worth as a stud." A mad glint lit Lord Rowan's eyes.

Sera laid her palms flat on the table and used the touch of the cool wood to centre herself. "You may have deprived me of my magic, but I make this vow... if you try to put Tomlin in this cell with me, I will kill him with my bare hands."

Lord Rowan never flinched. Although to be fair, her threat hadn't been directed at him, and he had already demonstrated little concern for those around him. Perhaps he saw Lord Tomlin as disposable. There were eleven male mages, after all.

His lips pulled back in a smug expression. "I'm not

a monster. You will be given a choice. Either Lord Tomlin or another less *pleasant* partner."

If he said Lord Ormsby, she would throw up.

"My intent is to create a Nereus, but if you prefer, we can see what you birth from an Unnatural father first." He gestured with one aged-spotted hand to the adjoining cell. "I believe you have met your fellow inmate. Perhaps once you have one child, you will be more amenable and desirous of more. I am told that is often the way with women."

Sera's stomach roiled, and she glanced once more at her cot and the container hidden underneath it. Should she lunge for the painted porcelain, or see if she could vomit on Lord Rowan's shoes? "You expect me to breed with *Lionel*?"

The grin widened. "Ah. You are on a first-name basis already. Excellent. I thought putting you beside him would allow you a chance to get acquainted and fully consider your options."

With a mighty effort, Sera pushed aside the revulsion and horrid images in her mind. "Let us for one moment entertain your mad idea and assume that I would let Tomlin do anything more than wipe the mud from my boots. What will you do with such a babe? You are an elderly man, Lord Rowan. Do you have another twenty years to see your plan to fruition?"

She doubted Lord Rowan would even give her an opportunity to know her child. The baby would still be bloody from its birth when he ripped it from her arms.

Would her offspring be given to Abigail to raise or to Lord Tomlin?

The thought of either one touching any child she bore seared words of resistance into her bones.

Lord Rowan may have thought to bully her into submission, but all he'd done was make her stronger.

Four

Lord Rowan's hands gripped the arms of the chair. "I don't have to wait twenty years to see my plan to fruition. A Nereus possesses almost unimaginable power. They can turn back the hands of time. Your babe will make me young again." His voice betrayed how desperately he wanted to recapture his youth.

Curiosity made Sera abandon her chair and pace before the bars. There were too many thoughts galloping through her head for her to sit still. "Our gift cannot heal bodies, no matter how talented we are. It is the one way in which we are lacking. Mages cannot heal people. We harm them. Only a few rare after-mages have a talent in the area of healing." How she longed for the ability to cure rather than curse. To create rather than destroy.

Lord Rowan shook his head, and his demeanour returned to that of the elderly scholar. "A Nereus can heal or harm at his whim. But sadly, such enormous power is coupled with an unreliability of the mind. They cannot control all that their veins contain, and it drives them quite... insane. Seventeen hundred years ago, the last Nereus in Britain nearly tore this country apart. It took legions of Roman soldiers, and all the druids in England at the time, to defeat the Nereus. That experience is what prompted the Mage Council to implement their unpleasant policy. If there are no women mages, there can never be another such creature."

Sera's mind leapt on this new knowledge. Finally, she understood what had motivated the repugnant killing of girls with power. All because of one mad*man*. She blew out a snort and entertained the idea of establishing a country free of men. One where girls could aspire to be whoever they wanted, education was free for all, and doctors were fully funded by their government so anyone could be tended in a hospital. What sort of culture would flourish, based on a matriarchal society?

But if she did find such a kingdom, she would lose Hugh. That reminded her that some men were worthy of a woman's love. She and Kitty would instead fight to fix their broken world for all the girls to come.

"Is that your plan, then, to create someone who will destroy Britain?" It seemed rather shortsighted and petty to Sera, all for the sake of being young again. Unless it was all an intellectual exercise to him, and he didn't care about the outcome.

"This country will not be destroyed. Far from it.

Once I have regained my youth, I shall settle the argument over the Regency. It is irrelevant who the lords and politicians think is more fit for the position, Queen Charlotte or the prince. I shall step forth and don the mantle. Mages were created superior to men for a reason, and we should never have been cast as servants of the king. Britain will grow stronger under my rule, and it will herald a new age of the British *empire*." He raised his gaze to the ceiling and lifted his arms, as though he already heard the roars of an adoring crowd as he placed the crown on his head.

Sera let out a sharp breath and rolled her eyes as her mind unravelled the tangled web of Lord Rowan's plan. He had waited decades for a woman mage, so that he might create a powerful vessel to allow him to seize control of the country. He was delusional, obviously, if he thought the peers of England would stand by as he usurped their precious line of succession. "You will still need to wait years for any such child I bear to grow, mature, and learn to master their gift."

The old mage barked in laughter. "I need to wait less than a year, assuming you prove fertile. I have no intention of ever letting your child use their gift. I will direct their ability and wield it as I desire."

She knew she was arguing with a madman but couldn't stop herself. Endless questions pressed into her mind, each answer spawning a dozen more ideas, all demanding to be satisfied. "How? You cannot expect a babe to cast with you."

He raised bushy white eyebrows. "Branvale really

did keep you in the dark. Your education is remarkably deficient in many areas."

Sera sucked in her lips to stop herself from leaping to Lord Branvale's defence. In hindsight, her guardian no longer seemed as monstrous as she had once thought him. In his inept and cold way, he had protected her from the true monster in her world—an elderly grandfather with a long white beard.

"There are two ways to use another mage's magic. One is co-operatively as we did when we froze the lake. The other is to take what you need by brute force. We seldom try that except in situations of dire need as, rather naturally, we fight against any mage who attempts to snatch at our magic. It will be easier with a baby, as it will not know how to shield or resist. It will be a simple matter for me to lean into its mind and take all I need. Over time, the child will become accustomed to my drawing off their power. Keeping your child in such a fashion also ensures I never succumb to the same madness that will inevitably claim the Nereus. But their short lifespan is no concern of mine. I will have what I need by then." He laced his fingers and a smug look formed on his wrinkled features.

Sera stopped her pacing to drop back into the chair, elbows on the table as she scrubbed her hands over her face. How calm he was as he proposed such a horror. He expected her to birth a child who would spend their entire existence in captivity, being used as a sort of magical larder. To be drawn upon to fuel the old man's desire to be young again and set aside the king to seize control of England.

A child who would never walk free but be eternally bound in chains of servitude.

Her heart ached for her nonexistent offspring, even as her stomach churned at the thought of letting Tomlin within six feet of her to attempt to conceive such a being.

"Nature knows such things should not be," she murmured. A human form could not hold such power. The magic consumed their mind. Lord Rowan had also overlooked the most obvious flaw in his plan.

"Do you really think I would allow you to do such a thing to a child of mine?" Her body and soul united in a protective instinct for a baby that would, in all probability, never exist.

"Events are set in motion, Seraphina. Either you allow Lord Tomlin to do what is required, or the bars between your cell and the next will be removed. When the lycanthrope claims you, there will be no one to protect you. But I can be magnanimous. Since it is the festive season, I will give you a little more time to decide which course of action you prefer." The old mage rose and turned to leave.

"On consideration, Lord Rowan, I have an addition to make to the previous promise I made you," Sera called out, referencing her earlier vow to kill Lord Tomlin.

He paused, the same indulgent smile on his face

that he'd worn when reviewing her work to decipher the Fae ruins. "Oh? And what might that be?"

He obviously expected her to promise that she would be compliant, that she would lie back and think of England as Lord Tomlin did his duty. She would disappoint her former mentor. Again.

She let her rage simmer in her eyes. "I promise that I will escape this place, and both you and Abigail will suffer the consequences of your betrayal and your *repulsive* plan."

He scoffed, but the smile faltered for an instant. "You are alone, without your gift, and imprisoned in a place steeped in magic, able to hold far more dangerous things than you. You are no threat. Only an annoyance. My plan will advance whether you co-operate or not. I am told it will hurt less if you comply."

With that, he stalked away, and the solid door clanged shut behind him. Sera's gaze slid sideways. Lionel crouched in the middle of his cell, his pale stare on the closed door. His hackles rose, and he emitted one last low growl.

Sera swallowed the tears that were trying to find a way free, burning them away with her will to resist every single part of Lord Rowan's mad scheme. "I'm sorry, Lionel. You and I will never be romantically entwined. But we could be collaborators if you can understand me."

The half-man, half-wolf shook himself, and the raised fur along his spine fell back into place. Then he tilted his head. One ear flopped over and the other stood taller. Sera took it as a sign of curiosity.

"Help me to escape, and I'll help you gain control over your shift." She had no idea whether either was possible, but she had hope, and that was enough.

He stared unblinkingly at her for so long that she wondered if he'd understood what she said. Perhaps his mind was too far lost to the wolf, and he couldn't speak.

Then he heaved a sigh. "Yes." He uttered the single syllable as a combined sigh and growl.

Satisfied, Sera walked to the side table and opened the drawer. Selecting a piece of paper and a pencil, she returned to the desk. Smoothing the paper, she started a list.

1. Escape
2. Fix Lionel
3. Exact revenge on Lord Rowan and Abigail.

No, she really needed to fix Lionel before she escaped; once she left the Repository, she doubted she would ever return to visit the lycanthrope. She crossed out the first two items and switched their order.

Lord Rowan had been wrong about a number of things. His biggest error was in thinking she was isolated. Now that she had shaken off her despair, aided in no small part by Lord Rowan's visit—not that she would ever tell him that—Sera knew she had never been alone. Her friends resided in her heart, just as she knew she was kept safe in theirs. A certainty settled within her that Hugh, Kitty, and Elliot were tirelessly trying to find her.

Not that she would sit around and wait to be rescued. She had escaped the clutches of one old mage, and she could certainly do it again. Only this time would be a little trickier.

Lord Rowan and Abigail had made a crucial mistake in thinking her cut off from her magic. Once, her gift had been like an oak tree. Solid and mighty. Its branches were her veins, reaching to her outer limbs from the central trunk. Whatever Lord Rowan had done, it had reversed that oak tree's growth. Turning back the hands of time, he had shrunk the tree until it curled upon itself as a small acorn. After she'd discovered the tiny, slumbering seed inside her, Sera set about determining how to wake it up. She had spent hours studying the dormant nub. She theorised that, like the oak that grew outside of mage tower, she had only to nurture the acorn of her magic into a sapling, and then into a mighty oak again.

That would require the helping hand of Gaia. But how to reach the earth goddess when she was surrounded by so much stone? Sera leaned back in the chair and tapped her bottom lip with the pencil, considering and discarding ideas until she settled on one in particular.

"Yes. That might work," she whispered. All she

needed was to ask a favour of Jerome when next the caretaker appeared.

She embellished the page bearing her list, adding the tiny acorn in the bottom corner. Then she drew a teeny sprout that broke free and spiralled up the page. As she filled the empty space with a riotous plant that wrapped a tendril around Lord Rowan's name and squeezed, a chill rippled over her skin. Sera rubbed the goosebumps away. Was it raining outside? Had that caused the temperature to drop? There might even be snow, depending on where in England the Repository was located.

A low growl from Lionel pulled her attention away from her work. The lycanthrope sat at the bars, the hackles up all along his back as he stared at something.

Sera followed his line of sight. A misty shape drifted along the corridor before their bars and back again, as though it wanted to attract her attention.

Abandoning her drawing, Sera approached and stopped when the shade halted its gliding. Now, it pulsed up and down, like an eager child bouncing on the tips of their toes.

"Hello." Instinctively, she reached for her magic to wrap around the spirit and help it solidify. A moment of panic followed when there was no answering pool of warmth in her palms. Drawing a deep breath, Sera steadied herself. She could do this like any normal person would when faced with a spirit. "I am sorry, but I cannot help you become more visible. You will need to concentrate very hard if you wish to communicate with me."

How much easier it would be if she had a way to part the veil between life and death, and clearly see the souls of those who lingered in the living realm. Or if she had old Ethel's gift to converse with the deceased.

The spirit stilled. Mist swirled within its outlines. Tiny clouds of matter bumped into each other and merged, growing denser each time until it solidified enough for Sera to recognise a woman. One without feet, as she seemed to hover a hand span from the ground. Dressed in a simple kirtle with a belt knotted at her waist, her hair of wispy cobwebs hanging down her back, she had an oval face and unnerving empty holes where her eyes should have been.

"Out," the woman croaked at her with a voice seldom used.

"I would love to get out if you could assist." Did Sera occupy the woman's cell, and the ghost planned to evict her? Or was she offering to aid an escape?

"Out." She raised an arm, and smoke seemed to drip from the limb as she pointed to the door at the end of the corridor.

"Before I can go out that door, you need to open this one." Sera rattled the locked door to her cell. She had tried to coax the lock into opening but had failed without tools or the slightest wisp of magic. That gave birth to another idea. She would ask Jerome for hair-pins. Once, she had seen Elliot use something like an unbent hairpin to open a locked liquor cabinet in Lord Branvale's house.

The spirit floated closer, and Lionel let out a long, high-pitched whine. Mist stroked along the bars and circled the lock mechanism. Sera held her breath. Could her escape be this simple?

Then the heavy metal door, with its array of rivets, banged open at the end of the corridor. The ghost emitted a shriek and disappeared in a burst. Teeny pieces of spirit drifted towards the ceiling like dandelion fluff. Once they reached the ceiling, they popped out of existence.

"Ah. I see Ruth has paid you a visit. She's normally rather shy and rarely materialises." Jerome carried two trays. He balanced them both on the chair, then picked up the large wooden bowl from one and slid it into the gap in Lionel's cell door.

Disappointment rolled over Sera at the interruption. Had Ruth been about to unlock her door? It had seemed that way—some part of the ghost had wrapped around the lock. Hopefully, now that she had made contact, she would return.

"Perhaps the novelty of a captured mage brought her here to have a stare." Sera took her tray and set it on the table. "Is she very old? She seemed quite insubstantial and took some time to manifest." The ghost's attire was from hundreds of years ago when women wore simpler gowns. But it could have been a style she'd adopted much later than that. Erin and her crow sisters were fond of kirtles.

Jerome picked up Lionel's tray and sat in the chair previously occupied by Lord Rowan. He appeared keen for conversation. "I don't know how long she's been here. She's not much of a talker. All I know is that Ruth roamed these halls before this house became the Repository. It was one of the reasons Queen Elizabeth and her mages chose this spot—it attracts such phenomena."

"There are probably powerful ley lines running through here. Where exactly is the Repository?" With no memory of her journey, she could have been in Mayfair or Yorkshire.

Jerome huffed and held the empty tray across his knees, his fingers curling around one edge. "You are only a few hours from London, milady."

"In which direction?" His words gave her hope. They were within easy distance of her rescuers. But her emotions must have played across her face.

"I could give you the exact address and it would be useless. No one can find the Repository unless they have been here before." He reached out and ran a hand along the solid stone of the wall.

"Then how does anyone find it?" Magic must shield the building from view. How annoying. But anything cloaked by magic would still leave a trace. A person just needed to know how to look with more than their eyes.

Jerome tapped the side of his nose as though he shared a great confidence. "A new visitor must accompany someone who already knows how to find us. After that, they can journey here on their own."

There was the fly in her soup. But not an irrecoverable situation. She remained confident that Kitty and Hugh would figure out where she was being held.

Eventually.

FIVE

SINCE THE CARETAKER was in a talkative mood, Sera returned to the day's latest visitor as she ate her meal. She didn't think it had been that long since Jerome had carried in breakfast, but Lord Rowan did like the sound of his own voice. The visit must have taken longer than she realised. "Is there more than one ghost here?"

Jerome's old eyes lit up, and he smiled. "Oh, yes. Felix, a Roman centurion, patrols the grounds. He never comes inside. He refers to the house as *the villa,* and I often wonder what it looks like to him. I think he recalls what stood on this spot at the time he died. Felix is an excellent gardener and keeps the hedges trimmed."

Sera wasn't sure whether the caretaker was toying with her or not. "You have a ghost gardener? How is he corporeal enough to pull weeds?" Objectively, the Repository was a fascinating place. Since she was here, she longed to be let out to poke into its corners and uncover its secrets.

Jerome screwed up his face. "I have no idea. All I know is that he can use his short sword to trim shrubbery, and that's enough for me."

"I would like to see that for myself. Will I be allowed to walk the grounds today?" It was worth asking, even if she doubted that Jerome would open her door. Her interview with Lord Rowan hadn't gone as well as the old mage probably hoped. Things like a window, fresh air, and clean clothes were reserved for biddable broodmares, not old nags that bit and kicked.

"No, I am sorry. Lord Rowan was most insistent you are to be kept confined. But I have written to Queen Charlotte, as you requested." He flashed her a sad smile.

That was something, at least. The queen would surely confirm that King George had never signed the order for Sera to be captured and held. Or overrule it if Parliament had voted for her to be the Regent. Thinking of the fierce queen made another worry surge up through her. Lord Rowan had said the queen had other worries on her mind and wasn't bothered by Sera's absence. What had he done?

One problem at a time, Sera. The queen might not have noticed her absence among the throng of courtiers, but she would not ignore a letter. The thought of how long it would take for a response made something Lord Rowan had said spark once more in her mind.

"Lord Rowan said it was the festive season. How

can it possibly be Christmas time already?" She set down her cutlery as cold fear curled through her. It had been mid-November when Abigail had called bearing her poisonous brew. Surely that had been no more than a few days ago? How could a month or more have slipped past unnoticed?

Jerome stared at the tray on his lap. "It is indeed December beyond our walls and blasted cold with it. You'd not want to go outside at the moment, milady. Frost would nibble on your toes."

She drew a steadying breath and picked up her fork. The solid metal in her hand gave her a focus before blind panic could surge forth. A *month* had passed while she had been drowning in an ocean of despair. It had nearly claimed her, but now that she was free of its grip, she would not return. "Since it is not the weather to go outside, could I have a ball, please?"

Jerome's brows crinkled in confusion. "A ball?" he repeated in a hesitant tone, as though he thought he had misheard her.

"Yes. Something small that can pass between the bars, if possible. I thought it might entertain me... and Lionel." She gestured to the lycanthrope, who slurped up the contents of his bowl and then licked the insides.

"You want to play ball with Lionel?" A deep frown furrowed Jerome's forehead, as though he still doubted the reliability of his ears.

"Since Lord Rowan intends to remove the bars between our cells, I thought I might try to engage with my fellow inmate first. A game might make the differ-ence between his tearing my throat out... or not." She tried to make light of the horrible fate that awaited her for defying the old mage, but a tiny hint of hysteria still crept into her voice.

Jerome's eyes widened. He stared at the foot-wide gap in the stone wall, with its thick bars that allowed the inmates to peer into each other's cells. "Surely he did not mean any such thing."

"To be fair, Lord Rowan gave me two options. I either submit to being raped by another mage, or I am thrown to Lionel as some sort of chew toy." Sera kept the quaver from her voice, as fear was overridden by anger. As much as she appreciated Hugh's steadying influence when her temper flared, sometimes rage *was* the appropriate response.

The caretaker's jaw dropped. Apparently, Lord Rowan hadn't shared his breeding programme with the person tending the bloodstock. "I—he—" Jerome's eyes wrinkled almost closed, and he pinched the bridge of his nose between thumb and forefinger. The colour drained from his already pale skin. Then he shook his head and slapped his palms on the tray on his lap.

Sera might have found an unexpected ally in the caretaker. Here was yet another flaw in Lord Rowan's hideous plan. Any more holes and it would leak worse than a sieve, and she would easily slip through. What the old mage intended to do turned the stomachs of honest folk, and that disgust would embolden them to help her. But she wouldn't push Jerome to choose a course of action yet. Let the revelation of what Lord Rowan proposed to do bubble and ferment inside the caretaker until his revulsion became stronger.

Instead, she returned to her original question. "So, could I have a ball, please?"

He blinked and took a long moment to respond, washing his hands over his face first as though trying to remove unpleasant scenes from behind his eyes. "Yes. Is there anything else you require?"

She had rather a long list of demands since the accommodation was barely adequate. But she'd pick the things she thought were most likely to be given to her. "Since I am not allowed outside, could I at least have a potted plant? Something living and green to brighten up my cell?"

Jerome's eyes widened for a moment, and he tapped his fingers against the tray. "We have a conservatory at the rear of the house. I could bring you something from there. Do you have any preference?"

"No. Just something... bushy." She made vague shapes with her hands. "I would also like a change of clothes. Lord Rowan abducted me but failed to pack any luggage."

"The Repository will provide what you need now that it has heard your request. Now, I shall leave you to your meal." He rose from the chair, tucked the empty tray under his arm, and strode back along the corridor, muttering to himself.

After eating the pie and drinking the tea (which had less milk in the pot this time) Sera paced back and forth. Jerome didn't return, but after some time, a gentle thud made her turn around. A red ball bounced along the corridor, thrown by an unseen hand. It passed between the bars and rolled into her cell. She scooped it up with one hand and glanced at the solid door, which had remained closed.

"Where did you come from?" she asked the toy. Roughly fist sized, it resembled the ones she created for children.

Had the Repository made one with its magic in the same way? Ideas burst into her mind—did the Repository have a soul at its centre, like Mistwood? How she longed to have her power returned to her and send it filtering through every stone and timber in the property, to see what she could find.

"Ball?" Lionel rasped, his little-used voice interrupting her thoughts. The shifter reached through their shared bars, his clawed hand swiping the air.

Sera tossed the ball, and it flew between the bars and over Lionel's head. The part-man, part-wolf let out a whoop and leapt backwards, chasing the brightly coloured projectile. A thud and a clatter sounded as the ball bounced off the stone—he must have tripped over his bowl. Then he reappeared with the toy clutched in his paws. With great care, he crouched low and placed it between the bars, and gave it a gentle push to send it back towards Sera. A keen look lit up his eerie gaze.

Sera picked up the ball and tossed it up and down a few inches. "I wonder how long we can do this?" she said, before throwing it over Lionel's head again.

As it transpired, lycanthropes were near inexhaustible when playing fetch. Her arm grew weary of throwing the ball long before Lionel showed any signs of waning interest. When she didn't throw it back, there was such a look of disappointment in his eyes it tugged at her heart, and she had to remind herself the man had taken the lives of three people.

"Tomorrow, we will play more. I am feeling oddly tired." She glanced at the squat teapot. Did it contain more than tea, water, and milk? Was something else responsible for the lethargy sweeping over her limbs? She hoped it was simply boredom and lack of activity that was making her tired.

Sera curled up on the bed and tugged the blankets over her. Sleep came quickly and blanketed her in an inky cloak that held no dreams or imaginings. When she woke some indeterminate amount of time later, a plant in a deep blue ceramic pot sat on the table. Rising, she approached and stroked one glossy leaf. Vaguely heart-shaped, the leaves had visible veins.

"A philodendron. How did Jerome get you in here?" she murmured to the plant.

Then her attention caught on the pile of folded clothing next to it. She shook out a clean green linen gown of a simple design, a chemise, and a shawl. They weren't hers, but they were fresh. How had both plant and clothes appeared in her cell? She did not sleep so deeply that the caretaker could have unlocked her door and crept in without her knowing. There must be unseen hands serving the needs of the inmates.

"Oh, I must learn your secrets now," she murmured to the silent stone enclosing her.

Imagining the Repository as another sentient building like Mistwood Manor gave her brain a mystery to puzzle over and pushed the despair away. If there were two such places in England, there might be more. Vilma had said she wanted to travel the world to find them. Sera couldn't wait to read of the new vampyre's discoveries.

Sera started her day with a wash and a change of outfit. First, she glanced into the adjoining cell, where Lionel was curled up on his bench. Then she stripped off her dress and underthings and washed herself with the tepid water in the jug. After a brisk rub with the cloth, Sera put on the provided clothing.

The dress hung loose and reminded her of the kirtle the ghost Ruth wore. The neckline was a simple slash straight across, and the long sleeves were wider at the bottom and brushed her fingertips. In a moment of whimsy, she thought it might have been similar to what Morag had once worn.

"We both defied king and council, and we will both succeed," she promised the long-deceased woman mage and reassured herself that she would prevail.

Picking up the plant in two hands, Sera set it in the middle of the rug. Then she sat cross-legged before the brilliant blue container. Leaning forward, she placed her palms on either side of the pot, closed her eyes, and concentrated on what she wanted to achieve.

In what seemed like a lifetime ago, Mother Nature

had augmented Sera's gift to enable her not only to complete the pointless task set for mages at the barren tower—growing a single blade of grass—but to exceed the requirement by sprouting an oak. In the cell, Sera was cut off from earth and water. But the plant from the conservatory still contained a spark of nature, even if in a smaller, more confined form.

She used the plant as a conduit, opening herself to any trace of the earth goddess that might linger in its soil. All the while, Sera murmured a prayer to Gaia, asking her to help her daughter in a time of desperate need. A faint tingle washed over Sera's palms and travelled along her arms to her core. Like a spray of stars, it encircled the acorn lying dormant inside her and the seed gave a tiny wiggle. Then the glittering tendril faded away like winter snow under the heat of the sun.

Exhausted, Sera opened her eyes and wiped a bead of sweat from her forehead. While it had worked to a certain extent, the philodendron wasn't large enough to free her magic. "I should have asked for an eight-foot potted palm."

Rising, she placed the plant back on the table, when a low growl from close by made the hairs on the back of her neck stand at alert. Slowly, she turned and approached the space shared with Lionel.

In the middle of the shifter's cell stood a massive wolf. His shoulder easily came to her waist. A frisson of fear rippled over her until she chased it away with curiosity. The creature was covered in thick black fur, interspersed with a lighter grey that shimmered like silver. So soft and inviting did the fur look that she stepped closer, wanting to bury her hands in it. Sera imagined that if she were lost during a snowstorm, she could curl into the wolf's plush fur and stay warm. This was so unlike poor Lionel in his trapped state, with sparse fur that made him look as though he suffered from mange.

What has triggered the shift in forms? There might be a full moon outside, but that implied she had completely lost her sense of night and day. She'd thought it was morning. She didn't need another reminder that the calendar had moved into December without her realising it.

"You are magnificent," she murmured to Lionel. Did he understand her when in his full wolf state?

The wolf growled again, its pale, unblinking gaze focused on her. His jaws were half-open, revealing gleaming canines and sharp incisors.

"I had hoped we could become friends and help each other escape our mutual predicament." What a shame she had missed the change. There might be something to learn from witnessing how the half-man had managed to unleash the entire beast.

Sera slid her hand into the pocket of her gown. It had delighted her to discover deep pockets on each side. One held a particular object she had picked up off the floor. She withdrew the item and held it up before wolf-Lionel.

The growling ceased, and she was certain the wolf

winked at her. Lionel padded to the bars and sat. One ear flopped over as he waited.

"There is no need to throw me to the wolves. They come when I call," she whispered to the sentient building. Then Sera threw the ball into the other cell.

The wolf barked and leapt, chasing the bright red sphere as it bounced off the walls. When he returned to the bars with the ball held in his jaws, he dropped it and then nudged it with his nose to roll it towards Sera.

They were still engaged in fetch when Jerome appeared with breakfast. He set the trays down on the bench and sucked in a breath at the wolf in one cell. A flash of worry crossed the caretaker's eyes. "Hello. I hope you did not argue with Lionel, milady, that he has changed?"

Sera shrugged. "When I woke, he was asleep in his half-state on his bed. Perhaps he dreamt of playing with the ball and this form seemed better suited to the activity?"

Jerome huffed in quiet laughter; his concerns alleviated. "Perhaps. I hope the plant and clothing are suitable."

"Yes. Thank you. I did not hear you enter my cell to deliver them." Sera wiped drool from the ball with her washcloth before returning it to her pocket.

Jerome smiled and slid her tray under the bars. "I didn't."

"Who tends to us in here? Are there ghosts bound in eternal chains of servitude?" The thought horrified her if the servants were not given a respite from their duties even after death.

"I've been here for quite some time and even I haven't figured that out yet. To the best of my knowledge, it is a combination of magic and some creature that is able to move invisibly and pass through walls." The caretaker pushed Lionel's bowl towards the wolf and then stood back as it pounced on the exposed piece of meat.

The ability to move invisibly and pass through walls indicated a ghost to Sera. She let out a frustrated snort. There was so much to learn about this place, and Lord Rowan had cut her off from her ability to peer under its floorboards and between the mortared stones in its walls.

"Is there a full moon outside that Lionel has transformed?" She cast her mind back, trying to remember what phase the moon had been in when she was abducted and where it might be in the sky now.

Jerome shook his head. "No. I wonder if your game has brought the wolf to the surface. I've never met a dog who didn't like to chase a ball."

A low growl came from the other cell, and Sera swallowed a laugh. "Mr Parr, I don't think he likes being called a dog."

Six

THE BEATS of her heart were the only way by which Sera could mark the passage of time. With each gentle thud, she kept her mind occupied and the darkness at bay. Fears and worries swirled deep inside her, but she refused to let them overwhelm her again. How long until Lord Rowan made good on his threats? He had said he would give her a little more time, but would it be days or weeks? With one hand over her chest, she tried to judge how many grains of sand remained in her hourglass.

To fill her time (whatever time meant anymore) she played ball with Lionel and continued to write on the sheets she thought of as her journal, detailing her observations about the lycanthrope and her interactions with him. She wrote descriptions of his appearance alongside his visible mental state, wondering if one influenced the other. Then, she started another sheet about the Repository, detailing all she learned and suspected, from ghosts who did gardening and unseen hands that cleaned her chamber pot, to what she could discern about the unique magic all around her.

The next time Jerome appeared, Sera rushed to the bars and curled her hands around them. "May I go outside today, Mr Parr, please? I want to dig my toes in the dirt and feel the sun on my face."

He huffed a laugh as he delivered Lionel's meal and then hers. "There's no sun outside today, Lady Winyard. Only a frigid, low mist and a few snow flurries."

"I don't care. Snow on my nose is as appealing as wind in my hair or rain on my shoulders." The weather was irrelevant. What mattered was going beyond the four walls that contained her. Sera took her tray and placed it on the table.

His shoulders drooped, and he glanced at the floor. "Lord Rowan has forbidden it."

"You mean the man who abducted me from my home, holds me prisoner against my will when I have committed no crime, and who plans to let either a mage or a lycanthrope force themselves upon me? He is the monster, with his repulsive scheme to use me as a broodmare so he can seize power in England for himself. He is hardly the person to be taking orders from, I would have thought, unless you agree with his intended course of action? Personally, I believe in doing what is morally right." She couldn't hold back the anger that coloured her words.

Jerome lifted his head and tensed his jaw, a multitude of emotions running behind his tired eyes.

"Please? If I do not have some time outside, I shall go mad. If I dash myself against a wall, I will be of no use to Lord Rowan." Not that Lord Rowan needed her mind—only the vessel containing it. For one tiny moment, she allowed the despair to surface in her gaze.

The caretaker thinned his lips, and his shoulders rose as he drew breath to deny her. Those were words she wasn't ready to hear, lest they break through the fragile wall holding back the wave of fear.

"You have already told me that escape is impossible, so what is the concern? I cannot go anywhere," she pleaded.

He exhaled an audible sigh, but as his features relaxed, she saw that a decision had been made. "Do you promise not to try to escape, and to return to your cell when asked?"

Now it was Sera who heaved an exasperated breath. "Let us speak honestly, sir. We both know I fully intend to escape the instant you let me out of this windowless box. But I promise that should my attempt fail, I will return to this cell when summoned back."

He chuckled. "Everyone tries to escape, their first time outside."

"How many succeed?" Did he keep a tally somewhere, recording the names of those who bested the Repository and its defences?

"None." He tugged on the keys attached to his belt.

That knocked the wind from her sails. The others

who had tried to escape most likely weren't mages with determined friends outside the walls. She would be the first to break through its many wards. Perhaps after she left, Jerome could erect a small plaque to mark the day she became the first successful escapee.

"Would you like to finish your breakfast first?" He gestured to the cooling porridge on her tray.

Sera pushed it to one side. "No. I'd rather touch the earth and see the sky."

The caretaker selected a brass key from the chain, unlocked the door, and swung it open. "This way, milady." He swept a bow as she stepped from cell to the corridor. "I will lead you to the front door. It is easy to become lost down here if you're not used to the twists and turns and the way the Repository changes."

Sera stood in the open doorway, the toes of her boots nudging an invisible line. She had no memory of her arrival at the Repository and the path taken to her cell. She couldn't imagine the slight Jerome carrying her unconscious body, but someone must have done it. What would she find beyond the grey, implacable walls? Like a confined bird unsure of whether it retained its ability to use its wings, she hesitated.

Was this who she wanted to become? A captive so used to her prison, she did not fly out even when the door stood open? Reminding herself of her bravado only a few moments ago and her promise to attempt to escape, Sera took one short stride and crossed into the corridor. "Lead on, Mr Parr."

Outside the iron door, they entered a wide hall that

was almost square. Lionel let out a howl as the door swung to, and he was left alone. His protest was abruptly cut off as the metal was sealed shut. Other riveted doors stood along each wall. Not a whisper or shuffle came from beyond and Sera could only guess whether they led to empty cells or any number of imprisoned beings.

"This way." Jerome gestured to a dark shadow beside one door.

Soft yellow lights high on the walls flickered on and off as they moved, illuminating only a few feet in front and a few feet behind them. Now she understood why Jerome had said he would escort her through the building. At times, they took a corner that she swore hadn't been there a moment before. When she looked behind, the hall had vanished. They took a curving flight of stairs upwards, only to step off at the bottom.

Along another dim hall they walked in silence until they arrived at the base of a spiral stair. The light grew stronger with each step and appeared more natural rather than magical. The stairs decanted them into a small foyer painted in restful, deep green tones. Muted light dappled the floor through two tall lead-light windows on either side of the front door. The windows depicted ivy, picked out in different hues of green glass, scrambling up the leadwork. With the dark wood panelling, the space gave Sera the impression of a forest glade.

Jerome gestured to a solid oak door. "It will allow you out."

Her hand shook as she grasped the brass latch and pushed down. The door swung inward to reveal a small porch on the other side. Beyond lay an expanse of green lawn dotted with patches of snow. A lime-chip drive as pale as strewn moonlight swept in a gentle curve towards an ornate iron gate. A stone wall encircled the property. Trees lined the wall like sentries, clipped to either pointed triangles or pillars.

"You might want this." Jerome took down a plain grey woollen cloak from a hook by the door.

"Thank you." Sera wrapped the soft wool around her shoulders and snuggled into its warmth. It was indeed still winter outside, so she had not been imprisoned longer than a season. Nor could it have been a year already. She doubted Lord Rowan would let her sit and do nothing for years when she could be gestating his Nereus. Or some sort of Unnatural experiment.

"I will be in my study when you are ready to return below." Here he gestured to an open door opposite the stairs rising to the first floor. "Most people head straight for the front gate," Jerome murmured as she stepped onto the porch.

Sera was not most people. If everyone headed for the gate, and everyone had failed to escape, then the gate was the *last* place she would try. Stepping down to the gravelled path, she headed to one side, her boots sinking into the soft grass and moist soil below. How she longed to take off her stockings and run barefoot across the lawn, but the winter chill threatened to bite at her toes if she did. Heading directly for the wall, she placed her hands on the stone and let her gaze travel to the top. It seemed to shimmer and move. She estimated it was at least twelve feet high, but when she tried to concentrate on the top stones, they blurred into the sky above.

Next, she ran her hands up and down the blocks, searching for handholds. When she found one and tested it with her weight, the granite shifted under her fingertips and her hand slipped loose. She tried in different areas and at different heights. Always with the same result. Once she found a crevice that seemed as though it should allow her to climb, the wall became as slick as a greased pole.

"Clever wall," she murmured.

There was more than one way to clamber over the obstacle. The surrounding wall was taller than the one that had enclosed the garden at her guardian's home. But no wall was unclimbable. Any child knew that all you needed was the right tree.

Sera paced up and down the front garden. The clipped yews offered no convenient dangling branches that would aid her escape. Perhaps around the back? But first, she would be remiss if she did not, after all, attempt the most obvious exit. She may as well get it over and done with before she looked for a tree to climb.

Striding along the driveway, she stopped before the closed gate. Wrought iron ivy clung to the bars and met in the middle. Sera reached out and as her hand neared the metal, her fingertips prickled in awareness of the ensorcellments used. Gritting her teeth against whatever spell kept the gate locked, she grasped the bar. A jolt shot up her arm and shoved her backwards. She landed on her bottom on the sharp lime chips covering the driveway.

A man emerged from the gatehouse built into the side of the wall. Bundled up in a green wool greatcoat and with a hat pulled low on his brow, he stared at her through the iron ivy. "Everyone thinks they can walk out the gate, miss. But if you're not allowed to leave, it won't let you."

"A warning tingle might be useful before it knocks someone off their feet." She picked a piece of gravel from her palm and stood.

Bundled up against the cold, the man rubbed his chilled hands together. "It does, if you go slow. Most of 'em just push a hand close to the bars and it's enough to scare 'em away. Not many grab hold all of a sudden like that."

"I don't do things half-heartedly." A grudging respect for the mages who had layered the spells over the property emerged inside Sera. But she was not defeated yet.

"Have a good day, miss." The gatekeeper chuckled to himself as he wandered back to his warm little cottage.

Sera turned and surveyed the house and grounds. Built of a pale grey stone and a plain rectangular design, its two storeys hunkered into the landscape.

The Repository of Forgotten Things looked like any other modest country estate built in the last two hundred years. There wasn't the tiniest hint of what it contained behind its rustic facade.

"Jerome mentioned a conservatory," she muttered as she walked back along the drive and then around one side of the house.

A shadow darted between two trees, and she slowed her pace. A form made of mist stood beside a triangular-shaped yew. This spirit was more corporeal than Ruth, who had visited her in the cells. The woman who was tethered to the house had to concentrate to make herself visible or to communicate. This ghost had a clear form. And feet—clad in leather and metal sandals. The leather strips of his kilt swayed back and forth with his movement. She could even make out the buckles on his shoulders that were attached to his metal breastplate. He had a square face and, somewhat aptly, a Roman nose.

"Good morning," Sera said, wondering if the spirit could talk.

"Domina." The centurion thumped his right hand over his chest. "I am Felix Densus, centurion of the Twelfth Legion of the Emperor Tiberius."

"I am pleased to make your acquaintance, Felix." How refreshing to talk to a coherent spirit rather than one that screeched at her. Why did he retain so much of his former self, when far younger spirits did not? It had to be more than the unique aura of the Repository, for that would have allowed Ruth to cling to more of herself. "Do you care for the gardens here?"

"I am stationed here until my legion returns for me. I have been entrusted with the safekeeping of the villa until the emperor arrives in this land." Lines furrowed his brow, and his outline shimmered as he pondered the return of his cohort.

"The villa?" Sera stared at the plain building and tried to imagine a grand Roman villa with white walls and a red tile roof in its place.

Felix nodded. "The emperor will visit one day, and everything must be ready when he does." He ran his short sword along the neat edge of the tree and a smattering of greenery fluttered to the grass. "Until then, I patrol the grounds, Domina. While you may take your exercise here, I am not permitted to escort you beyond the walls of the compound. It is not safe beyond for a lone woman."

The compound? The ghost must see the world as it had been when he died, and not the one he now haunted. But then why did he maintain the hedges? She couldn't imagine they had been standing along the walls when the Romans invaded England. Not that she was any expert on Roman gardens. Perhaps the villas of wealthy citizens did have such clipped topiaries in their gardens.

"Today, I am only exploring, so I shall not require your services, Felix." Nor did she think ghostly hands would be much use if she needed a leg up a tree.

The centurion bowed and dissolved back into a

yew, his short sword the last thing to wriggle into the greenery. Sera continued around the side of the house. To her delight, the rear did indeed have a glassed conservatory with a roof that curved back to meet the top floor of the Repository. She could barely see inside, so crammed was the interior with palms, orchids, and other humidity-loving flora.

The grass here was unkempt, and the ragged edge ran into longer grass with seed heads long since spent. The withered carcasses clung to stems in defiance of any icy blast. Trees were clustered closer together here. Surely one would provide access over the wall.

The back portion of the walled garden was given over to a thick forest, its deciduous trees with bare, intertwined branches looking like skeletons hanging onto one another. In summer, when covered with thick leaves, they would provide dappled protection for the ferns and flowers below.

She walked with a slow tread, savouring the sting of cold air in her nostrils and the scent of damp earth. With each tree she passed, Sera pressed a hand to the bark to learn how each differed from its neighbours. At one point, the densely packed oak, beech, and birch gave way to a small glade. A few headstones were dotted among the remains of wildflowers. Sera paused and clasped her hands together, wondering at the lives of the souls who were buried here. Had they become the ghosts haunting the house and grounds?

Another day she would attempt to read the worn lettering to see if Ruth rested among them. She pushed on to locate the wall once more. In a back corner, she found an ancient beech tree, its weathered silver trunk large enough to shelter a farm animal if hollowed out. Its form was gnarled and twisted from centuries of growth as it spread multiple branches out towards the Repository and... over the wall.

Sera left her borrowed cloak hanging on a branch. She would miss its warmth, but it would hamper her climb. Then she tucked up her skirts and scrambled up the wide branches until she reached the one that jutted out. A giggle welled up, and she chuckled to herself as she stood. With arms outstretched for balance, Sera walked along the branch towards freedom.

How odd that even this close, she couldn't see what lay on the other side. A thick mist obscured whatever house, garden, or farmyard abutted the Repository. The image was smeared as though rain had ruined a water-colour landscape.

"Must be the magical barrier, keeping the curious out from both sides." No matter. Once on the other side, she would soon figure out where outside of London they had taken her.

Closer and closer, she inched along the branch. The top of the wall was almost directly beneath her now. From up here, the stones were nearly a foot thick and provided ample room for a cat to sunbathe or a person to sit. She took a moment to consider her next course of action. It would probably be best to step onto the wall, and then try to climb down the other side. If both sides of the stone had the smoothing spell, she would have to drop and hope that snow and damp earth broke her fall.

Decision made, Sera drew a breath and stretched one leg down and forward to place her foot on the capstone. Her boot touched its solidity. Triumph surged through her limbs as Sera placed her weight on her leg and moved her other foot from tree to wall. With two feet on the wall, she squinted to make out the ground beneath her on the other side... and freedom.

SEVEN

As Sera's foot stepped over the wall, a bolt fiercer than the one emitted by the gate shot through her. An invisible wire made of lightning encircled her body, pinning her arms by her sides. She let out a scream of shock as stabs of blazing pain pierced her body. Then the protection ward flung her backwards. Through the chill air she tumbled. Her mind forgot she had no magic and instinct summoned a buoyancy spell to her scrambling hands. It took only the span of a heartbeat before she landed with a thud at the base of the beech.

Fortunately, the densely packed leaf litter provided an inch of protection from the solid ground. Winded, Sera lay on her back with tears trickling from her eyes and stared up through the skeletal boughs. Everything hurt, even the breath she tried to draw into her lungs. The seconds ticked by, and the tears froze on her skin. Wiggling her hands and toes, she reassured herself that nothing was broken. Then she uttered a string of profanities that would have made Elliot blush. Even if he had taught them to her several years ago.

She wanted to meet the mage who had constructed the bindings in the walls and gates. Her only problem was deciding if she wanted to buy the person responsible an ale or punch him in the face.

Since she was stretched out like a supplicant, an idea formed in her head. One that she should have tried *first*, and that shouldn't result in her being struck by a thousand tiny barbs of lightning. Ignoring the damp chill soaking through her gown, Sera reached out and dug her nails through the decaying leaves and into the dirt below. She imagined her fingers were roots, extending down through the earth. Once more, she closed her eyes and focused on the dormant acorn inside her. All the while, she whispered an entreaty to Mother Nature, begging for the goddess to come to her aid.

Perhaps it was the presence of the ancient beech that helped, with its roots spreading far and wide. Or it might have been because Sera clutched mounds of dirt in her hands. But this time, an answering tendril sprouted up from deep beneath her. With a gentle touch that soothed her bruised limbs, it swirled around her body and burrowed inside her. Like a light-seeking length of ivy, the tendril speared through to her core and coiled around her dormant seed of magic. The shoot sent from Gaia reared back and delicately tapped the kernel as though it gently knocked on a closed bedroom door to rouse a sleeper. A hairline crack raced around the seed's surface and, its task complete, the tendril retreated through Sera and sank into the earth.

Sera let out a whoop of joy and grinned, ignoring the chatter of her teeth from the cold.

Lord Rowan might have cut her off from reaching for her gift, but he'd failed to stop magic from reaching out to her. Now she had only to nurture the seedling within her. With a little time and tender care, it would grow into a mighty oak once more.

When she began to shiver, Sera rose, collected the grey cloak, and walked back to the front door of the house. After batting dirt, leaves, and melting snow from her clothes before entering, she reported to Jerome in his study.

A wry smile touched his lips at the sight of her. "I am sorry you were unsuccessful."

Today she was unsuccessful, at least in one respect. Tomorrow presented another opportunity.

He escorted her back to her cell, and Sera struggled to contain her good mood. "Thank you, Mr Parr. I wonder if tomorrow I might be allowed to sit in the conservatory? I'm finding myself a bit sore after trying to breach both gate and wall and would relish its warmth in my bones."

He chuckled. "I have no objection to that, milady, now that you have tested the boundaries of the Repository and discovered for yourself that she will not let you go."

"Is there a library here?" The idea occurred to her as Jerome locked the door behind her.

"Yes. Do you wish more books to read? If you have a favourite author or topic, I am happy to see what I can find on the shelves or request a copy for you." He gestured to the three volumes stacked by her bed.

"Oh, Mr Parr." Just when Sera was beginning to like the man, he failed to grasp the importance of a library. "It's not about just wanting another book to read. A library feeds one's soul. You breathe in all those words. There is a unique scent to leather, paper, and ink. To simply stand in one, and be surrounded by the worlds and ideas held within!"

As she spoke, Sera closed her eyes, spread out her arms, and turned a slow circle. In her mind, she stood in a library of her own construction. Shelves soared over her head. A narrow walkway would give access to the upper half. A ladder on brass wheels would be used on the lower level. What bliss.

He shook his head. "I was never a big reader. As a lad, we used to throw dice to entertain ourselves. I'd much rather study the form of a sleek greyhound. That is one thing I miss being in here—the dog races."

Sera stopped spinning and stared at the caretaker. "Can you not leave here, either?"

"One day, when I pass my position on to another, I will walk out of the gate and not return. Until then, I confine myself to the boundaries of the Repository." He patted the stone wall as he spoke as though he addressed an old friend.

That puzzled her. If you could leave a place, why wouldn't you? Even monks didn't spend their entire lives in the monastery and occasionally went out into the world. "Do you not wish to visit London, or see the attractions about town?"

A sad expression dropped over his face. "When you have been here a long time, it is painful to see the world advance beyond the gate. And so, I keep to myself."

"How long, Mr Parr?" she whispered.

He stood a bit taller and puffed out his chest. "Queen Elizabeth herself appointed me to this position when she created the Repository in 1560."

Sera stared at him. He had kept his post for over two hundred years. No wonder he didn't want to go out into the surrounding area. Any friends or family he'd once had were long in their graves. The Virgin Queen had sentenced him to decades of loneliness.

"Did you know of this when you took on the role?" What drove a man to accept a position that cut him off from the world and everything he knew? Or had the queen punished him for some terrible crime by banishing him to the Repository?

He heaved a sigh and sat on the chair opposite her cell. "The mages told me that time would move differently here, but they didn't know exactly how, nor did I care. I only wanted to escape that world. Over the years, I have learned just what it means when time moves *differently*."

"But surely you could have a greyhound as a companion. Or does the Repository not allow pets?" Any objection would be odd, given that Lionel was a magnificent specimen of a wolf and from what she understood, there were probably other such Unnaturals elsewhere on the property.

"I'd not keep a creature meant to run trapped in such a small garden." His words were tinged with longing and sadness. She wondered what canine ran through his memories.

She bit her tongue since the irony of his own statement had flown over his head. She was meant to run, yet here she languished. "There are smaller and less active dogs. A spaniel, for example, would be quite content to sleep at your feet."

"Perhaps I will ask for one. Or a cat." He winked at her.

"There is no cat here? *There* is an omission that needs to be remedied immediately. Every mysterious magical place requires a cat." Sera shook her head. Imagine a place like the Repository not having a cat to prowl the ever-changing corridors, or hiss at the ghouls as they passed through the walls.

After Jerome had gone, Sera settled on the bed and closed her eyes. Once more she delved deep inside herself to where the kernel of her power slumbered. A faint glow issued from the fissure and the tingle seeped into her blood. Even as she held the seed in her mind, the crack made by Mother Earth opened a fraction more, and the glow intensified.

"Soon," she murmured. She had only to be patient —not a trait of hers, but she would have to learn.

Lord Rowan's spell had been broken, and her gift awakened. It simply needed a little time to be fully restored and ready to answer her command. Rather like Elliot if he were roused too early in the morning.

Satisfied that it was only a matter of time until she reached her full power, Sera turned her attention to the spell used by Lord Rowan. If not for her connection to the earth goddess, she wondered if her gift might have been trapped forever. Where had the old mage found a curse that could strip another mage's power and place it beyond their reach?

As she contemplated what sort of revenge to wreak upon the former Speaker of the Mage Council, she decided there would be poetic justice in tangling him up in his own spell. She would need to figure out how to do it without Abigail singing the words that activated it once ingested.

Time lost all meaning as she tried to tease apart the components of the spell, but without her full gift, the effort exhausted her while yielding very little return. Casting a spell upon a mage left a mental imprint similar to a tattoo. Her body would be able to recall the effects long after she had banished it from her form. But it frustrated her that she had less magic than a seventh-generation aftermage.

"Patience," she scolded herself. It had taken her years to escape Lord Branvale, but she was certain she would be free of Lord Rowan's prison in a much shorter time. Days, she promised both herself and her friends.

Without her full gift, she couldn't use her mage silver ring to contact them. At least Lord Rowan had left her the necklace tucked under her chemise. He would have thought the pendant was nothing of importance. She curled the silver disc in her hand, the physical manifestation of Hugh's kiss. Touching the warm metal reminded her that she was loved.

She also still had the autumn leaf. Her key to Shadowvane and the Fae realm. As soon as she escaped the Repository, Sera would need to lie low for a time, until Lord Rowan tired of searching for her. She would travel to the other realm and confront Lord Branvale's secret correspondent—who had told her of the Nereus.

As Sera sat on the floor guiding Lionel through some deep breathing to relax his state, the familiar clang of the heavy door heralded footsteps along the corridor. Two sets today. Sera assumed that Lord Rowan had returned to lecture her, or to see if she had miraculously become meek and mild. Leaning against the bars at her back, she used them to rise to her feet while thinking of witty retorts. The words dried on her tongue when she saw her visitor.

Lord Tomlin.

"No," she whispered, her heart racing.

He wore a grey greatcoat over a brown jacket and looked like a country squire paying a visit to his tenant. There were even mud spatters on his boots.

"Lady Winyard," he muttered as he struggled to

pull his arms from the sleeves of his greatcoat. Once he wrestled himself free, he threw the bulky item on the chair. He ran one hand through his hair and stared at the slate floor, unsure what to do with himself. He shuffled from foot to foot.

Jerome stood to one side, his lips set in a thin line. Sera glanced at the caretaker, wondering what role he would play. Then she clasped her hands together and steeled her spine. Sadly, she was no magical match for Lord Tomlin in her current condition. The flow of her gift was a mere trickle. But she vowed one thing— he would not succeed in his disgusting task. The pencil on the table could remove an eye as easily as a spell.

Finally, the other mage spoke, but he refused to look at her, instead focusing on the toes of his damp boots. "Lord Rowan sent me. I am sure you find the task he proposes as objectionable as I do. But we have an unprecedented opportunity before us." Now he turned with a fevered light in his eyes. "Can you imagine passing augmented power to our offspring, instead of our grandchildren receiving a watered-down talent? And that strength never diminishes. I shall establish the first magical dynasty and my bloodline will be immortal."

Sera curled her hands into fists. He thought only of himself. Why were some men so hungry for power that it overrode basic morality? "No, you won't. For a number of reasons. Firstly, Mother Nature places limits on her mages for a reason." There would be no Tomlin dynasty of powerful mages. That was a tale Lord Rowan had spun to appeal to his disciple.

The old mage had made it clear that he would take any such babe to use its magic as soon as it was born. That part of the plan obviously hadn't been shared with Lord Tomlin. They were both to be used by the former Speaker of the Mage Council.

Lord Tomlin scoffed and waved a hand through the air. "Lord Rowan says it is true. The necessary horrid bit will only take a moment, and for that, I shall live eternally through my line."

Sera stared at him. *A moment?* Conflicting emotions rose in her. Relief that she wouldn't have to endure his company for hours. Then sadness for Tomlin's new bride. Hugh was a considerate and most *thorough* lover, who took his time to ensure she was utterly satisfied.

"What does your wife think of this venture?" Sera palmed the pencil off the table and held it in the folds of her skirt.

Jerome remained silent, his face unreadable. A low, warning growl came from Lionel's cell. Lord Tomlin kept glancing at the misshapen creature, now returned to his half form.

"At this juncture, I have deemed there no need for her to know. If you would, Mr Parr, let us get the deed done. I do have other demands on my time today." Lord Tomlin gestured to the locked door.

Sera's breath came short in her chest. Tomlin would most likely use magic to restrain her, so she would have to strike first. The pencil jammed into his eye or ear would slow him down. A knee to the groin would stymie his intentions. Her rage would summon enough of her gift to give the blow extra force.

Lionel continued to growl. The shifter, now in his full wolf form, pressed his snout through the bars. Saliva dripped from his canines as he fixed his attention on Lord Tomlin.

Jerome tugged at the set of keys hanging from his belt. He fanned them out on his palm and stared at them. "Blast these old eyes. It takes a while to find the right one. We don't usually open these doors once an inmate is in residence, you see, milord."

As Sera watched the caretaker fumble for the correct key, a far simpler diversion occurred to her. "While you are here, Mr Parr, I require more rags."

The caretaker paused in the act of trying to fit an obviously wrong key into the lock. "Rags, milady?"

Bother. He might not understand the reference. "Yes. I have soiled the ones you gave me yesterday, and I have nowhere to wash them in here. Since Lord Rowan cut me off from my magic, I have no other avenues available to me to deal with my monthly courses."

Understanding lit the caretaker's eyes. "Of course, milady. I shall fetch a fresh supply once I have unlocked the door for Lord Tomlin."

"Monthly courses?" Lord Tomlin repeated the words as though they were spoken in a language foreign to him.

Sera guessed he was utterly ignorant in matters pertaining to the female body. He probably believed a woman on her courses would curdle milk. "Yes, Lord Tomlin. I am bleeding."

"Bleeding?" The mage's face turned a puce colour, and his mouth opened and shut. He took a step backwards as though her condition were contagious. Or he expected a sea of red to wash under the bars.

His obvious disgust made Sera warm to the topic. "Most profusely, too. I imagine it is the stress of being imprisoned making my flow so voluminous and... *chunky*."

The colour drained from Lord Tomlin's face, and his chest jerked as though he was about to be sick.

"I am surprised Lord Rowan sent you. Women are not fertile at this point in their cycle. But I wonder if he thought to give you a bit of practice first? Or do you have previous experience in raping unwilling women?" She stepped to the bars, her hand curling tight around the hidden pencil. Anger blazed in her eyes as she dared him to reply.

He scoffed weakly. "Obviously, circumstances are not conducive to the required task. I shall inform Lord Rowan and return in two weeks' time." Lord Tomlin searched his pockets for a handkerchief and held it over his mouth and nose, as though he could smell blood. Then he grabbed his overcoat and stormed along the corridor.

"I'll show you the way out, milord," Jerome called. Light sparkled in his eyes, and he winked at Sera.

Once the door slammed, Sera tossed the pencil back on the table and turned to her companion. "Thank you, Lionel, for your protection. A shame you could not bite Lord Tomlin's retreating bottom."

The wolf pressed his body to the shared stretch of bars. Sera reached out and stroked the fur on his neck, soft as any finely spun silk. As she caressed the thick fur, her mind spun with the implications of Lionel's co-operation. There might now be a way to escape her fate.

Eight

Sᴇʀᴀ's pounding heart had returned to a steady rate by the time Jerome returned. His hand shook as he unlocked Sera's cell and swung open the bars. "I will not be a party to the horror Lord Rowan intends, Lady Winyard. You have bought yourself a little time while we wait for a response from Queen Charlotte."

"The queen has still not replied?" Worry gnawed at Sera. She respected the queen and her advocacy for the women in her court. What had Lord Rowan done that had silenced the queen on the matter of Sera's imprisonment?

"No. But after the events of today, I shall write again. We cannot waste a moment. I thought you might like to sit in the conservatory to gather your thoughts. I can have a tray waiting for you there." He gestured for her to follow.

"Thank you, Mr Parr. I would like that." She

rubbed her hands up and down her arms to remove a chill that had nothing to do with the temperature.

The caretaker showed her along narrow, dark corridors. Then up a steep set of stairs that reminded her of the servants' stairs in Lord Branvale's Mayfair mansion. The next corridor they turned into was wider, with light spilling through cut-glass double doors at the end. He pushed the doors open and Sera gasped.

The external view had not done it justice. While not large, the conservatory contained such a dense mix of greenery she thought she had stepped into a tropical forest. Palms in beaten copper pots had fronds that nearly brushed the high glass ceiling. Orchids with sprays of flowers were interspersed among ferns, gardenia, philodendrons, and many other heat-loving plants. Some hung from hooks and draped over the sides of their pots, dangling foliage like fingers trailing in a river. Water spilt from a plaque attached to the wall and bubbled into a pond no larger than a child's bath.

As she had seen, the conservatory faced the wild area of the Repository's park, its glass walls curving back towards the side of the stone building. A round table was positioned in dappled light and had two cane chairs with thick padded cushions.

"A tray shouldn't be too far away and will probably appear while you explore the conservatory. I shall leave you to your contemplations. I want to have another letter to the queen in the gatekeeper's hands within the hour." Jerome bowed and retreated through the cut-glass doors.

Sera inhaled the rich, earthy scent. Heat wafted over her skin. Plants were laid out in borders around the edge of the conservatory. A path curved around a bed in the middle, shaped somewhat like the number eight, with two rounded beds that met in the middle. She spent some time touching the plants, digging her fingertips into the soil to check moisture levels, and dead-heading spent blooms.

Only when her hands were dirty, and she had a pile of leaf litter to sweep outside did she drop into one of the chairs. Closing her eyes, Sera relished her surroundings and let the peaceful atmosphere sink into her skin. The gentle exhalations of plants calmed the anxiety that tore through her from Lord Tomlin's visit.

Quiet time in the conservatory was exactly what she needed to plot her next move, heal her gift, and nurture the seedling within into more extravagant growth. With her focus drawn inside her, it took some moments for Sera to realise that a chill had blown over her skin, chasing aside the heady warmth of the conservatory. Opening her eyes, she found the spirit of Ruth hovering a few feet away. The outline of a palm was clearly visible through her spectral form.

"Hello. You look a little more solid today. Let me see if I can help you communicate." As though she recovered from an injury, Sera's magic trickled slowly, almost sluggishly, through her. Yet she was still able to release a gossamer-thin tendril towards the ghost, giving her form a little more substance.

Magic scattered over the ghost like stardust, and

Ruth's features filled in. Her sockets were no longer empty, luminous green eyes regarded Sera with curiosity. The curve of her gown's neckline was distinguishable on her form. The rest of her body remained insubstantial mist lacking feet, but there was only so much Sera could do.

"Jerome says you have been here a long time." On her previous visit, Ruth had pointed at Sera and said *out*. Hopefully, she might now expand on that single syllable.

The spirit didn't answer. She drifted closer and the delicate fronds of a maidenhair fern shivered as she passed.

"Are you trapped here?" Did the magic that stopped Sera from climbing the wall also mean the spirits could not ascend to the next realm?

As she neared, more details about Ruth became clearer. Two small braids kept her hair off her face and tumbled down behind her ears. She bore an odd mark on her collarbone. Sera squinted. It appeared to be a tattoo of some sort. A squiggly O perhaps, or a rune of some sort?

Ruth raised her arm and pointed at Sera. "Witch."

Really? Sera rolled her eyes. Even in the Repository, she couldn't escape such nonsense. Before she could say anything, Ruth angled her arm to point to herself. "Witch."

Ah. Now that was interesting. "You're a witch, too?" She couldn't mean a mage, surely. Perhaps in life,

Ruth had been a powerful aftermage, the grand-daughter of a mage. Like Abigail.

"Book." Ruth pointed back through the doors to the main part of the Repository.

Sera took a moment to decide what that might mean. She doubted the ghost wanted a bit of reading material. Nor was it likely the Repository library held a book detailing how to break the wards encircling the place. "There's a book about you here?"

"Ruth. Book," she murmured, then drifted through a *Dracaena trifasciata*, or snake plant. The spiky shoots morphed into a sort of bodice on Ruth. All she needed was a ruffled fern to create a skirt to appear a spectre drawn from nature.

"I shall ask Jerome if I might have time in the library and look for the book about you." At least it would give Sera something else to do while she tried to find a way to break whatever spell held Lionel in his half state, and her power returned to full effect to allow her to blast her way out.

"Out." This time Ruth pointed from Sera to the overgrown garden beyond the glass wall.

"You can help me escape?" Sera dared hope that the ghost offered solidarity among magical sisters. Although if the spectre couldn't break free of the Repository, could she be of any real help to Sera?

"Free." Ruth floated closer to the curved wall and raised spectral hands. Where she rested her palms on the glass, it frosted around them.

"I would be most grateful for your assistance if you

can show me a way to be free." If the woman had haunted the spot for hundreds of years, she might know of a secret tunnel or door that led to the other side of the wall.

Ruth tapped on the French door and floated back and forth, somewhat like a dog anxious to be let outside.

Sera rose and flung open the double doors on the hibernating garden with its smattering of snowy patches clinging to the shorter bits of lawn. As Ruth left the conservatory, her form dimmed, and became less substantial. Closing the doors behind her to protect the humidity-loving plants, Sera stepped out onto the icy terrace.

"Where to now?" she asked the shade.

Ruth drifted towards the trees. As she moved farther from the house, she diminished in size until she was no more than a ball of wispy light, darting among tree trunks. Branches stripped bare of their leaves reached for Sera, snagging on her hair and clothing. She batted them away as they moved deeper into the overgrown part of the Repository's garden. Cold seeped into her bones, and she wished she had thought to bring the shawl.

The luminous ball danced over a particular spot of dense undergrowth in the corner opposite Sera's thwarted escape attempt. Brambles and ferns were intertwined over the space. Sera breathed the damp loamy odour of the earth as she pulled bracts away. The plants had covered something, using the structure to grow higher. Wrapping her hand in her skirt, she yanked on a stubborn rose cane and revealed a piece of stone.

"What is this? Perhaps the marker to a secret tunnel." Excitement grew inside her as she brushed aside foliage and broke off branches obscuring the object.

A faint trickle of magic allowed her to push the remaining shrubs and climbers out of the way. Before her stood a stone, about waist high and with a curved top. Covered in lichen and moss, it appeared that a few words were etched on the surface. Sera flattened her hands against the stone and whispered to the letters to make themselves visible. When she removed her hands, she could just make out:

Ruth Newell

1402 – 1448

Sera sat back on her heels. The stone marked Ruth's grave in the isolated and long-forgotten spot at the Repository.

"Is this what you mean by escaping—death?"

The wisp floated up and down. This far from the house, Ruth had lost both form and voice.

"That's not funny. Nor do I need to point out that dying wasn't an escape for you. Your soul is still bound to this place."

Then Ruth's whispered words echoed through her

mind. *Ruth. Book.* Perhaps there was something in the book that explained why the woman was buried in the isolated spot, and what had bound her soul to the house. Was Ruth merely seeking Sera's help to be free, rather than offering a way for the mage to escape?

Glancing around, she estimated they were in the back corner of the Repository. Two sides of the wall were visible through the skeletal trees. She would ask Jerome for some time in the library to find any book mentioning Ruth, then she would return.

As much as Sera wanted to help the spirit move on, her own escape had to take priority. While Lord Tomlin was woefully ill-informed about women's health, even he might not believe she stayed on her courses for weeks or months.

Standing, she rested one hand on the grave marker. "Now that I know this spot, it will be easier to find again. Let us return to the house where it is warmer, and you are more substantial."

Sera retraced her steps, taking note of the trees as she passed. The wisp floated alongside her. The light wavered like a guttering candle and before they broke free of the forest, it winked out.

Back in the damp heat of the conservatory, she found a tray with a steaming pot of hot chocolate, a mug, and a scone with butter melting off one side. After pouring herself a drink, she curled up in the cane chair.

Sera toasted the air. "Thank you."

Her mind itched for access to books to discover what sort of creature served the residents and inmates of the Repository. They moved without being seen and provided exactly what she needed. How many years would it take to unpick every secret of the strange building? Well, if she had to be trapped, at least there were ways to occupy her mind.

A pang shot through her heart. She missed her friends. What sort of life would she have if she never kissed Hugh again, or heard Kitty make a sharp retort, or tasted the divine cakes Rosie made? Good grief, she even missed Elliot and his impertinent remarks.

Ruth did not reappear. Had the spirit exhausted itself by venturing so far from the house? More than ever, Sera was determined to escape. Then, she needed a way to return to learn the secrets hiding in the walls that held her.

After a pleasant afternoon in the conservatory quietly nurturing the acorn inside her, the light dimmed outside, and it was time for her to return to her cell.

Jerome had said she would be guided back and issued warnings not to wander off, or she might become lost. While part of her wanted to challenge that assertion (the Repository didn't look *that* big from the outside), she had seen enough to wonder how so many long halls, twisty stairwells, and rooms could be crammed under its roof.

At the conservatory doors, she peered back along the gloomy hall and called, "Hello? I'm ready to go back now."

A scuttling made her glance down. A mouse sat at

her feet. It reared up on its hind legs, twitched its nose at her, then dropped to the ground and made a zigzag line down the hall. After a few feet, it stopped and turned to stare at her.

"I assume you are my guide?" She walked after the creature, and it continued on its way and around a corner.

"Makes sense, I suppose. Who better to know the layout of a building than those who live within its walls?" She followed her tiny guide along halls and down a flight of twisted stairs. At the bottom, the mouse continued in one direction. A dark corridor in the other tugged at Sera's mind.

Once the mouse trotted partly down the lit corridor, Sera placed one foot in the direction of the dark one. After a short distance, no more than three steps, the darkness fell so deeply over her that she couldn't see her hands in front of her face. Turning, she found the entrance had likewise disappeared. A moment of panic climbed up her throat. Which way?

Rubbing her hands together failed to generate so much as a spark. Now, that was a concern.

She had barely gone more than one or two yards. The corridor and stairs should have been obvious. Trusting her instincts, she took a careful footstep and walked into a wall. Impossible. Reaching out, her hands found that what should have been open space behind her was now a solid wall, too.

A squeak drew her attention. The mouse sat at her feet, its tiny eyes pulled into slits. Which she could see since the mouse glowed, its fur emitting a faint golden hue.

"I turned the wrong way," Sera muttered as the mouse squeaked again.

It took far more than three steps to return to the base of the stairs. They also went around a corner that hadn't been there when she'd ventured into the corridor. Lesson learned. At least for today. She didn't deviate again from the mouse's path.

Finally, they reached the heavy, riveted door that led to her cell. The mouse sat and waited as she pulled it open. Not many prisons operated on the honour system, asking prisoners to return to their cells without armed escorts. But if the prison could change around them and trap them in an impenetrable dark, it reduced the likelihood of unauthorised explorations.

Sera dropped to the padded seat of the chair that Jerome had left from Lord Rowan's visit. She wasn't quite ready yet to put herself back in her cage. While the heavy door typically locked itself once closed, she remembered a simple way to defeat some spells—stick to the ordinary.

On one of her forays into the forest, Sera had placed a smooth, rounded stone in her pocket. It now acted as a doorjamb so that the riveted door couldn't seal itself. Somehow, in a process that truly was magical, a faint breeze blew through the two-inch opening.

Lionel lay asleep on his back, one arm thrown up over his head. But this time there was no mix of canine and human features. His hand possessed long, elegant fingers. Rounded ears poked out from his shaggy hair. His chest displayed sculpted muscles with a triangle of dark hair at the base of his throat. Even his calves were well formed and would have turned heads when clad in silk stockings and knee breeches.

This was his human form. The books were right. Lycanthropes did have a physique worthy of being immortalised in marble. Of course, so did Hugh. Her hands warmed as she remembered the feel of his wide chest under her touch and how she could run a fingertip along the edge of a pectoral muscle.

Lionel hardly stirred and made no noise. If it hadn't been for the steady rise and fall of his chest, she might have worried he had expired during the night. Jerome had said that only in the deepest sleep did he return to his natural form. Was emotion the key to his troubled transformation process?

In sleep, Lionel was fully relaxed and shifted back to his human form. High emotion, like the enjoyment of playing ball or knowledge of a full moon, triggered the appearance of the wolf. Did some form of anxiety trap him between the two forms? Pondering that, she returned to her cell and waited for Jerome.

"Why are you stuck in between?" she murmured, not expecting a response. Had he been afflicted since he was first bitten, or had some other event affected his ability to change forms?

There was no doubt he could shift from sculpted human to magnificent wolf with ease. The problem was what happened in the middle. She had taught him a simple breathing exercise that helped. Each time they tried, he managed to peel away a little more of the wolf and become more human.

"Hurts," Lionel rasped.

Her head snapped up at the unexpected sound. Beside her, he had roused and moved to slump against his bars. He scratched long claws up his arm, leaving deep red marks.

"Hurts," he repeated.

"The change hurts?" She was growing a little tired of monosyllabic conversations. Why weren't supernatural creatures more articulate?

NINE

WHEN SERA EXPLAINED to Jerome that the stone wedging the door open allowed faint bursts of fresh air into their cells, he allowed it to stay in place. But he did make her solemnly promise that she wouldn't wander off on her own along the capacious corridors.

A day or two later (or so it seemed to Sera), Lionel lay on the floor with his arms stretched over his head. The lycanthrope drew deep, even breaths through his nose. As his body and mind relaxed, the sprouted fur disappeared back beneath his skin and his musculature filled out. No longer did he possess hairy knuckles when he curled his long fingers into fists and stretched them out again.

Breathing had been Sera's idea since he was able to resume his full human form in sleep and high emotion triggered the wolf. If anxiety had kept Lionel trapped in a half-form, pain from the incomplete shift had probably augmented his reluctance to change fully in either direction.

As she sat, thoughts swirled through Sera's mind with the faintly wafting breeze from outside, and with it, a daring idea took shape. "Lionel, what is your sense of smell like?"

"Excellent. Rain has fallen." His voice had a raspy edge due to long disuse, but he now managed to string together more words than his previous monosyllabic answers.

"Could you use it to find your way through the Repository to the outside?" She tried to keep the question light, even as her stomach clenched at asking it.

"As wolf. Yes." With a slow roll of his spine, Lionel sat up. His pale gaze fixed on her face. His jawline was square, with a faint shadow of stubble that made Sera realise he never shaved. Since he didn't have a razor for such an activity, either their invisible attendants shaved him at night, or the Repository wove some process that stopped him from growing a full beard.

A tingle started in her toes and crept up her calves. He could get them out. Sera knew her time was running out. Lord Tomlin would return, and who knew what sort of chains he might wrap her in, to advance Lord Rowan's revolting scheme. She was certain her body now contained sufficient magic to open the front gate. She could be strolling down the street in a matter of minutes. An hour at the most.

But could she trust Lionel?

"I would have to set you free." The lock of his cell

wouldn't be much of an impediment to her. Tiny mechanisms were her specialty, and she enjoyed crafting minute slivers of magic to coax them open.

"Yes." He thumped one hand to his chest. "Need out. Grass. Rain. Dirt."

The longing in his eyes matched her own, and she had wandered the overgrown forest guided by Ruth. For how many months or years had Lionel been cut off from all of nature?

"You hurt people." Sera's lips were dry as she said the words, and she moistened them with her tongue.

"They hurt first. Together. Free." He pointed to her and the metal door.

They hurt first. Did that mean he'd acted in self defence after men had hunted him down, and had merely been trying to survive?

Her breakfast rolled on an uneasy sea inside her. She had trusted Abigail and overlooked warning signs, and that hadn't ended well for her. But Lionel needed her in order to escape, and she needed him to guide her safely through the building, or they would both be lost somewhere far worse.

But what then? When they reached the serene foyer and opened the front door, could she unleash the creature on the world beyond the Repository's gate? If she made another mistake and those going about their lives in the surrounding countryside paid the price, she couldn't bear it.

Freedom could be a test, though. If Lionel turned on her in a dark corridor, well... her suspicions would be proven true. If they made it safely beyond the front door, she would consider what to do next. Stepping onto the clipped lawns was only one part of their escape. The lycanthrope had no way of getting past the gate on his own.

"You will need to be in wolf form to scent the air outside. Do you think you can do that?" Sera rose from the chair and approached his bars.

Lionel inhaled through his nose and closed his eyes. Then he placed both hands over his chest and curled his torso down towards his toes. As his form lowered to the ground, it shimmered and blurred. With a soft thud, two padded feet landed on the slate.

Sera stared at the sharp white claws extending from the pads and by the time she looked up, all of Lionel had shifted into the waist-high wolf. Keeping her heartbeat steady, she walked from her cell to the door of his. Kneeling before the lock, she placed a hand flat on the cool metal.

The wolf sat on the other side and tilted his head. Waiting.

With the tiniest tickle of magic, Sera coaxed the lock into releasing the mechanism. With an audible grate, the long-disused metal retracted and rasped against itself. The wolf nudged the bars with his enormous head and the door creaked open.

He padded out to the short corridor and lifted his head, nostrils flaring as he scented the air. Then he trotted to the heavy door and wedged his body into the opening to push through. He cast a backward glance to

Sera to ensure she followed and then disappeared through the doorway.

Sera had one pang of regret as she cast what was, hopefully, her last look at her cell.

"I hope Jerome takes my potted plant back to the conservatory," she murmured, before following Lionel.

Corridors twisted and turned. At one point, they walked in pitch blackness and her stomach lurched. Her senses were unsure which way was up or down. Sera kept one hand on Lionel's furry shoulder to anchor herself as he guided her through the unnatural night. They went up one set of stairs, only to descend another. Then at last the corridor turned and soft natural light filtered down a familiar narrow and steeply twisted spiral of stairs.

Hope flared inside Sera as she climbed to the top step and placed one boot in the dark wood and deep green foyer. Another wide set of stairs ran up the side of the space. The door to Jerome's office was closed. Before them stood the front door of the Repository.

Lionel had done it! His keen sense of smell had found a way through the underground labyrinth.

Excitement bubbled up inside her, along with surprise as she reached for the latch to the front door, and it opened without protest.

She stood on the sheltered porch while Lionel bounded forward. The lycanthrope was like any dog excited to be outside after a long confinement. He rolled on the grass. Dug a hole. Urinated on a tree. Then he raced off, chasing a leaf tossed by the wind.

With careful steps, Sera trod the lime chips towards the front gate. Her heart pounded as she approached freedom. Standing before the gate, she curled her hands into fists and concentrated on a spell that would allow her and Lionel to ease past the wards.

As she worked, from the corner of her eye, she noticed the change in Lionel. The wolf stopped his frolicking and came to sit on one side of the gate. His pale, predatory gaze fixed on her and made a shiver run down her spine. In that instant, she realised she had made a mistake. Lionel was no wolf in sheep's clothing attempting to deceive her. He was, literally, a wolf. One who had killed people under circumstances unknown to her.

Never again would she ignore the warning tingle at the base of her skull. In her rush to escape, she hadn't fully considered the wisdom of letting the lycanthrope free of his cell. As she murmured the spell under her breath to break through the gate, Sera decided that whatever happened next, Lionel would never leave the Repository by her hand. His fate wasn't her decision to make. She wasn't arrogant enough to assume their shared captivity meant she knew everything about the other creature, or his inner motivations.

Decision made, she altered the words that circled in her mind. When a trickle of magic pooled over her skin, she raised her hands and laid them flat on the metal. Sera whispered the incantation and braced her body for what would follow. The unpleasant tingle pressing against her skin turned into a sudden *whack!* and she was blasted backwards.

Sera landed on her bottom in the grass, her entire body stinging as though she had flung herself naked into a patch of nettles. Even her jaw ached. It appeared that using magic against the wards, even when she only pretended she was going to escape, had amplified its reaction. There was a nugget of knowledge that might be handy another day.

As she lay on the grass and stared at the clouds above, Lionel let out a snarl. The wolf pounced and landed at her feet.

"Sorry, Lionel. Apparently, I am not strong enough to open the gate. We shall have to think of another way." She shook her hands to release the tingle. Her words were a lie. When her hands had touched the metal, it had swayed under her gift and indicated a willingness to bend. While she chose not to risk the consequences today, if she used all her magic, she might be able to create an opening.

The snarl turned into a shout. A large hand wrapped around her ankle.

"Mine. Rowan. Promise." Under his intense emotion, Lionel had shifted back into his human form and, with a firm grip on Sera's ankle, pulled her backwards over the lawn.

While she had often used her magical skills to defend herself, once again the mundane was the better course of action. Sera kicked out with her other leg, catching Lionel smack in the head with her boot. He let out a grunt and loosened his grip.

"That's enough of that! I do not belong to anybody." Sera scrambled free and jumped to her feet.

Lionel rose to his full height and glared at her, anger burning in his pale eyes. Curling his hands into fists, his form shimmered as he changed back into the wolf and leapt at her again.

Sera flung up her arms and created a shield similar to the one that had protected her and her friends from the gryphon's attack. Lionel's claws scrabbled over the invisible barrier as he hit it, and Sera cried out at the weight. Planting her feet and using all her might, she was able to fling the heavy wolf away.

Shaking himself, Lionel appeared to be enjoying his exertions. With tongue lolling to one side, he was bunching his haunches to jump when a ghostly form stepped out from the clipped yew beside Sera.

"Back, you beast!" Felix shouted and held his sword high overhead.

Lionel snarled, ignored the ghost, and leapt. Sera cringed, doubting that a phantom would be any impediment to the lycanthrope. The centurion swept his sword through the air, even as the wolf's outstretched paws and claws passed right through the ghost's misty form.

The wolf emitted a high-pitched yowl and tumbled to one side. Bright red blood glistened along the length of the centurion's sword.

"Back, Lady Winyard!" Jerome came puffing along

the grass, a bundle curled in his hands. As he approached, he threw a silver net over the panting wolf.

Before Lionel could struggle to his feet, the strands of the net pulled tight around him and swept his legs out from beneath him. The creature thumped back to the grass, his sides heaving. He whimpered and caught Sera's gaze, as though he expected her to free him.

The wolf dissolved, and the naked man remained. A long gash in his side bled into the grass underneath him.

"Thank you, Felix." Sera still struggled to understand how the blade could be solid enough to inflict damage, yet the wolf was not able to touch the ghost's form.

"I admit that as a lad, I much enjoyed the gladiatorial games. Man against beast was always my favourite, and I spent many an hour practicing against an imaginary tiger or lion. Thank you, Domina, for giving me the opportunity to battle a most fearsome creature." Felix bowed.

Jerome trotted to the gate and had a hurried conversation with the gatekeeper, then returned with a disappointed look in his eyes. Sera was becoming accustomed to such a look from people she had let down.

"I am sorry, Mr Parr. I should never have let him out, but after Lord Tomlin came... I have so little time left." She curled her hands into fists and dug her nails into her flesh to hold back the tears of frustration. "I realised once I stood at the gate that he could never be allowed to leave here. I never intended to open it but had to pretend, so he thought I had tried and failed."

Jerome stared down at the bleeding man. "We will discuss that later. I have sent for the surgeon. This wound will need stitching. If I fetch a stretcher, can you help me carry him back to his cell?"

"Of course. Whatever I can do to assist." She had stymied Lionel's escape, but she'd never intended to see him seriously injured. Although he did deserve a tiny bit of punishment for trying to claim her as *his*.

While Felix oversaw them and issued commands, Sera and Jerome managed to slide the injured man onto the stretcher, still ensnared in the net. Sera picked up the foot end of the poles while Jerome took the head and led the way.

The centurion trotted alongside them. "I shall send word when the physician arrives."

"How will we get him down all those stairs?" Sera asked once they had manoeuvred their heavy load through the front door. They set him down in the foyer as they caught their breath. Their route didn't seem conducive to carrying a large man between them. Nor did she think her arms would last the entire way. How she missed Hugh's solid presence! He could have stitched up the man and carried him back through the underground corridors, too.

"The Repository knows when we need a more direct route." Jerome grunted as he bent to pick up his end of the stretcher again.

As he spoke, a wide-panelled door swung open in

the wall to reveal a sloping corridor beyond. The edges of the door expertly blended in with the surrounding wallpaper so that when closed, it became invisible once more. Grasping the handles of the stretcher, Sera followed Jerome into the pale light.

Instead of stairs, they took a series of ramps of varying inclines in between long stretches of corridor. She was panting and sweat ran down between her shoulder blades by the time they arrived at their cells. A bowl of warm water and cloths awaited them, a faint spiral of steam wafting from the water.

They set down their load, and Jerome gestured to Lionel, who appeared to drift in and out of consciousness. "Could you wash his wound, please, but do not remove the net. He will need to be restrained at all times. I must wait for the doctor."

"Of course." Sera dropped a cloth into the steaming bowl and set to wiping away the blood. Lionel sucked in a sharp breath as the fabric tugged on the edges of the sliced flesh.

"You have only yourself to blame. You should not have attacked me," she murmured as she worked.

The man growled but did not speak. Then he turned his head away. Before long, footsteps rang out again and Jerome returned with a man of a similar vintage who clutched a battered leather bag.

"Let's see what we have. Never thought a ghost would slice one of your residents, Jerome." The doctor raised one eyebrow at Sera, and she stepped out of his way.

"Felix defended Lady Winyard, but it was unfortunate the incident happened at all." Jerome carried a brass apple in his hand and held it up before the surgeon. "How long?"

"An hour, no more, from the looks of it," the doctor replied.

Jerome twisted the metal fruit, which revolved in the centre, and a ticking sound filled the air. Sera's skin tingled as a spell settled over Lionel. The lycanthrope drew a deep, shuddering breath, then his form relaxed. The caretaker released the net, wound it back into a tight ball, then slipped it into his pocket.

Sera sat on the chair outside as the doctor worked. He knelt on the cold floor as he passed a needle back and forth through flesh. Then he painted a thick, honey-like substance over the closed wound, before winding a bandage around Lionel's middle to hold the poultice in place.

Once satisfied, both men backed out of the cell. The lock fell into place with a loud *thunk*. Jerome picked up the apple. "Ten minutes left. Thank you, Doctor Blythe."

Jerome glanced at Sera with an unreadable expression and then escorted the doctor out.

Sera leaned against the arm of the chair and watched Lionel sleep. Her mind revisited the moment when his hand had closed around her ankle, and he'd uttered those three words. *Mine. Rowan. Promise.*

He had clearly been listening the day Lord Rowan had outlined her choice of breeding partner—Lord

Tomlin or the lycanthrope. She shuddered and let anger flow through her limbs. Why were women treated as chattels and breeding stock by men? The events of the day only hardened her resolve to live free of the dictates of men. If one walked beside her through life, it would be because she wanted him there.

Hugh. She breathed out his name and rubbed the ring on her pinkie in the faint hope he would sense her... wherever he might be.

TEN

SERA WATCHED the rise and fall of Lionel's chest until Jerome returned. The caretaker leaned on the bars, facing her. He crossed his arms over his chest.

There were many things she wanted to say, but *sorry* seemed to dissolve on her tongue. So she chose a different question to satisfy her curiosity. "What happened in the case of the men Lionel killed? Was it self-defence?"

The caretaker snorted. "Is that what he told you? They weren't all men. He killed two women and one man. Lionel had been stalking a village, snatching women. Two managed to escape with their lives and tell their horrifying story. Another two were not so lucky. The brother of one of the slain women headed out alone to find what had mauled his sister. A hunting party found what was left of him. It took five men to capture Lionel—and the only reason he wasn't strung up on the spot was that an agent for the Repository led the party to find him."

"Women?" Sera laid one hand over her mouth. How narrowly she had avoided disaster! Not for the first time she had proven herself too quick to act, too quick to anger. As a result, she had nearly made a terrible mistake. "I'm truly sorry, Jerome. You have to believe me when I say I never intended to let him out the front gate. Unfortunately, I realised my error in judgement once we were outside, and not before I unlocked his cell door."

"Done is done, and it is fortunate only Lionel was injured. But perhaps you now understand why some doors must remain locked." He gestured to the slumbering man.

She heaved a sigh and remembered how the ward had wavered and seemed seconds from melting under her touch. It still haunted her palms. So close. If she had sufficient time to recover her ability, she could create a hole she could climb through. Assuming the gate wards didn't blast her halfway across the lawn again.

"Please don't put me back in there," Sera whispered as she stared at her hands.

Jerome huffed. "Since you can unlock the door, it does seem rather pointless. Nor do I want to risk you becoming lost in the dark labyrinth down here. I understand why you did it, milady. I'll not be a party to the horror Lord Rowan intends. But I cannot command the gates to let you out until the order from the king is rescinded."

A faint smile touched her lips. If he left her free to roam, at least outside, she would have plenty of opportunities to test her returning magic against the gate. "Thank you, Jerome. That means much to me."

He smiled and gestured to the propped-open door, still using her stone from the garden. "Let's go have a cup of tea and warm ourselves by the fire."

They walked in silence through the twists and turns and stairs back to Jerome's cosy little study. Sera tucked her feet up under her in the armchair before the cheerful fire and gratefully accepted the hot, sweet tea. They sat in silence, both lost in their thoughts.

At length, Jerome lowered his cup and spoke to the flames. "I will have a room made ready for you upstairs. You can at least be comfortable while we figure out how to thwart Lord Rowan's repulsive plan."

"Please tell me it will have a window." It wasn't freedom, but at least now Jerome had become an ally.

He huffed a quiet laugh. "Yes. And a fireplace to warm you, and a proper bed."

Sera considered diving into an enormous bed piled high with soft pillows. "Oh, bliss! I shall sleep all day. No offence meant, Jerome, but those cots in the cells are torturous."

"At least you had a mattress, however thin. Originally, they were all stone such as Lionel sleeps upon." Jerome stood and poured more tea.

Sera's mind briefly flitted back to the cell, which

she hoped she never saw again except to retrieve her papers. "I fear something has happened to Queen Charlotte, that she has not replied to your letters."

"Doctor Blythe says that she is secluded at The Queen's House for the winter and is not receiving any visitors." The caretaker threw another scoop of coal onto the fire before settling back into his chair.

"But that doesn't explain why she can't answer her correspondence." Sera pondered what would keep the queen from wading into her favourite mage's predicament.

There were only two possible options. One, that she had never seen the letter, and two, that she was incapable of a reply. Some would argue a third option—that she agreed with the decree, didn't want to get involved, and had chosen to leave Sera to her fate. But that idea could be rejected. Queen Charlotte was a vocal and, some would say, troublesome woman herself. She would not sit quietly by while her mage was imprisoned unfairly and without cause.

"I fear Lord Rowan's influence has spread to the queen." If she followed that thread, since the old mage had no hesitation in silencing the bothersome women in his path, would he aim higher and poison the mind of a monarch to make it easier to remove him? "I need to leave here. I fear the king is in danger."

"Tomorrow, milady. Night has fallen. I'll not stand in your way if you wish to attempt the gate again. Although, as I told you, no one has made it out before their time yet." Jerome rose and walked to a square panel in the wall where a brass knob jutted out. When he tugged on the knob, a section hinged down, revealing domed plates inside the cavity. "How about some dinner? Then I will show you upstairs."

He carried the tray to the small round table and set out the dishes.

"Perhaps you can tell me who runs the kitchen, fills the coal scuttles, and empties the chamber pots," Sera said as she moved to a chair at the table. Closing her eyes, she inhaled the aroma of dinner and her stomach rumbled. The caretaker ate better than the prisoners below.

Much to Sera's frustration, even after over two hundred years to dig into the Repository's secrets, her dinner companion knew very little. Or perhaps he chose not to share the knowledge he had gleaned.

After the best meal she had consumed in some time, Sera followed Jerome up the stairs to a gallery that could have belonged to any country estate. Portraits of humourless men and women hung on the wall and passed judgement on those walking by. Their clothing ranged from Tudor ruffs to the excesses of King Charles. The carpet runner was in muted tones of blue and grey. Flickering lights in sconces lit their way.

One door was cracked open a few inches. Jerome stopped and pushed it open wider. "Here you are."

The room did indeed have a window. Sera peered below and delighted in the view back over the conservatory and rambling forest. A fire crackled in the hearth, the bed had been turned down, and her potted plant relocated from her cell to a sideboard. Her notes on the Repository and Lionel had also been moved and waited in a stack on the desk.

She bounced on the bed and grinned at Jerome. "Thank you."

He stood in the doorway. "I only ask that you don't go wandering the halls tonight and exploring. Some of the residents don't like having their doors flung open in the early hours."

"There are others in the rooms up here?" She had thought the Repository a prison, not a boarding house. Although when she thought about it, Jerome had to lay his head somewhere at night, and must have private quarters.

His lips twitched. "We have a couple of residents. They are secluded here voluntarily for their own reasons, and I would ask you to respect their privacy."

Still feeling chastised about how close to disaster she had come that day, she nodded. "I shall leave locked doors alone, I promise."

THE NEXT MORNING, a pale shaft of sunlight struggled across the floor and woke Sera. She stretched out her limbs and imagined a warm, muscular companion sharing the bed. Thinking of Hugh made a pang spear through her heart. "I will see you again. And Kitty," she murmured to the lonely room.

Flinging back the blankets, she padded to the fire. As she warmed her hands, a rap came at the door.

It took Sera a moment to remember she was incarcerated in a magical prison, and was not a house guest at a country estate. Opening the door, she found Jerome in the hall with a tray.

"Good morning. If you like, after breakfast I will show you the library. The Repository will allow you to leave your room and make your way to my study." He handed over the tray.

"Yes, thank you." Taking her breakfast, Sera carried it to the little table under the window.

She ate her porridge while watching the garden slumbering below. Birds dug for worms in the frigid soil. Droplets of water hung suspended on the ends of tree branches, and the perennials hibernated under their blanket of earth.

After breakfast, washed and dressed, she opened her door and ventured out into the hall. Sera walked a few paces and stopped, staring at a closed door. Curiosity nibbled at her. Was there some creature or unfortunate behind the polished wood? She strained her ears and ignored the pounding of her heart.

There! A shuffle as though someone turned the pages of a newspaper while they drank their coffee.

Her hands itched to knock on the door and introduce herself as their new neighbour. But she had promised Jerome that she would respect the privacy of the residents. Did that include peering through a keyhole? Best not to risk it. With a backward glance, she carried on to the stairs.

She knocked on Jerome's open door and saw the caretaker busy with paperwork at his desk. "I am ready to inspect the library. Then I intend to make another attempt on the gate." She wanted to free Ruth, but not without knowing more about the spirit. Who knew, her soul might have been imprisoned for some abominable crime and she might morph into a demon once beyond the wall.

Setting aside what appeared to be a handful of invoices, Jerome rose and winked at her. "Excellent. I'm sure those plans will keep you entertained until suppertime."

"You have a distressing lack of faith in my abilities, Jerome," she murmured as he showed her across the hall, and to the room tucked beside the stairs.

Jerome flung open the door. Sera stepped in and disappointment showered through her.

The library was an ordinary-sized room of only one level. Three walls were covered in bookshelves, laden with volumes on all manner of subjects. Some new, some old, some faded, and some pristine. One wall held a square window in the middle that looked out over the drive. The fourth wall held the fireplace and an inglenook on either side, where a person could curl up in the warmth. The pungent aroma of old books lingered—the mustiness of antiquity and old secrets, long forgotten.

"I expected far more books and still can't believe you don't have a cat," she muttered as she plucked a volume at random.

Jerome shrugged at her glare. "I did say I'm not much of a reader. These are the books I have collected over my time here. Perhaps my replacement will share your love of libraries and this place will grow to extraordinary proportions."

Sera paced the shelves, wondering where to start her search. "Are they in any order?"

He pointed to the left of the door. "I started there when I first arrived and worked my way around."

Sera's mind turned to Ruth. The ghost had said the word *book*. Would her story be contained in here, somewhere? Given that Ruth was already a spectre roaming the halls when Jerome had taken up his position, if it was here, her story would likely be among the older volumes.

"I shall leave you to your day. Come to my study at suppertime, and we can dine together again if you like." A hint of loneliness tinged Jerome's words as he made the offer.

"I look forward to it. I shall regale you with my day's adventures over supper." Sera's attention returned to the books.

While the library was devoid of dust, it also lacked any... *soul*. She had often wondered if a library borrowed its life not from the tomes on its shelves, but from those who frequented it. With no one to caress the volumes, or to bring stories to life in their imaginations, the library slumbered like the hibernating plants outside.

One day, someone who adored the written word and who often became lost in a good novel would arrive at the Repository and breathe life into the room. And Sera hoped that any new caretaker would add a second floor, a narrow walkway around the middle of the room, and rolling ladders on brass castors.

Until then, she lavished attention on the variety of books she plucked from the shelves at random. There was a history of the Tudor reign, a detailed biology book on different species of frogs (no mention of naughty grandson toads), and a number of ghostly tales that she assumed were fictional, but the text was unclear.

"Where are you, Ruth?" Sera murmured as she moved to the next section. She thought the long-dead woman might have materialised by now and pointed out which particular book was about her. That would make Sera's task much quicker.

"Perhaps a work about witches might mention her." As she scanned titles or flipped through pages, Sera spoke to the room as though it were a sentient being capable of listening.

The Repository seemed an unusual house, like Mistwood Manor, that had some unknown entity residing at its core. While a vain hope, there was even a slim chance that if she sweet-talked the Repository, it would open the gates for her.

The library contained a number of books detailing

the horrific witch trials of previous centuries. Women with a variety of aftermage gifts had been accused of terrible crimes. To Sera's mind, most of these seemed obviously natural events or else the product of overactive imaginations. How could a judge be so dim as to think them malicious actions?

Someone had gone to the trouble of noting whether the women were found guilty of killing a cow, souring milk, or suchlike, which was considered a secular crime; they were hanged. If a woman was found to be a witch (a ridiculous accusation that made angry sparks flare over Sera's knuckles), which was a religious crime, the unfortunate was burned.

"I must be searching in the right area," she whispered.

Her hand plucked a volume that seemed to have a different binding to its neighbours. The leather seemed rougher under her fingertips. Much to her disappointment, the book was about women's health and mysterious illnesses that cause hysteria in women. Like reading too many books, apparently.

She was about to return it to the shelf when the author's note caught her attention.

"The degeneration of a good woman's mind from exposure to learning meant only for men was observed by this physician in the case of Ruth Newell. I have found you!" Although how sad if Ruth had been the person studied, forming the basis of such a ludicrous statement.

Taking the book to the inglenook, Sera continued

reading. *"After goodwife Newell consigned her soul to Hell by flinging herself down the stairs, portions of her skin were removed—"* With a gasp, Sera nearly lost her grip on the book. *"—tanned and used to bind this volume of essays."*

Ruth hadn't meant a book about her life—although she was one of the case studies examined—or about why she had become a ghost. *Ruth book* had been meant literally. They had turned her skin into a book. Sera peered at the front cover. Now that she knew what it was made of, she could make out tiny hair follicles and what looked like a mole. Then her curiosity charged off, wondering what part of Ruth had been used. Her stomach? A thigh? Buttocks?

"Oh, Ruth. Is that why you are bound here because part of you resides unburied and unsanctioned on a shelf?" Sera knew of books bound in human skin. A few such volumes were kept in the library under Mage Tower.

She would ask Jerome over dinner if he knew of any impediment to her freeing Ruth. Then, once she was free of the Repository, Sera would visit old Ethel and ask the aftermage who spoke with spirits if she could help Ruth move on. Or she could bring Ethel to the Repository, which might achieve two objectives in one visit. They could help Ruth find peace and Ethel could make eyes at Jerome. They were both of a similar physical age.

Making a note of the book's location, Sera slid it back into place and selected a gothic novel, sadly not one penned by her dear friend Vilma Winters. The comfortable inglenook called to her while snow flurries blew past the square window. The visible signs of winter reassured her that she hadn't been imprisoned for months. The return of her magic made her sensitive to the way time flowed differently at the Repository. The lack of windows in the cells meant a prisoner could fall asleep and, instead of snatching eight hours of slumber, they might remain in the dream world for days without realising it.

As she had.

While her first few attempts to escape had failed, she was not deterred. Once the snow abated, she would tackle the gates—this time without a lycanthrope watching her with hungry eyes. And this time she would succeed.

ELEVEN

SERA TOSSED a scoop of coal onto the fire, then curled up once more on the padded seat in the inglenook and leaned against the wall. She opened Clara Reeve's *The Old English Baron* and decided that her life could be worse. Her incarceration meant a reprieve from the noxious-smelling chores Lord Ormsby kept allocating to her. Was anyone unblocking the drains in the East End, or helping the farmers gather seaweed to fertilise their paddocks? Probably not.

That made a new worry appear in her list of things to rectify. Who was aiding the common folk in her absence? Those who could afford magical assistance were given priority by her male colleagues—with the exception of Lord Pendlebury. But the last she'd seen of him, he had been off to the wilds of Scotland. Sera imagined spring would see her knee-deep in refuse once more as she mended neglected drains and waterways.

If one were of an optimistic and cheery disposition, her time in the quiet building could almost be regarded as a holiday. Of course, that required a monumental effort to overlook the disgusting machinations of Lord Rowan. She had better make it a very *short* holiday before the old mage returned.

With no clocks in the room and the sun obscured by thick clouds, she marked the passage of time in pages. Who knew, it might catch on as a new standard of time, with people saying such things as, *I'll meet you at ten pages past a chapter*. However, since people all read at different speeds, or rarely, like Jerome, it might result in people either being terribly late or horribly early.

"Perhaps we ought to stick to the standard measure of time," she murmured as she turned another page.

At that point, it occurred to her that she wasn't the sort of person who enjoyed too much free time. Her mind wandered in all sorts of odd directions if left to its own devices for too long. Yes, a prompt end to her holiday at the Repository was definitely needed. Whatever would she do next to fill the hours? At this rate, she would be taking Jerome up on his offer of needlework supplies.

She returned her attention to the story in her hands, but just as the hero was encountering another setback in his life, Jerome burst into the room.

"Milady, there is a carriage at the gate. I believe it is Lord Rowan's." He pointed to the square window surrounded by books.

Fear arrowed sudden and cold through Sera. She stood, the book tumbling to the floor from slack fingers. "No. It's too soon."

She had planned to skip out the front gate once the snow flurries had passed. Now, she had lingered too long in the little library. This wasn't the end to her relaxed stay that she had envisioned. Surely it hadn't been long enough? Lord Tomlin had said he would tell Lord Rowan to delay their plans by two weeks. It had been less than a week since the old mage had called upon her, followed by Lord Tomlin, and then she had tried to escape with Lionel, only for the creature to turn on her.

Now that she tried to count the days in her worried mind, she was not so certain it hadn't been two weeks.

She stood at the window, frozen in place, as the gates swung open, and the horses plodded along the gravel. As the vehicle approached the curve in the drive, she recognised the arms painted on the carriage door. It was indeed Lord Rowan.

"You must return to your cell." Jerome paced back and forth. "Or hide."

"Hide? Where?" Sera swallowed the sob of hysteria that tried to push its way up from her chest. She had to think and for that, she needed a clear mind. Lord Rowan would not win. With her last breath, she would fight him and whatever magical army he had at his back. Never again would he crack her spirit. Her blood bubbled with resistance and the panic was washed away.

"Stay in the library. He never ventures in here." Jerome rubbed one hand over the back of his neck as he thought quickly. "I will tell him that during your attempt to escape yesterday, you became lost in the shifting corridors below, and that I need time to locate you."

"He will use his magic to find me," she whispered as the carriage rolled to a stop.

"Lord Rowan hates being cold and inconvenienced. I am betting he will instruct me to find you, lock you up, and notify him when you are caged once more." Jerome moved to the doorway. Watery sunlight now streamed through the window and the lead work holding the panes of glass cast a pattern on the floor that was eerily similar to bars.

Sera didn't know what made her do it. Perhaps morbid curiosity drove her to take one look at her tormentor before she cowered in a corner or discovered if she could fit under the seat in the inglenook. It seemed less cowardly if she faced him first, even if only through the thick and distorted glass of the library window. Risking discovery, she moved closer to peer out as the man emerged from the carriage and stepped to the ground.

"That's not Lord Rowan," she whispered. The figure was too broad to be the elderly mage. Or did the distortion of the glass play tricks upon her? Hope tried to flare into life inside her, but fear poured icy water all over it.

Needing a clearer view, Sera rushed across the tiled

entrance and charged into Jerome's study with its larger window of finer glass. If Lord Rowan strode through the door, she would hide under the desk. With the better-quality panes in the study, the figure became clearer.

"No." The word slid past her lips, part denial of the evidence of her own eyes, and infused with yearning.

Jerome approached and stood next to her. "Who is that?"

"Someone I know very well. If it is indeed he." Still, she held her ground. Trickery had snared her once. What if Lord Rowan had cast an enchantment over himself to alter his appearance? She might run from the building, only for a trap to close around her.

Then two more figures emerged from the carriage and Sera made a decision. She spun so fast that one foot slid on the wooden floor. So impatient was she to get outside that her hands scrabbled with the latch, unable to make it work for long seconds. Finally, it released, and the door swung open.

With a sob of joy, she launched herself across the foyer at the man approaching the door.

"Hugh!" If this was a cruel trick by Lord Rowan, at least Hugh's face was the last thing she would remember. And those of Kitty Napier and Natalie Delacour the gargoyle, who stood on either side of him. Her mind accepted that Abigail and her grandfather might adopt the faces of her lover and best friends to trick her into obedience. But the inclusion of Nat in the party surely meant it was really them. However, the group had wrought such a miracle.

Sera found herself swamped in the strong embrace of Hugh. He angled her face and kissed her most thoroughly, leaving her knees weak and her heart skipping a few beats. She curled her hands into the thick wool of his overcoat to remain standing. There was no way Lord Rowan could kiss like that, even if he had used a glamour to hide his true appearance.

Pulling back, Hugh gently wiped away the tears spilling down her cheeks with the pad of his thumb. He stared at her as though drinking her in and couldn't believe she was before him. Then, before he could kiss her again, Kitty elbowed Hugh out of the way and flung her arms around Sera.

"I thought we'd never see you again," her friend cried against her hair.

Nat let out an audible snort. "She is fine. Just like I told you she would be. Nobody listens to Natalie."

Sera glanced up as the gargoyle crossed her arms and looked bored. She might feign indifference, but her presence among the group spoke volumes of her concern.

Love flowed into every corner of Sera's being. She had not been abandoned and left to moulder like a forgotten potato under a cupboard. She reached out and took Hugh's hand as she kept hold of Kitty, too afraid to let go in case her friends evaporated into mist.

She glanced from one beloved face to another. "How did you find me? Jerome says you cannot find the

Repository unless you have been here before, or come here with someone who has been here before."

Hugh let go of her long enough to tug up the sleeve of his coat. Diamonds sparkled on his arm, where a familiar Fae bracelet had stretched itself to accommodate a broader wrist. "All the court was told was that you had gone to the country for an extended period. Abigail declared that she did not know where you were, and then had Kitty forcibly ejected from her home. So we found another way to discover where you had been taken."

"She threw you out?" Sera stared at her dearest friend, and a rush of anger on Kitty's behalf surged through her.

Kitty shrugged. "Did you think I would just give up when I encountered a frosty *no*? Of course I pushed the matter with the horrid cow. But despite my best cross-examination, all Abigail knew was that her grandfather had taken you to someplace called the Repository, and she didn't know its location. Then she called two footmen to escort me from the premises."

What cross-examination technique had Kitty used to discover even that much information? But that was a tale her friend could relate once Sera was free. "I can't believe she had you manhandled."

Kitty winked and mischief burned brightly in her eyes. "I made sure to yell from the street that I would pursue my payment for the abortifacient potion she had swallowed. You should have seen the horrified looks on the faces of the society women passing by. Trying to dampen *that* rumour will keep Abigail busy for some time."

Sera pursed her lips to stop her laughter, then worry fought its way through her good mood. Hugh wore the bracelet that had wrought such a horrible effect on Lady Zedlitz and all whom she touched while wearing it. "I'm still not clear how you found this place. Did you use the bracelet on Lord Rowan?"

Kitty snorted. "Sitting idle has affected your brain, Sera. Think! Who brought you here? Do you really imagine that Lord Rowan had you slung over the pommel of his saddle?"

Sera stared at the carriage and mentally smacked herself on the forehead. "You compelled his coachman."

Hugh laced his fingers with hers. "Now that we have found you, we need to get you out of here. There must be guards somewhere about who will pounce and drag you back to your cell."

Kitty frowned. "Why are you just wandering around? This seems a most odd prison. Or are you allowed exercise time out of your cage?"

Now Sera took over the explanations. "There is no need for guards here. The Repository doesn't let prisoners leave. I have tried. Twice. There's quite a kick in the protective wards when you try to push through them."

"There is magic in the air. It stings." Nat narrowed her gaze at the stone walls enclosing the property.

Sera started a mental list of questions for her

friends. She imagined them all seated at a table before a fire in a cosy tavern, with a good ale and better food as they each told their part in the story of her escape. "As for why I'm not in a cell, Jerome let me out for good behaviour."

Kitty laughed so hard she doubled over and made a choking noise as she struggled to inhale.

Sera grabbed Kitty's arm in alarm as Hugh thumped her back. "Breathe, Kitty. My behaving is not such an outrageous idea," Sera said.

Tears of laughter were streaming down Kitty's face when she straightened up. "I need to meet this man who has managed to reform you."

"Being stripped of one's magic and confined in a windowless, cold cell gives one plenty of time for self-reflection. You don't know how desperate I was to get out of there," Sera whispered. A ripple of the old despair washed over her, and she drew a deep, steadying breath.

Kitty hugged her. "I am sorry. I cannot imagine what you have endured. Once we are free of here, you must tell me all."

"They took your magic?" Worry widened Hugh's gaze, and he slid one hand around her neck to stroke her nape. "I would not have thought it possible."

"It is. But I found a way to break it free from where Lord Rowan had imprisoned it." Sera reached out and clasped Hugh's hand in both of hers.

With escape so close, and her friends to assist, Sera blew away the feeling of hopelessness and concentrated on the task at hand. She also realised there was quite a chill in the air, and that she had run outside without a shawl. Apart from Nat, her friends were dressed in warm winter coats and hats. Her skin prickled with cold, and she rubbed her hands up and down her arms. "If you wish to meet my guard, follow me. It's blasted cold out here, and I need my shawl."

"I will stay here. I am curious and will inspect the construction." Nat advanced on the exterior stones of the house.

Sera drew Hugh and Kitty inside. The warmth and silence enveloped them as though they stepped into a library. A proper library, with towering stacks of books and a floor magically warmed under her toes.

Jerome emerged from his study, a grin of relief on his face that it had not been Lord Rowan emerging from the conveyance. "You did not tell me you were expecting visitors, Lady Winyard."

"Isn't it lovely of my dearest friends to pay a visit? Lord Rowan must have allowed it. Perhaps this is a peace offering to make up for what he has done." She smiled and let the caretaker draw the wrong conclusion. She liked Jerome, and while he was a sort of ally in her escape plan, there was no need to tell him *everything*. The less he knew, the less an angry Lord Rowan could extract from him later.

A frown flitted across Jerome's features, then the smile returned. "Indeed. Although he did not make any mention of it to me."

Sera leaned forward and lowered her voice. "I fear

his advanced age makes Lord Rowan rather forgetful. I thought I would show my friends around the grounds. I just came inside to collect a shawl. It's quite nippy outside. The snow has relented, but I would not be surprised if it returned before the end of the day."

"Shall I have a tea tray prepared for after your walk?" Jerome enquired, now acting the part of butler.

"If you wouldn't mind? We shall take tea in the conservatory, I think. It is always so warm and cosy in there, whatever the weather outside." Sera took the woollen shawl that had been in her room, now hanging from the hook by the door. Wrapping it around her, she tied the ends together in the small of her back.

Then she shooed her friends out the front door and pulled it closed behind her. Kitty wandered a short distance from the house, then turned to stare up at the silent Repository. The Boston ivy, a deciduous cousin of the evergreen English ivy, had dropped all its leaves, leaving naked fingers clinging to the stone. The thick glass obscured whatever resided behind the upstairs windows. Only the glow of a lamp indicated someone, or some*thing*, occupied the rooms.

"What prison serves tea in the conservatory? This is more like some ridiculously exclusive gentleman's club," Kitty muttered.

"Let us walk while we discuss the escape plan. I'd rather not have Mr Parr—Jerome—overhear. While he has been good to me, I am not entirely certain of his loyalties." The caretaker would remain after Sera fled the coop. She hoped the Repository wouldn't sulk and take it out on the elderly retainer. Or that Lord Rowan would lose his temper at the man who has given such loyal service for over two hundred years.

Sera slid her hand into the crook of Hugh's bent arm and snuggled into the warmth of his side as they strolled along the perfectly trimmed trees that guarded the wall. "Please tell me you have a plan for how to get me out of here. It will not be as easy as sitting in the carriage while the horses trot through the front gate."

The idea of being physically wrenched through the structure of the carriage by the magical wards made her shudder. Her body would be broken and even Hugh, with all his skill, might not be able to save her.

"Well..." Kitty began, but before she could finish, a figure emerged from between two shrubs, the greenery visible through his body.

Felix raised his short sword towards Hugh's nose. "Halt! Who goes there?"

"Oh, I say, an actual ghost!" Hugh took a step towards the centurion, but Sera tugged him back. Experience had taught her that while the ghost might be incorporeal, his sword was razor sharp and very real.

TWELVE

"FELIX, these are my friends come to visit—Miss Katherine Napier and Mr Hugh Miles." Sera introduced them to the apparition. "This is Felix Densus, centurion in the Twelfth Legion of the Emperor Tiberius."

Hugh blew out an awed breath that frosted on the chill air, and Kitty's eyes widened.

"This is highly unusual, Domina. I can only assume the emperor must have allowed it and the pigeon notifying me of this change of protocol must have gone astray. Carry on." He waved his sword and saluted with his fist to his chest as they passed.

"Sera, that was a ghost." Kitty and Hugh both turned their heads to stare at her guard.

"Yes. Felix prowls the grounds and trims the hedges. There is another called Ruth, but she seems confined to the house and loses her form if she ventures too far out into the garden." While the Repository was a fascinating place, Sera wanted to get away from it as soon as possible, and her friends weren't sharing their plan.

"Where is the conservatory?" Hugh craned his neck around the corner.

"You are not getting afternoon tea." Sera stopped and her friends halted abruptly.

Disappointment flashed across Hugh's face, and his stomach rumbled. Apparently, rescuing her was hungry work. Although she was rather fond of his robust appetites.

"While I desperately want to climb inside that carriage with you and leave, I cannot. The wards would rip me from the carriage and fling me back to the grass." While her magic was slowly returning, it was hardly a match for the ancient forces that enclosed the Repository. Nor did she have the time to wait for it to fully recover. Sera crossed her arms and glared at them. This might be a bit of fun for them, but it was her life at stake. And her sanity, as she recalled Lord Rowan's disgusting intentions.

Kitty squeezed Sera's arm. "Hugh and I will be leaving by carriage. Not you."

"You had better explain yourself. Surely my friends wouldn't be so rude as to visit and then wave goodbye, leaving me here. Sand is running through my hourglass, and we do not know when Lord Rowan will realise what you have done." Annoyance and frustration crept into Sera's voice.

"We would never leave you here," Hugh said with a serious tone to his words.

He opened his arms, and Sera stepped into them. With his arm around her waist, they turned and walked back to the carriage. The driver held the reins loosely, his eyes unfocused and his form still.

A shadow loomed over them moments before Nat, in her monstrous gargoyle form, landed on the grass with a soft thud. "The air around the wall tingles as high as I flew. I will adapt. It will work."

What would work? Sera waited for one of them to explain everything.

"Kitty thought that this place would have magical wards around it. That gave me an idea." Hugh grinned. "Someone once told me that gargoyles are impervious to magic. I hypothesised that any such protection spells here wouldn't stop your aunt. Nor, I believe, could they stop something held in Miss Delacour's arms."

For a moment, Sera couldn't speak or breathe. Her friends were brilliant. "It might not work."

"That's why I call it a hypothesis. Having travelled through the wards with us and further investigated from the inside, Miss Delacour seems confident she can have you over the wall before the magic of this place can yank you back." Only now did a frown cross Hugh's face as he contemplated failure.

Sera chose to believe in her gargoyle protector. If it failed... well, at least they had tried. "When?"

"Now." Nat shook out her wings, casting a long shadow across the lawn in the watery light.

"I have faith that you will fly free of this cage. We shall see you on the other side." Hugh placed a large hand on either side of her face and kissed her with a gentleness that made her heart ache.

Releasing her, Hugh mounted the carriage box and touched the driver to compel the man to follow his new commands. Then he and Kitty took their seats inside. The driver cracked the whip and urged the horses around the sweep towards the gate.

Sera stood before her aunt and looked up into her granite face. "Whatever happens, thank you for trying."

Natalie nodded, then she picked up Sera and wrapped her arms around her. Being embraced by the gargoyle was not unlike snuggling under a warm, heavy blanket. The world and her worries fell away. Sera pressed her cheek to Nat's solid granite chest, where the stone gave off the heat of stored sunlight.

"I will gain height first, then angle over the wall. We will fall some distance, as I need to shield you with my wings to cover you completely." Nat's words rumbled through her chest.

In the next instant, Sera's stomach plummeted as Nat leapt into the air. Wings with a spread of over twelve feet beat with a steady thrum, and the air grew even colder. Sera curled her hands more tightly into the ridges of Nat's stone form. Even though her aunt had a firm grip on her, it unnerved Sera, the way her feet dangled, and she couldn't stop her toes from wriggling in the attempt to find purchase on something solid.

They flew higher in the sky and Sera gulped frigid

air into her lungs. Then they jerked sideways, and the world went dark as Natalie wrapped her wings around her body. Sera was encased in a stone cocoon, shielded from view and, they hoped, from the magic surrounding the Repository.

Judging from the way her stomach roiled, they were dropping fast. If Sera had the time or ability to speak, she would have quipped that her aunt fell like a stone.

As she drew her next breath, something slammed into her body with all the force of a horse at full gallop. The air was knocked from her lungs and pain flared over her shoulders and rushed to her ankles. The wards! They were ripping her from Nat's firm grasp. It wasn't working!

"No!" Sera cried as she tumbled backwards. This was her only chance. A sob welled up in her chest and tears burned in her eyes.

"Sera, are you hurt?" Concern laced Hugh's voice and his hands warmed her chilled flesh when he touched her face.

She opened her eyes, confused.

Had Hugh not left the grounds of the Repository? Had he chosen to stay with her? "It didn't work." The words came out quiet and tinged with fear. She refused to cry. She had promised to keep fighting until her last breath.

He grinned. "Yes, it did. You are on the other side of the wall. Natalie burst through the wards like a cannonball and didn't have time to slow your landing."

"I'm free?" Sera sat up and took in her surroundings.

Part of her still expected a cruel trap. She sat in long grass in a meadow. A few feet away, the tall stone wall shimmered as though her eyes couldn't focus on its height.

"Yes." Hugh steadied her as she climbed to her feet.

Nat shook her wings, and a pebble flew past Sera's face.

"That stung and was annoying. But the magic did not stop me." The gargoyle crossed her muscular arms with a smug, satisfied look on her face.

It had worked. Hugh's mad idea to use a gargoyle shield had actually worked!

"I thought—Lord Rowan had—" Tears of joy and relief ran down Sera's face, and her knees buckled.

Hugh wrapped his warm arms around her and bore her up. "You're free, Sera."

"Need I point out that we are not that far from your prison, and it's blasted cold out here? Let's get her into the carriage and put some distance between us." Kitty gestured to the waiting conveyance and the driver, still under a compulsion spell.

"Thank you, Nat, for once again saving me." Sera hugged the gargoyle.

Natalie stroked Sera's hair. "When I took the blood oath, I did not realise you would be so much trouble."

Sera schooled her face into a serious expression. "I promise not to need rescuing for at least a month after this."

The gargoyle chuckled and placed a kiss on the top of her head. Without another word, Natalie jumped into the sky. In a few beats of her monstrous wings, she had disappeared behind the low cloud.

Not needing to be told a second time to get out of the icy wind, Sera climbed into the waiting carriage. Once they were all settled, Hugh rapped on the roof.

"We have horses waiting not far away. Then the poor driver can be freed of his compulsion and return to Lord Rowan. Now that we are free of that place, what was the old mage's plan for you?" Kitty eyed Sera with a speculative gaze.

Acid rushed up Sera's throat as she considered the fate that had waited for her in the Repository. Now, with the luxury of time and the prison behind her, she could tell her friends the horrible truth. "He intended to breed me to Lord Tomlin. Or a mad lycanthrope. Or both, if I lived long enough."

She expected words of outrage from her friends. But both stared at her in utter horror. Hugh's jaw worked, but no words came out. His hands curled into fists, and Sera wondered if he imagined hitting Lord Rowan, Lord Tomlin, or battling a lycanthrope in her name.

With his trace of gargoyle blood and rage flowing through his broad body, he could probably take on all three. There was a fight she'd like to see. His protective instincts made love burn hotter inside her—even if they were wholly misplaced. Which was part of why she loved Hugh so fiercely. He still leapt to her defence even when she was perfectly capable of fighting for herself. No, he would fight beside her. Never would he demand she stand behind him.

Kitty shuddered and put together the puzzle pieces that Sera had dropped. "Lord Rowan seeks to breed a Nereus. What would he do with such a powerful child? I doubt he would live another twenty years to train and groom his magical weapon."

Sera leaned back against the velvet interior and pulled the carriage blanket closer around her knees. "He intended to keep the baby a prisoner and siphon off its magic. Lord Rowan said he could draw its power into his body, to make himself young again. Then he intended to wield the poor mite like a tool, so he could reshape England as he pleased."

Hugh blew out a long sigh. "He's mad."

"Yes. I suspect he has also had a hand in whatever is plaguing King George. If the king is declared incompetent, it will be easier for Lord Rowan to seize control as Regent." How many lives were being ruined by the old mage as he pursued his scheme? Sera needed to free the king of whatever magical poison had infected his mind.

"A bloodless coup, instead of outright killing our king. Clever." Kitty fussed with the blanket. "I thought old people were supposed to take up gardening or letter writing, not plot to seize an entire nation for themselves."

"Lord Rowan has waited a long time for a woman mage to be born. He had Lord Branvale killed so that he could get his hands on me. I think my guardian, and whoever he worked with in the Fae realm, knew Lord Rowan wanted to create another Nereus. They did what they could to thwart him." As much as Sera loathed the bracelet that had suppressed her magic as a child, she now wondered if the conspirators had hoped to make Lord Rowan believe she was too weak to produce the powerful offspring he wanted.

"What of Abigail?" Kitty murmured the question with a sideways glance at Sera.

Her friend didn't need to say another word. Nor did Sera wish to discuss the exact details of what she intended in Hugh's presence. The surgeon had too kind a heart to contemplate revenge. Kitty and Sera, however, were cut from a different cloth. Sera clenched her hands into fists and a pale blue glow emanated from between her fingers.

"They took my magic from me," Sera whispered, part of her terrified that if she said it aloud, she might reactivate the hibernation spell.

"How?" Hugh asked, ever curious.

"Lord Rowan concocted the spell and Abigail delivered it. Just as she did with the poison she gave to Jake, to kill Lord Branvale. My magic was placed into a sort of induced hibernation, then hidden deep inside me and wrapped in a hard shell. They thought I could never reach it again. They were wrong." The blue flame danced along her knuckles when she turned her hand over.

Her former friend had betrayed her in a most terrible way. For all those years, Abigail had played her.

Sera had been so desperate for friendship that she had ignored the warning signs. Such a betrayal could never be forgiven. Nor could she let it go unaddressed. To grow into the mage she wanted to become, people had to know she was not one to be meddled with.

"She made her choices and will have to live with the consequences." And there would be consequences. Sera would make sure of that.

Kitty made a satisfied noise. "You are obviously not magic-less anymore. You said something about breaking it free?"

Her friends regarded her with curious eyes.

"Yes. With the help of a potted plant." The philo-dendron had held enough of a connection to Mother Earth that Sera had found a tendril of hope to spur her on.

"There is a story you must tell." Hugh's eyes gleamed with curiosity.

"Before I tell that story, we must finish another. You have not asked me to remove the bracelet." Sera reached across the carriage for Hugh's hand and slid his sleeve up to reveal the diamond-encrusted item.

"It is a dangerous thing, and I do not wish to utter the wrong words and compel you. I am quite fond of having two hands, and losing one would affect my ability to continue as a surgeon." He huffed a quiet laugh but worry simmered in his gaze.

Once, a man had unknowingly clicked the bracelet closed on his fiancée's wrist. She had demanded he remove it. Forced to act by the magic it contained, he had hacked off her arm with a cavalry sword.

"Lord Rowan's men ransacked your house looking for that. I suspect he was rather displeased when they returned empty-handed," Kitty said.

Worry gnawed at Sera. "Elliot, and Vicky, and Rosie.... are they unharmed?" Furniture could be righted, paintings straightened, rugs smoothed out, but people could not be replaced.

"Elliot was badly beaten but is recovered now. You have been missing for over a month," Hugh said.

A month. Sera sucked in a breath and stared out the window. "Time moves differently in that place. I thought it had been little more than a week, and at other times it felt like years. I am glad that Elliot's wounds have healed. But where did you hide the bracelets?"

Hugh grinned. "I placed them inside a cadaver. Then I stitched him up and attended his funeral. When we formulated our plan to rescue you, Kitty helped me retrieve the bundle from where their protector lay in his family's mausoleum."

"*Kitty*, is it?" Until now, Hugh had referred to her closest friend more properly as Miss Napier.

"Once you have broken into a crypt with someone, cut open a corpse's stomach, and rummaged around inside their body, it rather puts one on a first-name basis. Hugh does know how to give a woman a most marvellous time." Kitty's eyes brimmed with mischief.

"But what is the plan now? We have horses waiting, but Lord Rowan will certainly send men after you."

Sera knew exactly what she had to do. "I'm going to Somerset to cross into the Fae realm. You, Kitty, must return to London."

Kitty opened her mouth to object, but Sera silenced her with a lift of her hand. "You and your father must work to undo the damage Lord Rowan will wreak. He has the ear of the king, pouring his poison into his mind, and had an edict signed that authorised having me imprisoned. Until that order is revoked, I will never be safe."

"Ah, you need me for legal shenanigans. Very well." Having her own mission to undertake satisfied Kitty.

"I will accompany you to the court of the Fae," Hugh said.

"I do not know what sort of reception we will find there. But I would be grateful to have you at my side." Sera could have insisted Hugh remain in the mortal realm, but selfishly, she couldn't find the strength to deprive herself of his presence. Whatever they found on the other side, she would protect him from mischievous Fae.

"You must take news of Lord Arwyn Fitzfey to his mother. If she asks, of course." Kitty reminded her that Arwyn had been removed from the Fae realm when he was born and delivered to King George's doorstep.

After two hours, the carriage stopped. Peering out the window, Sera found another carriage waiting with four saddled horses tied behind. Both the driver and the groom wore the Napier family colours. A familiar figure slumbered against the carriage wheel.

"Elliot!" Sera called as she leaned out the window.

"Excellent," Kitty said as Hugh jumped down and held out a hand to assist each woman. "There should be fresh clothes for you, Sera, and a basket of food before we depart again."

Sera's footman climbed to his feet and grinned at her. "You didn't think I'd let you run off on an adventure without me, did you?"

She examined his face, to reassure herself that no trace of his beating at the hands of Lord Rowan's men remained. "I'm sorry you were hurt. What of Rosie and Vicky?"

"Both of them are settled at the Napier home, but ready to return to Soho whenever you are." He rubbed his jaw, and a flash of guilt flared in his eyes. "I tried, Sera, I promise. But it was damned unfair that there were three of them, and they jumped me while my back was turned."

Sera hugged him. "You did the most important things—you raised the alarm, and you looked after Rosie and Vicky. Now, is there still any food, or did you eat it all?"

THIRTEEN

Elliot huffed a laugh, but the guilt had not left his eyes. "You took your time getting here. What was I supposed to do while I waited? Starve?"

Sera swatted him. "I should have turned you into a toad months ago. That way, you'd eat less."

Inside the Napier carriage, Sera nearly cried with joy to find that Kitty had packed her favourite outfit. Neatly folded on the seat were her woollen double-breasted jacket with its swirling split skirt, black trousers, knee-high boots, and a fresh shirt.

After she changed clothes, Hugh released Lord Rowan's driver from his compulsion, with final instructions to return to Mayfair and not remember anything.

The surgeon scratched at his arm as they took the reins of the saddled horses. "Do you think that when we next stop, you will have time to examine my jewellery?"

Worry nibbled at Sera. She had seen what the Fae bracelet had done to Lady Zedlitz, although Hugh had only worn and used it for a matter of days. "Yes. But we will need quiet and no interruptions."

Kitty thanked her staff, and the groom gave the women a boost up into their saddles. They turned their mounts to the east, and the group set off on the next leg of their journey. They rode hard all day, determined to put distance between them and the Repository. Kitty only allowed them brief stops to water their horses and themselves before they were back on the road.

Sera discovered that their saddlebags held a variety of items, both edible and practical. As darkness fell, Elliot scouted out a suitable place for them to spend the night.

"While a pub would be grand and it will be blasted cold out here, I don't think we can risk anyone's recognising you," Elliot said as he gestured towards a stand of trees.

The trunks made a loose circle and fallen leaves covered the ground, offering a small bit of insulation between the frigid ground and their bottoms. They gathered up branches and twigs and soon had a fire blazing in the middle of the little glade. Blankets were laid out around it. As darkness covered them, Elliot was put in charge of producing dinner from the contents of the saddlebags.

Sera sat before the fire and took Hugh's arm in her hands. Pushing up the sleeve of his coat, she examined the bracelet, marvelling at how it had adjusted itself to fit perfectly around the surgeon's wide wrist. Even when she squinted, there was no sign of any clasp or seam to indicate where the piece opened or hinged. Peering underneath, she spied a thin silver tendril burrowing out of the gold and into Hugh's flesh.

So it had begun.

Thus far, they had witnessed only two ways to remove this particular bracelet. One involved death, the other dismemberment. Sera hoped to find a solution that left Hugh alive and intact. She was rather fond of his large, gentle hands. A similar bracelet on her own arm had sprung open once she had removed all the nearly invisible strands that grew from magical metal to burrow into flesh. She offered up a quick prayer to whoever might be listening, that this bracelet would respond the same way.

"This is going to hurt." She met Hugh's gaze, remembering the white-hot agony that had cut through her body as she tugged free each tendril. She had worn that bracelet for years. Hopefully, the roots of this one hadn't gone as deeply into Hugh's body as they had in hers.

"I shall hold still," he murmured.

"It will hurt *a lot*." For a moment, she wondered if she could go through with it and inflict such pain on the man she loved. But she had to, or he would never be free of the cursed thing. She could not risk his amputating his own arm, which she guessed might hurt just a teeny bit more.

He tensed his jaw and nodded. "Do it. It is the only way."

Sera drew a breath and reached out to her magic. Then she sent it swirling around the Fae bracelet. Tiny, almost imperceptible shoots appeared from each diamond chip embedded in the gold. They swayed to an invisible wind, reaching for her gift, wanting to feed from her power. Such a tiny worm to sink into another person and compel them to do the wearer's bidding.

Sera grasped one wriggly strand between thumb and forefinger. At the same time, she whispered a spell to freeze the roots. Once it chilled to her touch, she yanked it free of the bracelet and Hugh's skin.

Hugh sucked in a breath. "That packs a bit of a sting."

Sera dangled the frozen worm between them. "These don't have long roots, fortunately. The ones from my bracelet had spread throughout my body over all those years." She tossed the strand onto the fire and it sparked violet before bursting apart.

She kept working, luring the tendrils to the surface with a wave of her finger, then plucking them free. Most had not yet burrowed into Hugh but merely scraped the surface of his skin. But each time he had used the Fae bracelet to compel someone, a strand would have spread its poison through his arm to do his bidding.

Slowly, methodically, she kept tugging free the wisps of Fae magic. Then she struck one that had deeply anchored roots. Only Hugh's shallow breathing told her that he was keeping a tight lip on the pain.

"I'm sorry. It will be over soon." She was repaying his actions in freeing her with pain. Only by using the bracelet had they learned where she was being held. It wasn't fair that his devotion was being rewarded with the equivalent of a slender, white-hot poker.

The last thread proved to be the most stubborn. She suspected it had been the one unleashed when Hugh compelled the carriage driver. His co-operation had been needed for longer, which had given the magic a chance to establish itself inside Hugh's frame. She pulled the end free and wound it around her finger before reaching for more. For every inch that she drew forth, Hugh took a quick gulp of air.

Finally, the wagging tail broke free of the bracelet and the invisible seam in the metal split open. Sera froze the strand and threw it on the fire to burn with its companions.

Hugh let out a ragged sigh and shook the piece of jewellery free of his arm. A sheen of sweat covered his face from the exertion of holding still. Then he examined his skin, which bore bright red pinpricks where each tendril had pierced his flesh.

"There's an experience I never want to repeat." He rubbed his hand over the punctures and up his arm.

Sera wrapped the bracelet in a handkerchief and knotted the ends. "I shall try not to be interred in a magical prison again."

Hugh took hold of her left hand and pushed up her

sleeve, running his thumb over her scar. "I have a small amount of appreciation for what you endured. Alone. I do not know how you did it. You are the strongest woman I have ever known."

"What about my Aunt Nat?" Sera couldn't imagine a woman stronger than the formidable gargoyle.

"There are different types of strength. You have an inner fortitude and determination that is pure granite." Hugh smiled and raised her hand to kiss her palm.

"Ah. Perhaps we share a spiritual strength." The more she thought about it, the more she liked the idea. She imagined that something in her early days and the blood oath made by her protector meant some of the gargoyle's strength had soaked into her skin. It would explain what some called her *stubbornness*, which Sera preferred to think of as merely knowing her own mind.

Then she glanced at her friend, overseeing Elliot's efforts. Kitty was blessed with a strength of mind greater even than Sera's. One day, Kitty would make a formidable figure in society. One looked up to and respected... if Sera didn't get her killed before then.

Sera took the bundle of fabric with its tempting piece of jewellery and tucked it away in her saddle bag. There was no safe place in the human realm for the thing. Men would battle to use it once they knew of its existence and what it could do. To some, the price it demanded would be worth it to give them power over others.

With Hugh at her side, and free to touch her as he pleased without the risk of compelling her, Sera could relax a little. She had innumerable questions for her friends and picked the most worrying to ask first.

"What news of Queen Charlotte? I asked the caretaker at the Repository to write to her, but he received no response."

Kitty shook her head and took the bowl of stew that Elliot handed her. "She has not been seen about the court. Rumour has it that she is upset about the king's deteriorating state of mind. Lord Rowan has offered himself as special advisor to the Crown."

Hugh tossed a chunk of wood on the fire. "The king went to Cheltenham Spa for treatment, where the finest medical minds and aftermages tried to alleviate his symptoms. But to no avail. He continues to worsen."

"There is a reason for that. I suspect Lord Rowan has cast some ensorcellment to drive him mad. I need to get close to the king to confirm if there is a spell and figure out how to unpick it." Sera spooned a mouthful of stew into her mouth and savoured the spicy taste. Elliot was rather a good cook.

Kitty clicked her tongue against the back of her teeth. "We had better act fast to restore his health. When Parliament reconvenes, Fox and Pitt will battle over the terms of a regency. It appears both think it should fall to the Prince of Wales. They are merely arguing over the conditions around it."

"I thought Pitt supported the queen as regent?" Hugh asked.

Kitty swallowed her mouthful before speaking.

"No longer, alas. Something has occurred behind closed doors and alliances have shifted."

"I imagine that *something* will have Lord Rowan at its root. Wait and see—he will offer himself as regent and ruler of England. Or he would, if only some troublesome woman mage hadn't gone and ruined all his plans." Sera chuckled to herself. As long as she remained at liberty, Lord Rowan was stymied. Unless he found a way to unnaturally extend his lifespan, all she had to do was wait him out. Not that hiding and doing nothing appealed to her while others suffered.

Then another thought struck her—was he mad enough to seek out a woman mage on the Continent? There were a scant handful, living quiet lives in seclusion. Not that she could imagine Lord Rowan trying to abduct a mage from some remote castle in Europe. They were closely guarded, no doubt in case of just such an attempt.

"Did Lord Tomlin not woo and win you?" Kitty arched one eyebrow.

Elliot nearly choked on his dinner, while Hugh stared from one of them to the other.

Sera snorted. "He didn't even try. His idea of wooing was telling me it would take *but a moment*."

"A moment? I pity that man's wife," Elliot managed to say.

"That's exactly what I said." Sera took Hugh's hand as emotions played across his broad face.

"Are you saying that Lord Tomlin was *willing* to... assault you, without your consent?" Hugh's jaw tensed and a rare fire lit his eyes. "Only one swipe of my scalpel, and his line ends with him." The gentle surgeon was slow to anger, but it appeared the idea of harm to Sera would provoke him into action that ran contrary to his Hippocratic oath.

Sera ran her hand up to Hugh's muscular forearm. "There is no need. I told him I was on my courses, and he practically ran from the building."

"Let us suppose that you had entertained this repugnant scheme for one second—" Kitty began.

"Which is as long as he'd need, apparently." Elliot chortled.

Kitty shot an amused look at Sera's footman. "Once Rowan had this infant Nereus in his arms, how did he plan to contain it, if it is such a powerful being?"

"I think that part of his plan horrified me the most. The child would be kept a prisoner its entire life, while he used its power to make himself king." Sera scraped up the last spoonful of stew from her bowl.

"But if a Nereus is so potent, couldn't it just magic itself out of any prison? Even that Repository?" Elliot only fully joined the conversation now that he had cleaned his own bowl.

Hugh set down his spoon in his empty bowl. "Do you know why a full-grown elephant will allow itself to be tethered to a stake with a piece of rope it could easily break?"

Kitty and Sera exchanged glances and then shook their heads.

"Its captors do it while it is a baby. It tries to break

the rope and cannot. When it grows, even though it could easily escape, it never tries again. A child so used to being restrained and imprisoned from the first day it draws breath would never know of freedom—or even that it *could* break free."

Silence fell around the fire as they all tried to digest the unpalatable image Hugh's words conjured.

"Lord Rowan also mentioned that the human form is not capable of holding such magic as a Nereus wields, and their minds splinter. He said it was kinder to keep the child imprisoned. The damage the last Nereus did to England is why the council decided they could never risk the creation of another. Hence the murders of all mages born into a female form." Sera broke off a chunk of bread and chewed as she stared into the flames.

"Speaking of that, Lord Rowan has spread the word you're dangerous and not right up here." Elliot tapped the side of his head. "Now that you've escaped his clutches, he'll have the militia out hunting you."

"They'll not find me," Sera murmured. She drew the necklace from under her shirt. Stroking the silver disc, she let it drop and held up the autumn leaf. "We're going to Somerset, and I am crossing Shadow-vane into Faery with Hugh."

Kitty gestured to Elliot. "You are to help me, Elliot. We must try to have Sera's wrongful imprisonment overturned and keep causing trouble for Abigail."

Sera drew up a battle plan in her mind. They each

had a task to perform before she could confront and defeat Lord Rowan.

Sera leaned against Hugh's side. "You will probably fall head over heels in love with the Fae. They say that is what splintered King George's mind—seeing the full beauty of Princess Deryn."

"There is no danger of that. My heart already belongs to another." His murmured words burned hot through her body.

"We will monitor Lord Rowan and his treacherous granddaughter. I will also see what news I can ferret out about Queen Charlotte," Kitty said.

With decisions made, they settled down for the night. Sera snuggled against Hugh and the surgeon curled his larger frame around her. She set magical alarms around the edge of their camp, to alert her if any creature approached, and a canopy to protect them from snow or rain. Then, safe in the arms of the man who loved her, she surrendered to sleep.

SERA WOKE AT FIRST LIGHT, as Mother Nature painted the sky over her head. The discomfort in her body from a night on the hard ground was forgotten as she watched navy bleed into deep pink, before spreading into a dusky orange. Only when the others began to stir did she rise.

Hugh poked at the fire with a stick, a small kettle balanced precariously over the flames. A strong odour escaped from the spout in spurts.

Sera inhaled the rich scent. "Is that coffee?"

"Campfire coffee. My specialty." He grinned.

"If only we had some fancy mage who could conjure up breakfast for us," Elliot grumbled. He had never been a morning person, unless you counted the hours before seven.

"I could conjure you a spectacular feast. But it would be ash in your mouth. Magical food has no real sustenance to it." Sera sat cross-legged on the ground.

Hugh fumbled in his saddle bag and pulled out two small tin cups. "If you wouldn't mind?" He gestured to the kettle hanging from the handle hooked over a thick branch.

Sera wrapped a wedge of magic around the pot and tugged it free of the fire. It floated over the cups.

"A mere inch in each, thank you," Hugh said.

A thick brown sludge oozed out of the spout and Elliot made a horrified noise in the back of his throat.

Hugh then ladled fresh water from a small pail and stirred the mix before handing one to Sera.

Kitty had retrieved two more cups from her bag and Sera poured an inch into each of those as instructed.

Sera blew on the strong brew, and a wisp of steam puffed over the other side of her cup. Taking a cautious sip, she screwed up her nose. "I don't think I could ever permanently replace hot chocolate or a cup of tea with coffee."

Hugh swallowed his in two gulps. "You get used to it. And I find a strong brew keeps me awake through the night when needed."

Sera steeled herself and kept drinking. They all needed fortitude for what lay ahead, and she most certainly would need her wits about her when they stepped into the Fae realm.

FOURTEEN

AFTER THEIR BREAKFAST of what Elliot called, with obvious disgust, *gruel*, they packed away cups and bowls and doused the campfire. Sera went to each horse and laid a hand on its broad face while she murmured a strength spell. They still had farther to ride than a horse, unassisted, could travel in a day. It was a risk, using her small store of magic to aid their journey, but she needed to be in the Fae realm and beyond Lord Rowan's reach as soon as possible.

There was one other magical task that she deemed an appropriate use of her recovering magical abilities. After Abigail had had Kitty ejected from her home, Kitty had loudly demanded payment for an abortifacient. That had no doubt already begun the reputation-destroying rumour that Abigail was with child.

Sera called to the birds and when they circled above her, she whispered an enchantment that would strengthen the rumour. The birds would be her messengers. As they flew over London, each *deposit* they left on rooftops, monuments, and the roads would release another whisper about Abigail's scandalous and unseemly behaviour. It might not work, but any trouble Sera could cast back at her former friend was worth it, in her opinion.

Once she had completed her tasks, they mounted their horses and rode hard all day, stopping only briefly when they found a river from which to drink and to relieve themselves. They pushed the horses until Hugh spoke up, concerned for their wellbeing.

"They are drawing strength from me, and will recover with a good overnight rest," Sera called over her shoulder as they cantered on along the packed earth roads. She would need more than a good night's sleep to recover, as the equines were tugging every spark of her gift from her body. This time, if she drove herself to exhaustion, she feared her gift would not return stronger, but she might extinguish her flame permanently.

The sun had nearly completed its journey across the sky when they neared their destination. Sera rolled her shoulders. What she wouldn't give for a hot bath and a soft bed! Up ahead appeared a squat stone cottage crouched under an ancient oak. The tree had a circumference that, if hollowed out, could have stabled two horses. Its boughs stretched over the roof of the cottage and would provide a shade umbrella in summer. In winter, it appeared that bony hands reached for the chimney on the other side.

Oddly, the cottage had no windows facing the road. The timber of the solid door had weathered to silver over time, and the cast-iron hinges were rusted in places. They dismounted, and Kitty let out a yelp.

"I can't feel my bottom." Kitty clung to the horse for support as her body remembered how legs were supposed to work.

"I'm sorry. You will be able to spend the night here. You can take a slower pace back to London and overnight in a tavern—if you can find one that meets Elliot's high standards." Sera stroked her mount and let another trickle of magic flow into the horse's tired muscles.

"As long as it serves half-decent ale, I don't care," Elliot grumbled as he dismounted and arched his back to relieve his tight muscles.

They tied their reins to a low-hanging branch of the oak. The exhausted horses lowered their heads to nuzzle for grass under the smattering of snow. Sera stretched her legs, walking to the edge of the meadow and peering at the other side, which was shrouded in a deep mist.

"Shadowvane," Sera whispered, and the name sent a shiver running over her skin.

"Is this it?" Elliot asked, his face screwed up in a scowl. "I thought we'd be going to Stonehenge. Isn't that the fancy doorway to the Fae world?"

Sera winked at Elliot. "Stonehenge is the distraction that keeps people away from here."

The footman scoffed. "It's a bloody big distraction."

"Which is probably why it works so well." Hugh stood on Sera's other side and scanned the field.

"Are you sure about this?" Kitty took Sera's gloved hand and squeezed.

Sera leaned into her friend. "Yes. If I can, I will use the mage silver ring to signal you. But I don't know if they will work once I am in the Fae realm. If we don't return..." Words clogged Sera's throat. How to tell her friend that she loved her with all her heart? And would never have reached this point without her unwavering support, sharp mind, and keen instincts?

Kitty grabbed hold of Sera's hands and spun her to face her. "Don't you dare. Not a single word of failure, or about not returning, will pass your lips. You will return, my friend, you simply must. I cannot endure London society without you. Also, I doubt the Fae want an argumentative and stubborn friend journeying across this field to rescue you."

"I love you, Katherine Napier." Sera threw her arms around Kitty and hugged her tight, some part of her dreading she would never see her again.

"I love you, Sera. Now let us stop all this emotional twaddle. There is work to be done." Kitty wiped her eyes with the heels of her palms and gestured to the field.

Worries multiplied in Sera's mind. If there was no way to communicate between realms, neither of them would know what the other faced. Nor could they warn each other if events reached such a point. No, wait.

That wasn't right. There *was* a way for messages to be relayed between the Fae realm and the human one.

"Paper!" Sera exclaimed, startling a bird in the tree above.

Kitty arched a dark eyebrow at her friend. "Paper?"

"Yes. I will ensorcell a piece of paper. Whoever Lord Branvale has been corresponding with is in the Fae realm, and their messages appear on paper. Which means I have a way to communicate with you." Then doubt assailed Sera. "If we have any paper, that is." Only now did she recall her stack of notes about the Repository left sitting in her room.

What followed was a frantic search of their saddlebags.

"Will this do?" Elliot pulled a folded sheet from his jacket pocket and waved it in the air.

Sera snatched it from his hand and shook it loose. On the front was an advertisement for a dancer at a tavern in Soho. "I hope you weren't keeping this as a souvenir?"

He ran a hand through his hair and dropped his gaze. "We all have to make sacrifices in these difficult times."

While wrinkled and creased, and bearing a few spots and stains of unknown origin, the back of the handbill was blank. "It will do. Thank you for your sacrifice, Elliot."

Holding the sheet in one hand, Sera raised the other and whispered under her breath. Drawing a line in the air, she sliced the paper in half just above the dancer's navel.

"Can you put her back together again afterwards?" Elliot sighed and his shoulders drooped at the sight of the beautiful woman, now in two pieces.

Kitty elbowed him hard. "After this, Sera and I will organise a private performance for you."

That idea cheered the footman immensely.

Sera added *dancer* to the list in her head of things to do when she returned. Although she suspected Kitty was keeping an actual list. That would save Sera from having to remember everyone she needed to thank once she had defeated Lord Rowan and favours needed to be repaid. Or dancers hired.

Placing the two halves facing each other, Sera cast the spell that would allow words written on one piece to appear on the other. A swipe of the hand would clear away the text to enable a response to be written. Given the shabby state of the page, she then added a protective charm to the fibres to extend the paper's lifespan.

"It's done." She folded each half into smaller squares and handed one to Kitty. The other she tucked inside her stays, close to her heart.

Then she surveyed the meadow where the hue of the grass changed from the winter green close to the cottage to an emerald sheen as it marched into the horizon. "Isn't it beautiful?"

A sweet perfume like honey arose from the soil as her boots trod the fertile ground at the edges. Birdsong that she had never before heard came from beyond the mist. Like a siren song, it urged her to keep walking and cross the meadow. Winged insects drifted from one spectacular bloom to another, sounding like a thousand fairies humming in a forest under the light of a full moon.

"Beautiful, but deadly. And treacherous. Reminds me of Abigail," Kitty muttered.

As much as Sera wanted to stride across the exotic landscape and cross into the other realm, there were still words that had to be said. She could afford a few more minutes with her friends.

Elliot waited behind them with the horses, his feet firmly in the human realm and a rare worried look in his eyes.

Sera marched back to him. The first thing she did was retrieve the Fae bracelet from her saddlebags and shove it into a deep pocket of her coat. Next, she addressed her loyal footman. "You are in charge of the household, Elliot. I trust you to take care of Rosie and Vicky and not eat all the cake. I will return, so don't go moving my clothes out of the big bedroom, either." Then she flung her arms around the man, who was far more than a servant. "Thank you," she whispered as unshed tears misted her vision.

Elliot hugged her tight. Then let her go to hold her at arm's length. A wan smile lifted the corners of his mouth. "Come back in one piece, will you? That would save me the trouble of finding a new employer."

Kitty slapped him on the shoulder. "Don't you worry about being kept busy, Mr Brynn. You and I have plenty to do in London. We might even have a set of livery that will fit you."

Elliot grimaced and cast a pleading look at Sera. She bit back a laugh. Quite apart from making Elliot wear a footman's uniform, Kitty would work him hard. He might even have to get used to rising early for the meetings at the Napier home. She had a sneaking suspicion that her right-hand man would be immensely relieved to have her back, so he could return to his more relaxed working conditions.

"The cottage is unlocked. You can stay here tonight and head back to London in the morning." Sera approached the lonely little building and pressed a hand to the solid oak door. The latch lifted, and the door swung inward without a single squeak or protest. Sunlight from the setting sun cast a golden glow through the single window that faced the meadow and bathed the interior in a cosy warmth, despite the chilly temperature outside.

"What is this place?" Kitty asked as she stood on the threshold.

Inside were two single beds with bright coverlets in autumnal hues. A table and chairs sat beneath the window. A fire was laid and ready to be lit, with two faded armchairs on either side of the fireplace. A thick rug covered the floorboards.

"The cottage is for the watcher, who is supposed to stop anyone from stumbling into the Fae realm. I believe the post is currently vacant, but the cottage remains ready in case it is needed. It is like a much smaller cousin of the Repository, I suppose." Sera knew a little about the person who was supposed to guard the portal between realms. The matter of the vacancy had been raised at one of the Mage Council's meetings and curiosity had driven her to find out a little more about it. Much like Jerome's position at the Repository, the role of watcher came with magical conditions.

"Brilliant! A proper bed." Elliot dropped the saddlebags on the bench that ran along one wall.

Sera cast a spark at the fireplace. Her friends would be warm and comfortable tonight. As for her and Hugh... who knew what sort of reception they would find on the other side?

"We will be able to watch you from here until the moment you... disappear." Kitty gestured to the window, set at the perfect height to give someone at the table a clear view over the meadow.

Hanging on a hook behind the door was a worn, brown leather satchel. Sera took it down and, with a promise to the cottage to return it later, she emptied her pockets into the bag. She also grabbed what items she thought they would need from their saddlebags. Once she had everything she might need in the Fae realm, she passed the strap over her head and settled the satchel at her side.

Then, she glanced at Hugh. "Ready?"

He nodded and took her outstretched hand. With a final wave to her friends, they left the cottage and walked across the field. Despite everywhere else being cloaked in the depths of winter and plants in hibernation, all around them were flowers in full summer bloom. Some had petals that appeared to be made of fluffy, pale grey clouds. Others seemed alive, their blooms swinging towards their movement. One had ink-black petals that curled over a honey-coloured stamen. Another sprouted what appeared to be tiny purple antlers or silken vines.

In the golden shafts of the gloaming, butterflies glided across the meadow in all directions, their wings like tiny kaleidoscopes of colour as they flitted from bloom to bloom. Dragonflies raced above the blossoms, their iridescent bodies sparkling in the descending twilight. The air was alive with buzzing bees and singing birds, at odds with the wintery conditions back at the cottage.

Sera curled her fingers more tightly in Hugh's grip. How easy it would be to become lost in the beauty of the place. Did time slow here, the way it did at the Repository? It certainly obeyed a different rotation of seasons. Or it might always be the end of summer in the meadow. She wracked her brain, trying to remember any stories of young people who had wandered into Shadowvane and emerged as geriatrics, unaware that years had sailed past as they chased butterflies or drank nectar from rare flowers.

Trees edged the meadow, creating a majestic backdrop for the beauty at centre stage. The long branches of willow and the pale trunks of birch swayed in the wind like graceful dancers. Fading light filtered through their leaves, and bare branches became fingers rippling across the land.

"What happens now?" Hugh asked as he reached for a black flower that appeared to be made of the softest velvet.

Sera wasn't entirely sure. She had only read accounts of how mages travelled between realms, and most seemed to use portals hidden in forests or disguised as rocks. She thought they stepped through from one side to the other as easily as one stepped from room to room inside a house. The opportunity for her to use a gateway hadn't presented itself—until now.

But Shadowvane was different. Here, the two realms butted against each other, and the edges overlapped. Two types of magic rubbed against one another and created unexpected results. There was no doorway. From what little Sera had learned, it was more like passing through a storm.

"We hope the offer of safe passage was genuine."

As though it knew where it was, the autumn-leaf pendant vibrated against her skin. Sera tugged it free of her warm layers. The metallic leaf glowed in the last caress of the disappearing sun and emitted a tune that harmonised with the music of flowers, birds, and insects. She closed her hand around it and thought of the person who had corresponded with her guardian, asking them to guide her and Hugh safely to the Fae realm.

The gentle breeze across the meadow grew stronger and stronger. It circled them as it intensified, growing in strength with each pass until a vortex whipped up around them. The swirling mass contained fallen leaves, snatched petals, twigs, and dirt, all of it plucked off the ground and mashed together until a wall of detritus penned them in.

"Is this supposed to happen?" Hugh shouted, throwing up one arm against the spinning litter.

Sera nestled close to him, sheltering in his embrace. They couldn't move without her using her magic to burst through the vortex. Assuming the wind was the method by which they would travel to the Fae realm, if they ran away from it, she would never know what lay on the other side.

"The token is our safe passage, but who knows what the Fae consider safe?" Sera yelled as the noise of twigs banging against each other and the roar of the wind grew louder.

The whirlwind circled them, the dense matter it contained now completely obscuring their view of the meadow, the sky, and their friends watching from the warmth of the cottage. Closer and closer it drew. The force of it tugged at them, threatening to separate them. Hugh tightened his grip on Sera's hand and wrapped the other around her waist. Sera curled her fingers into the cloth of his coat sleeve for extra security and clutched the strap of the satchel over her chest. She didn't want the dangerous bracelet flung across the meadow.

Their bodies were buffeted like small boats on a turbulent ocean. The very air seemed pulled from

Sera's lungs, and she coughed. When she dared to inhale, it rasped full of grit down her throat. Her skin tingled with the electrical charge in the air.

"Hold on!" Sera screamed as the mass dropped over them like a fisherman's net, and her feet were swept out from under her.

FIFTEEN

SERA's head pounded and light forced its way between her tightly closed eyelids. "Not again," she muttered.

If she opened her eyes and found herself back in the little cell in the Repository of Forgotten Things, she might just scream and have a mage-sized tantrum out of sheer frustration.

"Drink this," a soft voice said as something cool and moist was pressed to her lips. "Sometimes the wind is capricious, even if you were offered safe passage."

Sera pushed the glass away and sat up. She had heard stories that warned her to never eat or drink anything in the Fae realm, lest you be trapped forever. Her hands and feet scrambled at the slick floor until her back pressed against something hard and cold. Opening her eyes, a slender woman with lilac hair pulled back in a tight braid and the most stunning features knelt beside her. A crystal glass was held in her outstretched hands. Her pale brows were crinkled in a quizzical expression.

"Hugh?" Sera cast around for her companion.

Hugh leaned against the mirrored wall not far from Sera. They sat on a grey marble floor. Veins of silver and onyx wound their way through the cool slab and seemed to pulse as though the floor lived.

Hugh clutched a half-empty glass in one hand. He swiped his other hand across his mouth and Sera guessed he had just downed most of the liquid. She held in a sigh. Perhaps she should have warned him about not ingesting anything *before* they entered the Fae realm.

"You can eat and drink safely while at the Seelie court. You will come to no harm here." The woman's hair reminded her of a stormy sky with its streaks of grey and purple. Her eyes were likewise a blue that swirled to purple close to the pupil. Her shoulders were draped in a grey woollen cloak that had the softness of silk. Underneath she wore a paler grey gown of simple construction. She extended the glass towards Sera again. The golden liquid inside sparkled as the light passed through it.

"Telling me it's safe to drink sounds like something the Unseelie would do." Rather than trusting the unknown woman, Sera sent a trickle of her magic through the drink, trying to discern whether it contained anything she might regret drinking later. Not that she ever had much luck in detecting Fae magic.

"I understand why you might not trust my words,

my lady. I am Sinead. I am to be your guide while you are in our realm. You are under the protection of the queen, and none can harm you without incurring her wrath." Sinead sat back on her heels.

As Sera still hesitated about taking the drink, a cough wracked her torso, and she spat up a small bit of twig. That decided it. Her throat felt like she had licked a tree. Besides, if Hugh were trapped here because of what he had drunk, she would stay with him. She took the glass as Hugh downed the remains of his in one gulp and gave a satisfied burp.

"What is in this? It's mighty tasty?" he asked Sinead and dangled the empty glass from between two fingers.

"Honeyed mead with a few locally grown herbs," the Fae woman replied.

Sera sipped hers more cautiously. Recent events had taught her not to trust anyone. But the sweet flavour swirled over her tongue and eased the dry rasp in her gullet. Before she knew it, her glass was also empty and the ache in her throat had gone.

"Thank you," she murmured to their guide.

"If you are sufficiently recovered, the queen awaits you." Sinead took the glasses from them and handed them off to a woman standing behind her, who wore a crisp white apron over her dark grey dress.

Sera assumed the second woman was some sort of servant. More curiously, she appeared to be human. That led her to wonder if many humans lived in the

Fae realm, or had the maid been trapped and indentured to earn back her release?

Rising to her feet, Sera reached for Hugh's hand. Her gift flowed sluggishly within her, and she dared not use any more. Instead, she drew on the quiet strength of the man at her side and stood a little taller.

Only now did she take in the full wonder of her surroundings. The vortex had dropped them straight into the Fae court. They appeared to be in a grand presence chamber within, she assumed, the Fae palace. Everything around them gleamed with an otherworldly splendour. The silver veins in the marble floor sparkled like a tiny mercury river. The mirrored walls set on opposite sides of the chamber reflected the room into infinity and made the space seem endlessly vast. High above, an enchanted ceiling resembled the sky outside. Twilight streaked across it in hues of mauve and softest orange. Purple clouds drifted by, and a flock of oddly shaped birds flew in a *V* towards their roosts.

An intoxicating blend of exotic florals permeated the air, heightening the senses until Sera felt pleasantly drunk on the spectacle of beauty surrounding them. When she reached out to the earth far beneath her, she discovered the very stones of the palace thrummed with a subtle power, a pulse that created a tingle in her blood and revived her flagging gift a little.

This was a place of formidable and dangerous beauty, where the laws of mortals held no sway. Every part of her stretched taut with a warning. But she needed Fae help if she was to learn more about her history, save King George, and bring down Lord Rowan.

Hand in hand, Hugh and Sera walked through the gathered Fae nobility towards the raised throne at one end of the room. The ladies of the court were ethereal visions, their willowy forms draped in gossamer silks of scarlet, azure, and emerald. Their flawless faces were framed by cascades of hair—silver, lilac, frosty blue, and palest gold. Headdresses adorned with gems caught the light, and exotic butterflies were nestled in their hair as living combs.

"As beautiful as they are, none are as striking as you," Hugh murmured, and he grazed her knuckles with his thumb.

Sera tucked the lovingly spoken words away in her heart. Hugh was clearly delusional if he thought her more attractive than the Fae, who would make angels weep at their own inadequacy. But Hugh loved her, and obviously love did funny things to the mind. Or it affected his vision. Which was a worry for a surgeon, if his eyesight failed him. But his words reassured her that he wouldn't decide to stay in the Fae realm, or transfer his affections to another.

The highborn Fae lords cut dashing figures, clad in velvets and silks with intricate embroidery, brocade, and fur trims. Their chests glittered with medals from unknown battles, and chains of precious metals and stones were draped across their coats. As they stood conversing in small groups, they puffed on bejewelled hookahs.

In Sera's opinion, she much preferred Hugh's physique, the breadth of his shoulders, and the strength in his hands. Mentally, she estimated that the surgeon could toss any one of the dapper Fae lords across the room. Should they need to make a quick escape, that was, and the Fae men blocked the doorways.

Everywhere Sera turned, catlike eyes glinted with mischief and secrets, and the nobles cast wary glances at them. Were these people friends or foes?

With every step they took towards the queen, a new fantastical sight emerged. A lavender-haired Elven child in a silver tunic stalked past on stilt-like legs, clutching the jewel-studded leash of a live peacock. Two dwarven servants in velvet livery pushed a copper wheelbarrow containing life-sized marquetry chess pieces, the pieces carved from amber and jade to resemble the courtiers.

The court was a spectacle of strange and alien beauty. A seductive glamour woven with peril and sharp edges. Every new wonder inspired both gasps and shudders. Before they reached the queen, a headache had taken up residence behind Sera's eyes. It was all simply too much to take in, and her vision began to hurt with the mere act of *looking*.

"Keep your wits about you, Hugh. Whether Seelie or Unseelie, the Fae are known for mischief and tricks," Sera murmured to her constant companion.

"Perhaps you should have brought Kitty. She is better armed with wit," he whispered in reply.

Sera squeezed his hand. "We shall muddle through

without her. I'll not make any promises with a Fae until I have consulted with my solicitor via the ensorcelled paper."

Near the dias holding the throne, a trio of satyr musicians with curling gold horns and hooves like polished ebony strummed lutes and pipes, filling the air with a haunting melody. Nymphs draped in diaphanous pink and sea-foam gowns danced barefoot, trailing flowers and vines that entwined and blossomed with their graceful movements.

When they stood before the queen on her obsidian throne, Sera dropped a deep curtsey and Hugh bowed. They waited for several long heartbeats before she spoke.

"You may rise." Queen Deryn spoke with a soft, lilting voice. Upon her hair of silvery gold, her crown of platinum and diamonds cast dazzling rays of multi-coloured light. She was resplendent in an emerald gown covered in peacock feathers, whose knowing eyes seemed to wink at Sera.

"Your Majesty, I am Lady Seraphina Winyard, mage of England. This is my companion, Mr Hugh Miles, royal surgeon," Sera said.

"We know who you are, Lady Winyard. News of your exploits has reached our ears here in this realm." The queen leaned her cheek on one curled hand, her elbow on the rolled arm of the throne, carved to resemble a peacock's head. The bird's tail feathers fanned out behind the queen and formed the back of the throne.

Sera wondered which rumour in particular had penetrated as far as the Fae court, and whether that was good or bad. Or perhaps her anonymous correspondent whispered in the queen's ear.

On their ride to Somerset, Sera had pondered what to say to the Fae queen. In the end, she decided on the direct approach. There was no point in wasting her time if the queen was going to reject her appeal for help. "I have journeyed here to seek your assistance, Your Majesty. There is a mage who intends to overthrow King George and seize the crown for himself."

Queen Deryn tapped a fingernail against the arm of her throne, while she appeared to watch the dancers. "Why would events in the human realm interest us?"

"Because this mage intends to create a Nereus, to draw on its power for his own ends." Not that Lord Rowan could achieve that part of his plan now. Like dominoes, Sera would keep knocking over whatever the old mage tried until the entire plot collapsed in a heap.

The queen drew in a sharp breath, and when she turned her head, her gaze fell to Sera's belly. "Have you brought such a creature here?" She hissed the words in such a way that they shivered down Sera's spine.

Such a reaction indicated that the Nereus was not unknown to the queen. But how much did she know? The idea flitted through Sera's mind that Queen Deryn herself might be her correspondent.

"No. Nor will I ever, if you grant me your aid to defeat him." Sera didn't want to contemplate a future where Lord Rowan emerged victorious. The consequences would reach for her and all those she loved.

The queen tented her fingers, her elbows resting on the arms of the ornate throne. She tapped her index fingers together and regarded Sera over the steeple they made.

"Again, why should we become involved in human politics?" Her words held a chilled edge.

Sera kept a tight grip on Hugh's hand. "Someone in your court is interested enough in our politics to have spent years corresponding with my former guardian, Lord Branvale. They know more about the plot reaching for the father of your son. Or does the fate of Arwyn not concern you?" Sera met the queen's gaze. The other woman's pupils had widened at the mention of her son's name. Had she willingly given up her child to be raised in the human realm, or had the babe been prised from her arms?

Interest flared in the queen's golden eyes, and her hands curled around the peacock heads. "You have brought news of our son?"

"I shall tell you of Arwyn, if you tell me where to find the person I seek." As cruel as it was to keep news of Arwyn from his mother, Sera needed to find the person who wielded a pen over the enchanted paper.

The queen sat back and narrowed her gaze. For a moment, Sera wondered if she had overstepped some invisible boundary. Then a radiant smile broke over the monarch's face. "We were informed that you were a canny one. Very well, a trade it is."

A demure smile crossed Sera's lips. "I believe Your Majesty takes precedence, and should go first," she murmured.

The queen arched one delicate brow as she regarded Sera. Then she made a noise in the back of her throat as though she found something satisfactory or worthwhile in the view. "The one you seek is rarely within the walls of this palace. They prefer to spend their time out in the gardens. Sinead will lead you to where they can be found."

Sera reined in her excitement. She was so close now. All the answers she sought would soon be in her possession. "Thank you, Your Majesty. For my part, I am privileged to call your son my friend. He has grown into an exceptionally handsome, intelligent, and kind man." Sera left out the bit about Arwyn's revolutionary ideas and his support for the idea of dismantling the monarchy and placing control in the hands of the people.

"It greatly saddened us when our father had our child removed from our realm. A half-breed royal is not permitted here." The queen's voice softened as she recalled the pain of having to give up her child.

Sera glanced around her. From appearances, it seemed half-breed nobles were not so uncommon. Rounded ears, such as she and Hugh sported, appeared on a few of those assembled. Nor did they have the perfect beauty of the full Fae peers, whose faces were so startling that one could not gaze upon them for too long.

"It seems harsh to remove a baby from his mother. Was there no place for Arwyn here? I know he longs to make your acquaintance." Sera walked a delicate line, not wanting to cause some diplomatic incident by telling the queen how to run her court.

"Only a full-blood Fae may sit on this throne or have a seat at our council table. Our lives are bound by laws that have existed for millennia. It was considered... unwise to have a potential threat to our throne without an occupation." Queen Deryn's hands tightened on the arms of her throne.

Sera swallowed a snort. If they thought Arwyn might usurp the throne because he was bored, they should have given him a role. If their rigid rules had been around for that long, they were probably well overdue for a change. Someone had to be brave enough to carve a new path. Like two women, the closest of friends, who refused to bow to society's expectations that they sit quietly and do their needlework. Perhaps one day, the path Sera and Kitty intended to forge would benefit other women who would follow them.

"King George has placed Arwyn among his councillors, and often seeks his first-born son's advice." At least her king had not cast his son out into the cold. Arwyn had not chosen to be born; it was the willing actions of his parents that had created him. Why should he be punished for something he did not do? While diplomacy was not Sera's strong suit, she was wise enough to keep those thoughts firmly inside her head.

A coldness dropped over the queen's face, and her lush lips thinned. "You will be shown to the gardens, then to your rooms. Tonight, you will join us for dinner. Tomorrow, we will discuss other matters. In private."

Before Sera could say anything, Hugh's stomach rumbled, and she stifled a laugh. They had journeyed quite a distance and without any luncheon.

"Thank you, Your Majesty." Sera dropped another curtsey as the queen rose.

Silk rustled as the entire court curtsied or bowed as Queen Deryn left the presence chamber, trailed by her ladies. The satyr musicians followed, still playing as their hooves tapped on the marble floor at the rear of the entourage.

A tingle of excitement wormed through Sera's body. *Now,* she would meet her correspondent.

Sinead came forward and inclined her head. "If you would follow me?" Their Fae guide walked at a sedate pace from the presence chamber.

Sera resisted the urge to blow out a snort. Would she follow? Her bigger concern was holding back the temptation to use a trickle of magic to prod Sinead into moving faster.

Hugh's shoulders shook with restrained humour as he fell into step beside Sera. He was well acquainted with her impatience.

From the presence chamber, they turned along a wide hallway. The air was permeated with a faint perfume that changed from orange blossom to the spice of cinnamon, then the bright aroma of newly cut grass.

Mouldings at the juncture of walls and ceiling glinted with gold and silver. The runners on the floor were iridescent as though jewels had been magically turned into thread. Some of the portraits were ensorcelled, their occupants moving to more comfortable positions. One Fae lord stopped to converse with a painting of a noble with his hunting dogs, and laughter rang out over some joke they both shared.

Their guide led them through an archway, across a covered colonnade, and into a garden that brought a gasp from Sera. The palace was curved around the grounds, offering towering walls that protected the lush growth from the worst of any winds. The scale and lushness surpassed the fabled gardens of Versailles. They could become lost in such a garden for weeks and never tread the same path twice.

Sixteen

When Sera regarded the extensive gardens with a more critical eye, she saw that it was all so geometric and tightly controlled. That somewhat diminished the soul of the garden, in her opinion. How she loved a wild, untamed garden that sprawled and seeded wherever it wanted. In the garden she planned for Westbourne Green, she would create shadowy, quiet spaces nestled in the gentle embrace of tall hedges and trees.

Despite the human realm's being in the depths of winter, the Fae world balanced on the edge of summer as it prepared to leap into autumn. Sinead slowed her pace, as though she knew Sera required time to savour the sights and scents. Hand in hand, she and Hugh strolled slowly through the large, intricate Fae garden, divided into outdoor rooms by tall hedges or stone walls.

The first room they traversed was a colourful rose garden with neat rectangular beds bounded by clipped buxus and filled with every shade of rose imaginable. The air was heavy with their sweet perfume. Bees swarmed frantically among the blooms, gathering pollen before they headed back to their hive for the evening.

The next garden room held a fountain at its centre, water spilling from the mouth of a stone fish into a rounded basin. Ivy climbed the sides of the pond, its leaves shimmering with moisture. Statues of graceful nymphs dotted the lawn, grinning playfully down at clusters of purple and white lilies that sprouted at their feet. Butterflies danced over the spreading orange blooms of coral flowers and yellow marigolds.

Through an archway in the yew hedge, they entered a herb garden. Even here, order reigned, the beds laid out in neat rows to house the aromatic plants. The heady scent of rosemary mingled with thyme and basil. Chives and parsley grew in abundance, stalks heavy with fresh green leaves. Ladybirds crawled over sage and lavender heads nodding for attention.

"While I am enjoying the tour, we will soon run out of daylight. Where is my correspondent?" Sera called to Sinead. The sun dipped to the horizon and delicate strands of vibrant orange and deep pink were painted across the sky.

"We are nearly there." Sinead would say no more.

The next archway was lower than the others. The dense foliage brushed against their bodies as they pushed into the adjoining space.

"Oh," Sera breathed. At last, the hard edges and

sharp lines were left behind. Before her was the untamed beauty that called to her heart.

They crossed a wildflower meadow. Her feet sank into the damp grass. Ivy and wild grapevines, their dark green leaves shining after a recent rain, spilt over arched trellises made of willow cuttings.

In the far corner, sheltered by the surrounding hedge, stood the largest rowan tree Sera had ever seen. It must have been at least fifty feet tall and over two hundred years old to have reached such a height.

Sinead gestured to the tree. "I shall leave you alone."

"With a tree?" Hugh asked, glancing from Sera to the receding figure of their guide.

Sera plucked a strand of timothy grass with its fat, long-seeded head, and waved it like a wand. "Perhaps the person we seek is hiding behind it?"

The gnarled trunk and thick branches of the rowan were a rough contrast to the soft lushness that surrounded it. Deep red hollyhocks, catnip, and daisies grew wild at the tree's base. Curious, Sera walked around the tree, one hand trailing along its bark.

Hugh met her on the other side. "Perhaps it is a Fae joke? As if I asked you to pass me a left-handed scalpel?"

Sera didn't consider it amusing to have her limited time wasted. She walked back to what she considered the *front* of the ancient tree that looked out upon its corner of the Fae gardens. She was about to mutter something rude about Fae tricks when a hint of movement caught her eye. In the shadows of a knot, she glimpsed a face peering out at her. Then it vanished back within the trunk of the rowan.

"Oh! Not hiding behind the tree but *in* it." She wracked her brain for what sort of creature or person would blend so seamlessly with the bark. Only one sprang to mind.

Dryad.

How did one lure such a creature out of a tree? If it were a squirrel, she would offer a nut. Sera didn't have anything edible in her possession that might entice a dryad. But she had something else.

"I am Seraphina Winyard. I have journeyed here to find you." Sera pulled the token from under her shirt and held up the metallic leaf—the guarantee of safe passage sent by her correspondent.

The knothole morphed into an eye that regarded her. The iris was a mossy green and fringed by impossibly long and thick eyelashes, like rushes edging a pond. With a slow movement, the eye blinked. At first, nothing else happened and Sera wondered if the dryad had heard her. Then a rustle came from the rowan. The fissures in the bark raced along the trunk and formed an outline. Piece by piece, the being shook itself free of the trunk and formed into a willowy dryad. Her hair flowed down her back in leaves of crimson and gold, matching the rowan's autumnal colour and that of the token. Her clothing was made of papery fabric the colour of tea.

As the dryad moved farther away from the tree, her appearance altered and shifted.

Hugh drew in a sharp breath of wonder as, before their eyes, she changed until she resembled a human woman. She could have been somewhere around thirty years of age, her body past the bloom of youth and an ancient wisdom in her deep green gaze. Her hair changed to a russet brown, and her dress turned from leaves into fine linen.

"I am Elowen. We have much to discuss." The dryad gestured to a stone bench nestled between two topiaries and with its back to the hedge.

Hugh still stared, his face one of open wonder. It had been quite the week for him—first ghosts and now a transforming Unnatural. If Sera could have squeezed in a visit to Lionel, the surgeon might have expired from excitement. Perching on a stone that resembled a cairn, he patted down his pockets and drew forth a small journal. Then he began scribbling notes.

Sera tried to sort through what she knew. How on earth had the woodland creature been dragged into human events, and Sera's life in particular? Had she perhaps been present when Sera was born, like the gargoyles working alongside her father? "How did you come to know who I am?"

"All of this land, human and Fae, know of the girl mage born and allowed to live." Elowen's voice had a soft, pleasant tone. Like listening to the gentle murmur of water in a peaceful creek.

That a female mage had been allowed to exist was a

most unusual thing. Although in hindsight, Lord Rowan had probably rubbed his hands with glee and, Sera assumed, only put on a dour face when sitting at the Mage Council's round table.

"There is a difference between knowing of my existence and instructing my guardian to snap a cruel piece of jewellery onto my wrist to dampen my powers. How did you know of Lord Rowan's intentions?" How did dryads learn of human politics? Perhaps birds carried news from parliament and court, and gossiped while roosting in trees in the evenings. Sera had used avian messengers to further spread Kitty's gossip about Abigail, after all.

Elowen's eyes smiled but not her lips. "I have not always resided here. Once, I walked the streets of your realm in this form, and thought I would make a home there."

Sera couldn't imagine a dryad strolling the thoroughfares of London. What sort of company did she keep? She must have had some close friends if she thought to set up a home. Then an idea exploded in her head. A dryad was a type of Unnatural creature. Bonds of love might have made a woodland creature think about settling somewhere other than her natural habitat.

"You're Lady Branvale," Sera breathed in a soft tone, not quite believing it to be true and expecting to see confusion in the other woman's eyes. But she had to be. It was far too co-incidental otherwise. Her former guardian had spurned his bride on their wedding night

when he learned of her Unnatural state. And here, beside her, sat a being crafted from nature herself.

Pain flared in Elowen's eyes, then she glanced down at her hands, clasped over her gown of moss-green linen. On her left hand was a thin golden line, etched around one finger as though a golden ring had merged with her skin. "I thought he loved me enough to accept who I really am. Sadly, I was wrong."

How many years had it been, and yet her voice was thick with the heartbreak of rejection? Love truly worked in strange and mysterious ways. Sera hoped that Elowen had loved a man entirely different from the cruel and cold one who had ruled Sera's childhood.

"Is that why you are here, in the Fae realm?" Sera asked.

Elowen's hands tightened, then with a sigh, she cast them wide and curled her fingertips around the edge of the stone bench. "The human realm does not accept us. Here, the Fae live alongside all kinds of creatures and beings. They do not judge."

Sera could see the appeal of seeking refuge among the Fae. To settle in a realm where no one saw you as any different from another, despite the form you took. To be judged on your actions, and not your appearance or wealth. Or gender.

"You left our realm. But I don't understand why you involved yourself in this whole—" How to describe the abhorrent plot that Lord Rowan had hatched the day Sera was born? "Mess." Yes, *mess* seemed to fit it best. For she would certainly make a mess of things and ensure that Lord Rowan, and Abigail, rued the day the idea sprang into his head.

Elowen took Sera's hand and turned it over, tracing the lines on her palm. "All living things should be worried if a Nereus walks this earth again. None of us will be safe from its reach."

"What do you know of the Nereus? Did you hear tales of it?" Sera grasped for more information about the child of two mages. While her interest could only ever be an intellectual one, the mage library was oddly silent on the topic of such a powerful being.

"The earth remembers, long after humans have forgotten. While I had not yet sprouted, I am connected to those who saw the destruction the Nereus wrought upon the land. Forests burned. Rivers dried up. Crops failed. And all because a child threw a tantrum." The dryad traced a fingertip along Sera's lifeline.

A child powerful enough to dry up rivers and set forests ablaze would have been unimaginably powerful when they reached their full potential. All that magic squashed into a human form that, if Lord Rowan was to be believed, would fracture from the pressure. "Did the child gain control as he grew older?"

Elowen let go of Sera's hand and stroked a dangling vine of jasmine. At her touch, the plant grew a bud that opened to release the heady scent. "The Nereus did not reach adulthood. Your mages, or druids as they were called then, defeated him before it was too late. Even those who created the creature had realised their error by then. His mother laid the trap that captured and subdued him."

"Where did it happen?" Hugh asked.

"Scotland. On the shores of a cold and endlessly deep loch." Elowen rippled her fingers through the air as though she dragged them through chilly waters.

"Perhaps we could visit the site one day, Hugh. If we can find it." Would any trace remain of such a fierce battle? The land might have healed its scars, but Sera suspected traces of magic might still linger in rocks and soil. Or water.

"How old was he, when it happened?" Elowen said he had not reached adulthood. In Sera's mind, she imagined someone much like she had been when she escaped Lord Branvale's home. A young man about to turn eighteen and grasp his full power.

"I believe he had just reached his first decade." Elowen plucked the jasmine flower, and then the vine turned and crawled back over the trellis.

"Ten?" Sera gasped and glanced at Hugh, unsure she'd heard the dryad correctly.

Hugh had stopped scribbling notes and was listening intently to Elowen's tale.

All the mages of England had been needed to defeat a *ten-year-old child*. Sera closed her eyes as she imagined the battle playing out. A boy forced to fight his parents and the older mages. Had he brought a favourite toy to wherever they'd set their trap?

"I cannot imagine the pain his parents must have felt at having to kill their son," Sera whispered.

"I did not say they killed him. I said he was defeated."

"Was he imprisoned?" Sera tried to picture what had happened to the Nereus. Did the amassed mages have enough power to bind the boy's magic? What horrid existence had they sentenced him to? Then another thought wormed into her mind. Could the child be the magical being that powered the Repository? Although that had been created under Queen Elizabeth and the Nereus was captured centuries before that.

"The loch keeps hold of its secrets," Elowen murmured and declined to say any more on the subject.

Sera wondered what that meant. It only made her more determined to find the lake when her current problems were resolved. She turned her thoughts back to her predicament and the information she sought in the Fae realm. "When you wrote to Lord Branvale, did he know it was you?"

"Yes. He wanted me to return so that he could *cure* me." Pain echoed in her words.

Lord Branvale's love had driven his monstrous actions. Or had it ever really been love, if he sought to so fundamentally alter the person he claimed to love?

Everything she learned made emotions swirl fast through Sera. Like a river swollen by heavy rain, she struggled to contain herself, in case they broke free and overwhelmed her.

There was excitement, though, at finding someone who could finally provide her with longed-for answers.

Then came anger at how she had been manipulated and controlled for years.

She held out her arm and tugged up her sleeve to reveal the scarred imprint of the tree carved into her arm. "Did *you* give the bracelet to your husband that he snapped around my wrist when I was five?"

Elowen let out a sigh that sounded like a gentle breeze rustling through leaves. "Yes. Our queen's father, King Levian, sat on the throne then. His mage suggested the bracelet and found it among their store of ensorcelled items. I gave it to a messenger to carry to Branvale."

"Did the king's mage tell you what it would do to me?" Sera asked the question that had weighed on her mind since the day she had freed herself from it.

The dryad looked away, and the fading sun caressed her skin so that she glowed like bronze. "Yes."

"Did you not care about the suffering you caused a child?" Sera's voice broke on the words.

Hugh rose and moved to sit beside Sera. He slid one arm around her waist to protect her from old pain. Her hand curled into a fist. The pretty piece of jewellery had done far more than suppress her magic. It turned her into a weak and inferior vessel, to be taunted by the others. It had made her doubt herself and her own gift.

"You nearly destroyed me." If not for Kitty and her unfailing belief in her, Sera might have curled up in a ball and never sought to escape. After Lord Branvale was murdered, Lord Rowan might not have met any resistance as he slipped a new leash on her. She might even have been glad to go to her new prison.

Elowen regarded Sera, her eyes shining with unshed tears. "We suffered alongside you. Gaia herself cried for what had to be done. There was no other way that left you alive. If Lord Rowan thought you weak or powerless, we believed he would abandon his plan. For as you now know, two *powerful* mages are required to make the abomination."

That explained Sera's connection to Mother Earth. Had it always been there, or had the goddess reached out to soothe her troubled daughter? Sera slumped against Hugh, unable to speak as a torrent of memories washed over her and swept her away. The dryad cared about a mad mage's schemes of power, not about a small child, cut off from those who would have loved and supported her. Alone. Her magic suppressed.

She drew a shuddering breath as those days in the cold cell at the Repository sought to steal her back. Hugh wrapped both arms around her and held her close. Only his solid presence reminded Sera that she had battled all those who had tried to keep her down… and each time, she arose like the phoenix, to burn more brightly than before.

"I am forged in fire," she murmured.

"Yes. And your sacrifice has served to protect all those who call England home." Elowen stood and walked a few steps on the grass. Vivid blue cornflowers sprang up around the trailing hem of her dress.

Sera pushed despair and loneliness back into a

small box deep inside her. "I will stop Lord Rowan, either with your help or without it."

"He is powerful and has whispered his poison into many ears. You will stand alone on the battlefield as you face all of England's mages." Elowen tilted her head to regard Sera.

Lord Rowan's whisperings had already resulted in Sera's being incarcerated. She had much to undo at court. Not that she cared what most courtiers thought of her, but she longed to keep Queen Charlotte's goodwill. Elowen touched on what worried Sera the most. One or two mages she felt confident she could defeat. But the entire council?

"I am not alone. I have my friends, and that makes me more powerful than Lord Rowan realises." Sera took Hugh's hand and held it close to her chest.

"Would you risk their lives?"

Sera's fingers tightened as she considered the danger she would throw in the path of those she loved. Could she stand by as they perished beside her? A denial was trembling on the tip of her tongue when Hugh stood.

He grazed his curled fingers along her neck. "Sera would never ask it of us, but there are many like me, ordinary folk, who would fight beside her."

Elowen hummed, and the haunting melody rolled over the meadow. Dragonflies flocked to her and three glided around her head. "Perhaps, then, you are the one who can reach Ebonfyre."

SEVENTEEN

SERA ROLLED the odd name around on her tongue. "Who, or what, is Ebonfyre?"

Elowen walked towards the rowan tree. "Ebonfyre was imprisoned, as you once were, by the Nereus. Only the one who can unlock their cage can summon their assistance."

Sera blew out a snort. She wasn't sure she wanted to set something free that had been confined for over fifteen centuries. Look what had happened when she'd opened Lionel's cell door, and he'd only been trapped for years, not millennia. "I shall ask Queen Deryn about Ebonfyre over dinner."

A smile tugged at the corners of Elowen's lips. "Good. It is time they were free. I will be here when you are ready to talk more." The dryad spread out her arms, as though she would embrace the tree trunk, then she simply melded with it until only the blinking eye of the knothole remained.

The sun had sunk below the horizon and the gardens were washed in a deep golden glow as Sinead guided them back through the twists and turns of foliage. By the time they reached the palace, the glow had faded to the grey of descending night. Lights of pale mauve lit the opulent halls and gave all the furnishings an eerie appearance.

They followed their guide until she stopped before two panelled doors. Sinead placed a hand on one side and pushed the door open. "This is for you, Lady Winyard. Mr Miles will be accommodated farther down the hall."

Sera took Hugh's hand. "Mr Miles will be *accommodated* with me." For two reasons—one being her distrust of the Fae. The other being... personal.

"As you wish. I hope the room is sufficient for two." Sinead gestured for them to enter.

Sera bit the inside of her cheek. The suite was larger than the entire top floor of her little house in Soho.

The central piece was an enormous canopy bed that could have slept a family of six. The posts held aloft drapes of gossamer silks in violet and cobalt blue. Bolsters made from the softest feathers nestled against a headboard of intricately carved wood. The timber was so pale it gleamed silver and luminescent. Sera wondered how she would sleep at night in that glow— although it would be convenient for reading.

Wingback chairs upholstered in midnight velvet faced a grand marble fireplace where flames danced in an enchanting array of colours that complemented the bed hangings. An ornate desk inlaid with mother-of-pearl sat near the balcony, where views of the palace garden awaited. That reminded Sera that she needed to dash off a quick message to Kitty so that her friend would know they were safe—at least for the moment.

Gauzy curtains billowed gently in the breeze, bringing with them the sounds of fountains and the chatter of roosting birds from the verdant paradise below. Two armoires with their doors closed over the secrets they contained stood against the walls. The floor was covered in a multitude of plush rugs in the hues of dusk. They overlapped like clouds butting up against each other.

"This will do," Hugh announced. Then he hurled himself backwards over the end of the bed and a satisfied sigh wafted from him.

A small smile tugged at the corners of Sinead's lips as she watched his delight.

While Hugh made wrinkles in the bedding, Sera wandered through a decorative arch to the next room and found a bathing chamber. The walls were lined with bright tiles depicting a fantastical garden, rich with flowers, butterflies, and insects that reminded her of Shadowvane. A copper bath sat in the middle of the room, large enough to accommodate two comfortably.

"Oh, to have a bath." She picked up a brilliant blue bottle that sat on a shelf and shook it. Bubbles formed within.

"There are bath salts and oils, to scent the water."

Sinead appeared at her shoulder. "I can have the water drawn. There is time for you to bathe before supper."

"Yes, please." Sera's magic had waned after the day's exertions. No need to expend it on pulling forth water and heating it if the Fae had a way of doing it. She didn't know what lay ahead and needed to conserve what little remained of her gift so that she might be prepared to defend herself and Hugh if necessary.

"I will also see to it that suitable clothing is found for you both," Sinead said, tucking her hands into the billowing sleeves of her gown.

Was that a hint of reproach? Sera glanced down at her outfit, which suited her Nyx persona. It was her favourite, although she did concede that it was probably not appropriate for dinner with a queen. What would Kitty say if she were here?

"We are in Queen Deryn's debt for her hospitality," Sera murmured.

What price would the queen demand in return, though? From what she had read of the Fae, everything came with strings attached. There would be a price to pay. She only hoped it was one they could afford, or else that there was a way for them to escape the magical realm unscathed.

"I shall have the bath filled. Once you have bathed, the servants will assist you to dress." Sinead bowed her head and slipped from the room, gesturing for the waiting maid to enter.

While their bath was readied, Sera sat at the desk

and pulled the ensorcelled paper from its place tucked into her stays. When she smoothed it out, it already contained a message from Kitty.

What is happening? We have returned to London, and I worry.

"Kitty and Elliot are back in London already," Sera said to Hugh, showing him the message.

He frowned. "How is that possible? It is at least two days' ride from where we left them, and it has only been a few hours since we crossed over."

"Time flows differently here. We must take care not to linger too long." The Repository of Forgotten Things might draw on Fae magic to slow time in the human realm. Oh! she realized suddenly. It might even be situated over a portal to the Fae realm. There was a theory to explore if she ever returned.

Sera rubbed her hand over Kitty's neatly formed letters to clear the page. Taking up a quill, she quickly scratched out a message to her friend.

We are safe. It has only been a few hours here.

My anonymous correspondent is Lord Branvale's wife—who is a dryad!

. . .

Kitty's reply came almost immediately and Sera's heart ached that she had worried her friend so. Kitty must have been hovering over the page, waiting.

> A dryad? I have many questions, but I shall contain myself until I see you again. Do not dally so long that I am ancient when you return.
>
> Tomorrow, I begin my mission to speak with the queen. Father is working to have that ridiculous edict overturned.

"I do not doubt that Kitty and Mr Napier will succeed in having you freed from any risk of being returned to the Repository. Then we can study the ghosts there." Humour sparkled in Hugh's eyes.

Sera slid the folded page under the desk blotter and then walked out onto the balcony. Night had fallen, but a thousand stars lit the sky. In the gardens below, luminous insects flitted back and forth and ensorcelled lights on poles cast a soft lilac glow.

Hugh stood behind her and wrapped his arms around her waist. Sera turned her head so that she might rest her cheek on his upper arm.

"We have had an eventful day, and I am rather looking forward to supper," he said.

Sera smiled against the fabric of his sleeve. A tall, broad man, Hugh had lots of empty spaces that required stuffing with tasty morsels.

"Your bath is ready, my lady. Do you require assistance to bathe?" Sinead spoke from behind them.

"No, thank you," Sera called over Hugh's shoulder.

"We shall return in an hour to help you dress," Sinead said. Shortly after, the door of the room closed with a gentle *snick*.

Sera kissed Hugh's cheek, then broke free of his embrace to walk back into the bedroom. She peeled off her clothing and left it tossed over the footstool in front of an armchair. Naked, she padded towards the copper bath, unplaiting her hair as she walked until it tumbled down her back. The tiled room was lit only by the soft glow of magical lights in sconces on the walls. At a later time, she wanted to investigate how Fae power differed from her own. She had only gleaned a tiny bit from the bracelets.

One foot at a time, she stepped over the side of the bath, giving a contented sigh as she sank into the steamy water. It lapped at her skin, infused with the soothing scents of lavender and chamomile. Sera leaned back against the cooler metal, enjoying the silky feel of the water and the way the bath seemed to melt her aches away.

The tiled floor and walls surrounding her were a work of art, formed of tiny, hand-painted tiles that depicted a lush garden in spring bloom. Every detail was meticulously rendered, from delicate petals and leaves to tiny birds taking flight under a sunny sky. At night, with only the Fae lights for illumination, the garden seemed to come alive with shadows and mystery.

Sera gazed up at the towering, vaulted ceiling, made from a mosaic of glass tiles through which filtered the pale silver light of the moon and stars. She breathed deeply, overcome with a sense of peace in this place of beauty. Her gaze travelled back to the painted garden tiles, noticing minute details she hadn't observed before. She closed her eyes, losing herself to the soothing song of the night garden that drifted through the open windows.

Feet padded across the tiles, and the whisper of fabric hitting the floor followed.

"Do you mind if I join you?" Hugh's voice was hesitant, almost nervous.

Sera opened her eyes and drank him in. He was a banquet that she was hungry to partake of. "Of course you can. This tub is big enough for both of us."

She sat up as he climbed into the bath to face her. Hugh's substantial form displaced enough that a small waterfall sloshed to the floor. Sera stifled a giggle as he glanced over the edge, worried he had made a mess. The floor of the bathing chamber had a slight depression that allowed spilt water to swirl down a small drain.

Sighing with pleasure at the hot water, Hugh leaned back and stretched out one long leg on either side of Sera. She put aside thoughts of propriety and stretched out her toes to brush his thighs. His hands found her legs under the water and began to knead the tension from her calf muscles.

"You have a remarkable touch and always seem to know just what I need. Are all surgeons as talented as you?" she murmured, letting her eyes drift closed again. The steady motion of his hands was soothing and incendiary at the same time.

"I am only this attentive to my favourite patient," Hugh said.

Though his hands on her legs were gentle and unhurried, Sera could feel a delicious ache beginning to build inside her. She ran the tips of her toes up his inner thighs, eliciting a low growl.

"I believe Sinead said she wouldn't return for an hour," Sera murmured.

"That should be sufficient time to ensure we are both thoroughly... clean." Hugh switched to massaging her other calf.

Sera smiled, eyes half-closed. Bath time was much more enjoyable with Hugh. The warm water was no longer the only source of the heat flooding her body, and the song from the garden became a duet, awash in sighs of pleasure and muted laughter.

After a long and *heated* bath, Hugh and Sera emerged from the water flushed pink. As they towelled dry, a soft knock sounded at the door.

"Come in," Hugh called, wrapping the towel around his waist as Sinead entered. The human maid who followed her was now accompanied by a human valet. Both carried armloads of clothing in hues of deepest blue.

Hugh was shooed back to the bathing chamber by Sinead. "A shave is required, sir, before dinner," the valet murmured as he followed Hugh.

Sera was treated like a doll as the two women fussed over her clothing and hair. The maid braided the sides of her hair but left the back to tumble free. Thankfully, they didn't lace her into stays. Instead, a chemise of pale blue made of the softest cotton was dropped over her head. Next was a gown of midnight silk, dotted with little knots of silver thread. The long sleeves were bell-shaped and flared out from the wrist, the points dangling nearly all the way to her knees. The neckline was high, covering her collarbone. Sinead fitted a silver belt around her waist to cinch it in.

"Oh, it's beautiful." Sera brushed one hand over the tiny adornments.

"You are beautiful," Hugh said from under the arch.

He hadn't been dressed like a court dandy, but more like a rakish highwayman. Black trousers were tucked into polished black boots. A swallowtail coat of blue velvet fell to his knees at the back, under which he wore a waistcoat of a darker blue covered in the same tiny silver knots as Sera's gown.

"You are very handsome, Hugh. You should dress like a Fae noble more often." She held out her hand to him, and he tucked her fingers into the crook of his elbow.

As she gazed into eyes filled with love, a rumble emanated from his stomach. Before she could make a comment, hers answered.

"It has been quite a long time since breakfast," she said with a laugh.

Sinead led them back through the hallways that Sera was sure moved like those in the Repository, as she didn't recognise any of the twists and turns from their journey to their rooms. Eventually, the hall opened into a banqueting room of a similar grand opulence as the presence chamber, but on a slightly smaller scale. The long table could comfortably seat a hundred. Fifty high-backed chairs were lined up and down each side. A sparkling peacock throne made of silver stood at the far end of the table and awaited the queen. The centre-pieces of the table were tall crystal vases holding black branches laden with crystal berries that tapped against each other like delicate wind chimes.

Sera was shown to a seat on the queen's left, Hugh, a few places farther down on the same side. They all remained standing as the queen swept into the room. Pale cream rose petals erupted from under the edges of the long train of her silver gown, and they were quickly swept away by a footman. Once Queen Deryn was seated, she waved a hand inviting everyone else to do so.

Hugh's eyes were wide as he surveyed the strange and wondrous dishes. Silver bowls contained mounds of colour-changing grapes and apricots that rippled from green and orange through to blue and red with each bite. Tiny faerie cakes were dusted in crushed butterfly wings and edible gold leaf and released intoxicating clouds of spice and nectar with each mouthful. Pomegranates of ruby and garnet contained jewel-like seeds that burst with sweet juice on the tongue.

When the queen tapped her fork against her goblet, a procession of servants carried in hot dishes of roasted meats; roasted potatoes; and a dizzying array of vegetables, some roasted in savoury herbs, others sweetened with honey and lemon. There were baskets of fresh bread rolls, still warm from the oven. Sera broke one apart and sighed at the delicious, yeasty aroma.

Preferring plainer fare, she piled her plate with vegetables. When she glanced at Hugh, he was chewing on the roasted leg of some creature which reminded her of a painting of a young Henry VIII enjoying a feast.

Wine flowed from bottles of Venetian glass, the liquid gleaming with jewel-like intensity. Sera only sipped from her goblet, not wanting to dull her wits when surrounded by the Fae. The little she tasted danced across her tongue and seemed to fill her head with snatches of faraway music.

"How do you find our hospitality, Lady Winyard?" Queen Deryn asked, her gaze skimming over the wine-glass she held.

Sera swallowed a mouthful of potato dripping with butter and thyme. "Both Mr Miles and I are greatly appreciative, Your Majesty. I found Elowen in the garden, and she answered some of my questions. On the subject of my request for assistance, she advised me to enquire of Your Majesty about Ebonfyre."

The clear tone of crystal rang out as the queen dropped her glass to the table and it touched the side of her plate. The conversation around the table was silenced as effectively as though the queen had let out a scream.

"We do not talk about Ebonfyre at the table." The queen's words were clipped.

"I'm sorry, that was not conveyed to me. When might we talk about it?" Sera asked.

If the queen thought Sera would drop the topic, she obviously didn't know much about the determined young mage.

"Tomorrow. You will be brought to me." The queen regained her composure.

Sera's hands curled tighter around her cutlery. That was hours away, and assumed the queen saw them in the morning. What if they had to wait until tomorrow night? How many days would that be in her realm? Years could glide past, and who knew what they would find in England when they stepped through that side of the portal?

"I do not have the luxury of time, Your Majesty. Could we not discuss the matter after dinner?" Sera assumed the Fae women would retire to some gorgeous parlour somewhere to gossip about each other, and the men, after their meal.

The queen's haunting gaze narrowed. "Do not

think to dictate to us how things are done. We will see you when it is convenient for us. Musicians!"

At the royal command, the musicians to one side began to play, and the queen turned to the lord on her other side.

Frustrated words tried to surge up Sera's throat. She took a gulp of her wine and swallowed them down. Tomorrow, then.

EIGHTEEN

THE MEAL ENDED when the queen pushed back her chair. There was a clatter of cutlery as everyone dropped whatever they were eating and hurried to stand. Queen Deryn glided past her courtiers lined up by their chairs and disappeared through the door by which she'd entered. Sera grabbed a bread roll and cupped it in her hand since she had nowhere to hide it.

Sinead stood by the doors and waited. Hugh reached for Sera's hand and turned it over when she didn't lace her fingers with his. He chuckled and moved to take the other. "You need pockets. I managed to fit three of those delicious bread rolls in my jacket."

"Now you know why I prefer to wear breeches," she replied as they approached their guide.

Laughing courtiers left the banqueting room and turned to the right. Sinead gestured for them to go to the left.

"Can't we follow them? Is there not coffee and

cheese to finish the meal?" Hugh's gaze followed the brightly coloured lords and ladies, their laughter tinkling like frost in the depths of a hard winter.

Not a flicker of emotion passed behind Sinead's eyes. She merely gestured once more. "That can be provided in your room."

At that moment, soldiers in dark grey and black, who had been blending with the shadows, made their presence known. They didn't move towards them or make any gestures. They simply made Sera aware that they were *there*. Lurking. Shadowing their every move.

Sera tucked her hand into Hugh's elbow and beamed at Sinead. "That would be lovely. I have certainly been detained in more inhospitable cells, and without the luxury of Hugh's company."

The surgeon frowned and cast a glance behind him as the armed men retreated into their gloomy corners. "We are prisoners?"

Their guide walked a few steps along the hall. "The queen is concerned you might become lost in the halls if you were to wander off on your own."

"Jerome said the same thing about the Repository," Sera murmured as they fell into step beside Sinead. Apparently, magic-infused buildings with minds of their own were more common than she'd thought.

When they entered their room, a tray laden with crackers, cheese, and a polished silver coffee pot sat on a low table before the fire as though some invisible servant had overheard Hugh's words. Another similarity to the Repository. Although Sera doubted ghosts had carried the tray; it was most likely provided by one of Sinead's assistants.

Hugh shrugged off his velvet jacket and headed for the coffee pot, where steam curled from the slender spout.

"Do you require assistance to undress?" their courteous guard asked.

"No, thank you." Sera just wanted to pull off her shoes, strip naked, and curl up in bed.

"Very well. I hope your sleep is restful. I will bring your breakfast once you wake." Sinead retreated from the room. A moment later came the gentle click of a key turning in the lock.

Sera snorted. As if a locked door could stop her if she wanted to roam the halls at night. Not that she would this evening. Exhaustion crept over her, as though her body knew that days had passed in the human realm, and she hadn't slept.

"Would you like coffee or cheese?" Hugh asked as he poured into a small golden cup that appeared like a child's plaything in his hand.

"Neither. I am going to crawl into that bed and see if I can slow down my frantic mind." Sera stripped off the starry gown and chemise and soon had a pile of Fae clothing on a chair. Her own had disappeared, hopefully, off to be cleaned and returned.

Hugh created another pile as he undid the buttons of his waistcoat with one hand—the other holding a cracker with a slab of cheese balanced on top. Next, he divested his pockets of bread rolls and piled them on the tray. He had a moment of conflict when it came to boots and trousers. Those items required *two* hands.

Sera climbed into bed and nestled down among the numerous pillows, squirming to make herself the perfect spot. Then she watched Hugh undress from under her lashes. He padded towards the bed naked, clutching a single bread roll. He placed it on the bedside table before slipping under the blankets.

"In case I need it during the night," he said when Sera cast him a curious look.

Sera's tiredness retreated with the well-crafted surgeon next to her. Her mind detoured from mulling over events of the day, instead suggesting things they could do other than sleep that might require a midnight snack to replenish them.

"Perhaps you should have brought over the entire tray," she murmured as she moved to straddle him.

Hugh stroked his hands up her thighs. "I think I can make you forget about bread and cheese."

And he did.

Bright shafts of light fell across the bedroom and Sera stretched her arms over her head. Her body, and her magic, were rested. Perhaps she still ran on human time and had just had the equivalent of two straight days of sleep.

The first thing she did after climbing out of bed was to check the ensorcelled paper for any messages from Kitty. Sadly, her friend had no news to impart, except to say she continued to try to gain an audience with either Queen Charlotte or King George. The royal couple had disappeared from public view. Kitty and Elliot were intent on sneaking into the country estate where Their Majesties were supposedly spending the winter, to seek them out.

Sera dashed off a note to reassure her friend that they hadn't been poisoned or stabbed at the Fae court and that she had a private audience with the queen that day. With or without assistance, she hoped to be back in the human world before a week had passed.

A rap on the door heralded the arrival of Sinead with her two assistants in tow. One carried a tray of delectably smelling breakfast, another had clothing piled high in his outstretched arms.

"Good morning. I trust the bed was satisfactory?" Sinead stood with her hands tucked into the long sleeves of her gown, an open expression on her face.

Sera started to answer, but Hugh shot her a glance laced with humour and lingering heat that made the words dry up in her throat. "The bed was most satisfactory. Thank you," she managed.

"I will fetch you after you have broken your fast and dressed," Sinead said as the servants set down the items they carried.

After their guide and her followers had left, Sera

plucked a grape from a bunch and threw it at Hugh's head. "She meant was the bed satisfactory for *sleep*!"

Hugh caught the grape as it bounced off his forehead and held it between his fingers. "It was good for that, too." Then he popped the grape in his mouth and grinned at her.

Having Hugh at her side buoyed Sera's mood. He had a way of making her believe she could do anything. By the time Sinead returned, they were both dressed and had satisfied appetites.

When Hugh moved to join Sera, Sinead held up one hand. "Only Lady Winyard has an audience with Her Majesty."

A prickle of worry travelled through Sera. Was this a ploy to separate them?

Hugh squeezed her hand, then addressed Sinead. "Is there a physician I could watch or assist while Sera is with the queen?"

A brief, quizzical look crossed behind Sinead's eyes, then she nodded as though she listened to an unseen message. "There is a clinic for the lower classes that you may observe. Dalmor will take you there."

Hugh placed a quick, gentle kiss on Sera's lips, and then he went his separate way, accompanied by Dalmor, their male attendant. As the two men strode out into the corridor, Sera noted a bread-roll-shaped bulge in at least one pocket of Hugh's jacket.

Sinead escorted Sera along halls that became narrow, with a ceiling that was only twice the height of a normal one, instead of three or four times higher. The silence seemed thicker, and a tingle prickled at her skin. Magic sparkled in the air here, like glittering dust motes. That led Sera to wonder why she had not met any Fae mages. Or had they been around her, but she hadn't perceived them? The Fae bracelets gave off no hint of magic that could be discerned by humans. Their mages might be similarly cloaked from her notice.

At length, her Fae guard, as Sera now considered Sinead, paused at a panelled door. The wood was carved with a tree growing on one side, its branches reaching across the door and protecting the delicate wildflowers growing in its shadow. She rapped gently on the wood.

"Enter," a voice called.

Sinead opened the door and gestured for Sera to pass her. "I am not worthy, and will remain here," she murmured.

Sera stepped into Queen Deryn's private domain. The queen's study was a cosy yet regal space that reflected her status as both a monarch and a lover of knowledge and magic. The walls were panelled in rich, dark wood carved with intricate flora and fauna designs like that on the door. A large arched window to one side flooded the room with warm sunlight, which glinted off the gilded frames of paintings depicting the realm's most scenic vistas.

In the centre of the room stood a magnificent desk, carved from a single massive slab of polished ebony. Its surface was inlaid with whorls of silver that seemed to shift into mysterious patterns when no one was looking.

Stacked on the desk were leather-bound tomes of history, magic, and folklore, along with scrolls sealed with the crimson wax of the royal seal.

A pair of high-backed armchairs upholstered in plush crimson velvet stood before the large marble fireplace, whose carved stone mantel was adorned with curios like geodes, crystals, and the skulls of strange beasts. A silver bell hung within easy reach, ready to summon servants to stoke the fire or bring refreshments.

This was a place of deep power and deeper secrets, though its small touches of comfort betrayed the queen's appreciation for simple pleasures amid the grandeur of her rule. Overall, it felt like an island of warmth and mystery, where the queen could ponder affairs of state or pore over arcane texts in perfect solitude.

"Your Majesty." Sera dropped into a curtsey as she stood before the queen.

"Come. Sit." Queen Deryn gestured to the armchairs.

Sera waited until the queen's bottom touched the velvet before she perched on the edge of the chair. She rested one hand on the rolled arm and waited for the queen to open the conversation. How etiquette rubbed at her, and she longed to bombard Arwyn's mother with a multitude of impertinent questions.

The queen tilted her head and regarded Sera with a curious gaze. "You came here for assistance. Why should we meddle in your affairs? Our two realms are separate. We do not involve ourselves in human affairs, and you do not interfere in ours."

With one finger, Sera stroked the arm of the armchair and drew patterns in the velvet as she considered her options. She could try to play the coy diplomat and probably get nowhere, or she could take a bolder approach. She knew which path Kitty would advise her to take.

"With all due respect, Your Majesty, you involved yourself *intimately* in human affairs when you took King George to your bed after his coronation nearly thirty years ago."

Silence fell in the room and Sera realised it bore another similarity to the Repository. There was no tick of a clock. She couldn't remember seeing any timepieces in her room, either, or elsewhere in what she had seen of the palace.

"Our *affairs* are our own and none of your concern." The queen sat upright and glared at Sera.

"Yet our affairs are intertwined. Your son stands at his father's side. Lord Rowan is intent on removing King George from his path to power, and I do not doubt that Arwyn will be next." King George had a multitude of legitimate children with his beloved Queen Charlotte, but his half-Fae son held a special place in his heart. Some whispered that he should be heir regardless of his illegitimacy, being the child of not one, but two reigning monarchs.

Queen Deryn rose and stalked to her expansive desk, the fabric of her grey and silver gown swirling around her like a cloud. Into a crystal goblet, she poured an amber liquid from a golden carafe on the corner of the desk. She took a sip before turning back to Sera.

"While we always harbour within our breast a mother's concern for her child, our greater concern is for *all* our children. Our subjects. We will not see them harmed by Lord Rowan's despicable plan to create another Nereus." The queen returned to her armchair.

Sera considered that an easy concern to allay. "Then lend me assistance, and I shall ensure that plan never bears fruit."

Queen Deryn laughed, and it chilled Sera to the bone. "You are in our realm, Lady Winyard. We have before us two ways we can prevent a Nereus from ever being created—keep you here for the duration of your short lifespan or end it now."

When Sera curled her hands into fists, sparks flared up her arms. "I was given safe passage," she bit out.

"Safe passage *to* this realm. You were not promised safety *in* this realm. That is at our command." The queen maintained a calm demeanour as she discussed whether to execute Sera or not.

Sera jumped to her feet and stood with the window at her back. She imagined the queen's words as slender ropes being bound around her body and pulled tight.

"You cannot stop me if I wish to leave, nor can you harm me." She raised her hands above her head until her fingertips pointed to the ceiling. She channelled the dark side of her magic and the shadows answered.

Midnight shapes flickered and flowed over the walls, gathering around her as she crafted her soul-stealing crows to circle her protectively. Their ebony wings blocked the light coming through the window and cast eerie images on the lush carpets.

Queen Deryn sucked in a breath and rose to her feet. "You walk in darkness."

"I am told my vein of magic is *tainted* by the twilight world. Try to harm me or Hugh, and you will learn how powerful casting from the underworld makes me." Sera held one hand straight in front of her and summoned forth an ebony flame that danced on her palm.

Ignoring Sera, the monarch paced back and forth before her fireplace, her hands clasping and unclasping as some internal monologue raged in her head. At length, she stopped and stared at Sera with the clarity of a decision made in her gaze. "It seems you are the one we have sought for generations. Dismiss your shadows, Lady Winyard. We shall discuss how your aid to us can be of reciprocal benefit."

By clenching her hand into a fist, Sera extinguished the black flame. A wave of her hand dismissed her soul-sucking crows. Warily, and with her thoughts guarded, she returned to her chair. "You said 'reciprocal'. There is something you need from me."

"Once, this realm had a mighty guardian. One commanded by the Seelie monarch to protect our people. But when your mages defeated the Nereus, such power was unleashed that it created fractures in our realm. The blast trapped our guardian within one such fracture." Her hands tightened on the goblet until her knuckles turned white.

"What sort of guardian?" What creature could protect an entire realm? It would either have to be enormous, such that it could blot out the stars, or incredibly powerful.

But not powerful enough to withstand the effects of a Nereus, even from another realm.

A sad smile flitted behind Queen Deryn's golden gaze. "One who would be a fierce ally if your need were dire enough. We could command it to stand at your back when you face Lord Rowan."

"Ebonfyre." Shadows skittered in the corners when she murmured the odd name that Elowen had shared with her. The name intrigued her and made her think of the black flame that minutes ago had hovered above her hand. "You would offer this guardian's help to me?"

The queen placed her goblet on the table beside her chair and leaned forward, the interest clear in her eyes. "If you can free them, yes."

So far in Sera's life, nothing had been easily won. She had battled for freedom, respect, and those she loved. What was one more task if it gained her a mighty ally in her next fight? Especially if its presence could save her friends.

"How do I free Ebonfyre?"

The queen smiled, and Sera had the feeling a trap had just closed around her.

"Our mages have tried but cannot access what is

needed." Queen Deryn rose and walked to an ornate cabinet. She opened its doors, reached into the inky depths, and pulled out an object, which she placed on the side table next to Sera.

A box. Admittedly, a very pretty box, with brass corners and intricately carved runes. But it was still just a box. And Fae mages couldn't open it?

"There is more to this than meets the eye," Sera said. She traced a fingertip along the rows of runes. Only now did she wish she had spent more time studying with Lord Rowan. He would know what it said. She picked out words she knew. "*Open. Answer. Flying* or *soaring*? No, that's not right."

"You are studying our language?" Queen Deryn tilted her head again to examine her.

"Your language was hidden in the bracelet that suppressed my magic. I wanted to understand the spell used. But I am not fluent. This is some sort of message." She tapped one phrase and tried to puzzle out the words.

"It is a riddle. For centuries this box has remained shut, its secret sealed within. Solve the riddle, break the runes to open the box, and take hold of what you need to free our guardian."

The queen made it sound so simple.

"If the blast from defeating the Nereus trapped Ebonfyre, where did the box come from?" Sera struggled to understand what had happened all those centuries ago.

"That is a mystery our finest scholars have sought

to unravel. The box was found not far from where Ebonfyre lies trapped. Some power crafted it in the Nereus's final moments." Queen Deryn's hand hovered over the surface, as though she didn't want to touch it again.

A fiendish puzzle sounded exactly like something an immensely powerful ten-year-old might create. Had the child known that the ripples from their battle had ensnared Ebonfyre and in those final moments, had crafted a way to release the guardian?

That made another thought leap into Sera's mind. How did they know it was a way to free the creature, and not some terrible weapon that would destroy whoever opened the box?

Nineteen

"What do the runes say?" Sera asked. Her fingertip hovered above the carved marks, but like the queen, she didn't touch them.

If the box exploded when opened, the monarch was putting herself and her entire court at risk. Unless it only affected the hand that lifted the lid, which might explain why they had waited generations for a mage like Sera to do it. Why risk a Fae mage when there was a troublesome human one available? Particularly one whose life the queen had suggested ending just minutes ago.

The queen sat back down, then recited the riddle from memory.

> "To open the seal, the answer lies not in sight,
> But in what is left when light takes flight.
> In the void where shadows dwell,
> There you'll find the key to quell
> The magic that binds this box so tight."

· · ·

Sera snorted. It wasn't a particularly difficult riddle—even a child could solve it with only a little effort. She had expected something fiendishly hard from the Fae, who were renowned for their love of tricks and riddles. Or, she pondered, the danger might lie not in the words that delivered the solution, but in the actions that followed. An unwary hand might pop the lid without realising the consequences. That only made Sera more reluctant to open the container.

"The answer is night or darkness," she said. "Why did you say I might be the one you sought? Why hasn't one of your mages opened the thing?"

The cunning look returned to the monarch's face, and Sera wondered how vast a difference there really was between the Seelie and Unseelie. Both used shrewdness to get what they wanted from unsuspecting humans.

"Working with the night is impossible for our mages. Our magic is crafted from light. We do not touch the dark. We understand that even among your kind, it is unknown. Until you were born."

Sera bit her bottom lip. On that, the queen was misinformed. Her predecessor, Lord Dewlap, had worked dark magic, and the shadows had perverted his spells and tainted his ability. That taint had been passed to Sera. Or their line might always have embraced the night. More research would be needed to determine whether the power that flowed through Sera had always differed from that gifted to the other eleven mages.

"Your little puzzle box needs a mage bathed in darkness to unlock it." Sera let out a sigh. This explained why the queen's attitude had altered after Sera had summoned shadows and crows to protect her.

And the dark flame. *Ebonfyre.*

This was the queen's lucky day. Sitting across from her was a mage with a line of magic that drew from the velvet of night.

Then she remembered Elowen out in the garden and her correspondence with Lord Branvale. Had Queen Deryn always known that Sera differed from the others in more ways than her gender? Queen and dryad might have plotted this all along, making yet another group who sought to control her life. But the monarch's reaction to magic drawn from the void seemed genuine as though she'd had no prior warning.

"What of the Unseelie? Don't they possess such mages?" Sera still wasn't keen to touch the box without knowing more about it.

A shudder ran through the queen's slender body. "Yes. On rare occasions, a night-wielding mage is born among them. But we are not handing them the key to releasing our guardian. They would bend Ebonfyre to their own nefarious ends and never again would a Seelie monarch sit on our throne. At times, the power in our realm shifts between us. For two of your centuries, our father ruled this land. Then his crown fell to our head. In the past, if an Unseelie came to power, the box was hidden far beyond their reach."

The power shifts between Fae factions reminded Sera of England's history and the War of the Roses. Monarchs weren't always assured a secure seat on the throne.

"How do I know this releases some trapped guardian and isn't a weapon that will harm me? How do you even know that it has *anything* to do with Ebonfyre? It might be some Unseelie trick to release destruction on your court."

Sera recalled an old proverb along the lines of *Be wary of Fae bearing gifts*. Or unusual boxes.

The queen laughed, a light, delicate sound that reverberated around the room. "Despite all our hospitality, you still do not trust us."

The queen seemed in need of having her memory prompted. "Only a few minutes ago you suggested either holding me prisoner in this realm forever or killing me. Neither option engenders trust or gratitude."

"That was before we saw a demonstration of your gift. We have read the reports, of course, but we needed to see the shadows brought to life before our own eyes." She lifted the goblet from the side table and drank deeply, as though the conversation had brought about a great thirst.

That confirmed the queen had known of Sera's ability. Her skin prickled that yet another faction meddled in her life. Why couldn't everyone just leave her alone to control her own destiny, and stop scribbling in the margins of her tale? Once she defeated Lord Rowan, she would inform both crown and council that henceforth *she* would be the only author of her story.

"In their efforts over the centuries to open the box, many times our mages have taken it to where Ebonfyre is imprisoned. They have detected a connection between the two. Something within the box struggles to be free when near our guardian. Mages and scholars have studied both and concluded that this container either holds an object that can release Ebonfyre, or it possibly contains their soul." As she spoke, Queen Deryn gestured around the room with her goblet.

Only now did Sera pay closer attention to the landscapes adorning the walls. One showed a procession of Fae heading into a dense forest. At its heart lay a small clearing with what appeared to be a dark void in the centre. Was that the fracture that had ruptured in the Fae realm when the Nereus was defeated, trapping Ebonfyre in the inky shaft?

More importantly, Sera simply didn't trust the queen. The more the Fae ruler pushed for Sera to open the box, the more she resisted. She needed Hugh's calm counsel, or Kitty's insightful view.

"Assuming this thing contains a way to release Ebonfyre, as soon as it is done, I am returning to my realm to free King George of whatever spell Lord Rowan has cast over him, and ensure the old mage is soundly defeated." Sera pushed off the arms of the chair to stand.

Something about being in the Fae realm raised the hairs on the back of her neck, and she wanted to return home as soon as possible. Being in a constant state of guarded readiness was exhausting. But more than that, she worried about what had happened to King George and Queen Charlotte; loyalty to the English monarchs pulled her home.

The queen stood, and only the ghost of a smile tugged at her lips. "Then we have an agreement. Release Ebonfyre and you will be given safe passage back to your own realm."

Sera was obliged to negotiate. "Safe passage home *and* Ebonfyre assists me against Lord Rowan and the Mage Council." How she missed Kitty and her quick-witted legal brain! But the queen wasn't about to give her the chance for a long chat with her friend. At least she'd caught that a few missing words from a sentence had nearly seen her heading home without a way to defeat her enemies.

"Never in my memory have the Fae fought your mages in such an open fashion." Queen Deryn rested one hand on the marble mantel.

"And that will remain true. No Fae will fight beside me, only Ebonfyre. Or are you telling me that Ebonfyre is a Fae mage?" Now that she re-examined her conversations with both queen and dryad, no one had told her who, or what, Ebonfyre was. It could be a miniature pony with a fierce temper, for all she knew.

"Ebonfyre is... not a Fae, nor do they have a human form." Long nails tapped on the mantel.

"Then I don't see a problem. If you want your guardian freed, then they must answer my call. It is entirely possible that the other human mages will assume Ebonfyre is something I have conjured, rather than an actual creature." Once she had seen Ebonfyre's form, she could create an illusion version to fool Lord Rowan.

Another idea struck her. Ebonfyre could be a gryphon, such as the one Lord Dewlap had created by touching dark magic. That would explain why Sera and the magical vein she shared with him were needed to open the box.

"Yes, that might be satisfactory," the queen murmured. "Very well. We are agreed. Safe passage and you may summon Ebonfyre one time only."

"Agreed. Now I shall examine the box in private before opening it." Sera picked it up and tucked it under her arm.

The slight smile returned to the queen's face, and the unnerving feeling that Sera had walked into an unseen trap returned. "We will be told once you have unlocked the box, and our warriors will take you to Ebonfyre."

As Sera approached the door, it swung open to reveal Sinead patiently waiting in the hall. Her head was bowed as though she dozed while standing upright. Sera's approaching footsteps made her straighten. "I shall escort you back to your room."

"Is Hugh still occupied?" Sera asked as they walked back along the silent corridor.

The other woman's features went blank for a moment, then she blinked. "Yes. I am told he is assisting our physician with a broken bone."

"I'll not disturb him, then." For the rest of the walk, Sera wondered whether Sinead possessed magic, or a mage controlled her and allowed her to talk soundlessly to others. The Fae mages were curiously absent from court, from what she had seen. How she wanted to watch one cast and learn what differences or similarities they possessed.

In her room, Sera placed the box on the desk, sat down, and simply stared at it. While the solution was simple—darkness—the inscription said nothing about *how* shadows had to be used to unlock the lid. Nor had she decided whether she wanted to discover what lay within.

"Kitty," she murmured. Sera rubbed her thumb against the mage silver ring on her pinkie and thought of her friend. She wasn't sure if the rings worked with the two of them in separate realms, but she needed to talk to her friend.

Sera pulled the ensorcelled piece of paper from where it stayed hidden between the pages of a poetry book on the desk. A line of text marched across the dirty paper.

> *I am at Kew. The king and queen are being kept apart. I am formulating a plan to sneak in to see Queen Charlotte.*

HER FRIEND WOULD THINK of something. The biggest problem Sera could see would be avoiding detection by Abigail. The treacherous woman served as one of Queen Charlotte's ladies and would recognise Kitty immediately and raise the alarm.

With the side of her hand, Sera wiped the page clean and then took up a quill.

> *Queen Deryn wants me to open a box. She claims it contains something that will release the Fae guardian, whom I can call upon to help me defeat Lord Rowan.*

KITTY'S RESPONSE was quick and to the point.

> *Sounds like a Fae trick. Ask one of them to open it.*

KITTY's first instinct mirrored Sera's own. Beneath those words, she added:

> *They cannot. The queen says only a mage who can <u>touch the dark</u> can open it. They have been trying for centuries.*

WHILE SERA WAITED FOR A REPLY, birdsong drifted through the open windows, along with the fresh fragrance of the roses and lavender below. When she glanced down at the sheet of paper, words flowed across it in a steady hand.

> *Can you defeat Lord Rowan and the Mage Council with no other magical assistance? Obviously, I, Hugh, and Elliot will be right beside you. But we cannot match magic with magic.*

HOW SHE WANTED TO REPLY, *of course!* But she did not possess such arrogance, even if she believed herself the most powerful mage England had ever seen. Outside of a Nereus. She had not forgotten that it had drained her to the point of collapse to defeat Lord Tomlin during a staged battle to entertain the king and his guests.

In an actual magical fight, she would face at least six mages, led by Lord Rowan. They would combine their power, and while Sera would battle with all she had, she would not last long against them. Nor would she be able to protect her friends from whatever magical or physical weapons were aimed at them. With a heavy heart, she replied honestly.

No. I would drain myself, possibly to death, in the attempt.

How that sentence taunted her with its admission of failure before they had even tried. How it gnawed at her that she would be unable to protect her friends. If she could command Ebonfyre only once, would she use the guardian to defeat Lord Rowan, or ensure her friends' survival?

Then you have your answer. You must open the box. But please take precautions! Remember that Deryn is Arwyn's mother, and he is the most trustworthy and honest person I know. Come back to us with this guardian and a tale to tell.

Sera rested one hand on the polished wood and traced a line of runes. Kitty made a good point. Arwyn had a gentle and honest nature. Could a trickster mother have created a man with such dignity and integrity? Abigail's actions had made Sera doubt everyone. But not everyone was as dishonourable as that noblewoman.

"You'll not make me doubt everyone for the rest of my life, Abigail. For that would be delivering you a different sort of victory," Sera murmured to the empty room. Of course, if the box did explode or release some horrid creature that attacked her, she would re-evaluate her stance on trusting anyone else ever again.

There were precautions she could take, like throwing up a shield when she prised the lid open. Then, all she had to do was take whatever it contained to where Ebonfyre was trapped, release them, and they could head home. What might be a day or two for her and Hugh would be closer to a week for Kitty. She nodded to herself, satisfied with her decision.

Very well. I will write as soon as it is done.

Then she added a postscript.

> *I love you. Once this is all over, you
> and I should have a different sort of
> adventure. I'd like to see Italy and Egypt.*

As GIRLS, they had talked of travelling the world. She wanted to share that experience with her dearest friend.

> *I love you. WHEN we go to Italy
> you must promise to straighten that tower in
> Pisa. It's shoddy construction and the way
> it leans, quite ruins drawings of the place.*

LAUGHTER BURST through Sera's worries. She could well imagine Kitty instructing her to fix the monuments they visited on their grand tour. And Kitty would probably also insist Sera fix the drains wherever they went, to improve sanitation for the locals.

Tucking the piece of paper away safely once more, Sera stared at the box. The riddle stated that darkness was needed to crack the lid. But how were shadows to be used? There had to be more to it than placing the box in a dark room, otherwise it would have opened while it was in the cupboard.

"Darkness is key," she murmured, and the words clicked inside her. "Oh! Perhaps darkness *is* the key."

With that idea in her head, she examined every tiny

bit of the polished wood, searching for some sort of keyhole. While she was pressing each seam, rune, and brass corner to see if anything hidden was triggered, the door opened and Hugh walked in.

The surgeon bristled with good humour. His shirt sleeves were rolled up to the elbows, and dots of bright red were spattered across the snowy white linen.

"Did you have a productive morning?" Sera gestured to the blood spots marring his shirt.

Hugh rubbed at one with a fingertip, to no avail. "Yes. I helped the Fae surgeon set a rather nasty broken leg. Their anatomy is remarkably similar to ours, although their bones seem much lighter, which accounts for their tall but slender builds. I was able to impart my method for setting bones. I think it will knit cleanly and won't hamper the lad's ability to run once it's fully healed."

Warmth filled Sera's heart. Wherever Hugh went, he tried to help the sick or injured. "I am glad you were able to help. I had an interesting private audience with the queen."

"What do you have there?" Hugh peered over her shoulder at the object on the desk.

Sera reached up, took his freshly scrubbed hand, and pressed it to her cheek. "Something that apparently will free an ancient Fae guardian upon whom I may call to aid our cause. Or it could contain a horrible poison, explosives, or a Fae cephalopod that will latch onto my face."

"Well, I would suggest opening it outside in case it

contains poison or something that will blow up. That gives us the best chance of escaping to a safe distance. If it's an octopus, though, you are on your own. That is a scenario outside the scope of my training." He turned his hand in her grasp to stroke her face.

Sera scowled at him. "Whatever happened to unconditional love and support?"

"I am sure Kitty will tell you there is an exception for cephalopod attacks somewhere in the fine print." Hugh kept hold of her hand as she stood.

She balanced on her toes to kiss him. "I shall follow your advice and open it outside. I think the field with the old rowan tree is the perfect spot."

Elowen had suggested Ebonfyre. If the box contained anything truly horrible, Sera would be warned should the dryad not want it opened anywhere near her home.

TWENTY

SERA FLUNG open the door and startled Sinead, who appeared to have had her ear to the panelled wood. If she had been eavesdropping, that would save Sera having to explain what she wanted to do. "Could you show us through the garden to Elowen's meadow, please?"

"Of course." The Fae woman waited for Hugh to join them.

Hugh swiped the wooden container from the desk and carried it under one arm. Sera reached for it and clutched it to her chest. She didn't know why, but a proprietary feeling crept over her the longer she spent with the box. Holding onto it also gave her a chance to let her magic ripple over it and see what else she could learn about the thing. It wasn't particularly large, nor was it very heavy. When she gave it a shake, nothing rattled or shifted inside. Now that she thought about it, it probably didn't contain something that would explode, or it would have done that the first time she shook it.

Once free of the palace, they wandered through the gardens at a slightly faster pace than on the previous day. Sera began to suspect Sinead might want to get away from whatever resided in the box. Or perhaps she was merely tired of having to supervise Sera's every waking moment.

"Where are the mages to the queen?" Since it would take some time to reach the corner with the rowan tree, she may as well pick at Sinead for information on the way.

"Three are currently at court. The others are either at their own estates or elsewhere in the realm, as directed by the queen." They entered a low, circular maze. The hedges only came to waist height and allowed the person strolling the gleaming lime chip paths ample opportunity to plot their route to the other side.

Three Fae mages roamed the palace. Somewhere. Did they hide in the library, or had Sera passed one in the hall and never known it? "Were any at supper last night?"

Sinead turned and winked. "Yes. One." Then her smile fell away. "One is sequestered for health reasons and is not about court any longer. The third did not wish to sit at table with humans."

Was the mage's objection to humans the fact that she was a woman mage, or a human woman mage known to embrace the shadows?

"I found my work in the clinic this morning fascinating," Hugh said. "Queen Deryn makes her physicians available free of charge to all, regardless of their status. The sick and injured have only to turn up. Nurses assess the most urgent cases to be seen first. It works somewhat like our hospitals, but much cleaner and more efficient."

"Perhaps you can institute stricter cleanliness policies in our hospitals when you return?" Sera pulled a lavender stalk in passing and waved it before her, letting the sweet fragrance waft in the air.

Hugh gestured to the flower in her hand. "They use lavender oil, too. It burns in little holders dotted around the wards. They say the scent helps relax the patients."

"I imagine it also masks other, more unpleasant odours." Sera placed the lavender on the box as though it were an offering to whatever rested inside.

"I am keeping notes and intend to advocate for change at our hospitals when I return. If simply getting other surgeons to wash their hands is cause for battle, I can only imagine how they will react to the entire ward, and the operating theatres, being kept clean." He shot a rueful smile at Sera.

"Enlist Kitty's help. I am sure the hospital administration will cede to cleanliness under her instructions." Sera nudged Hugh with her elbow.

"That would be setting the cat amongst the pigeons. Or the kestrel after the mice." He huffed a quiet laugh, no doubt imagining the utter panic of the male doctors as Kitty instituted order, efficiency, and strict cleaning routines.

Soon they pushed through the overgrown hedge into the wildflower meadow. The leaves on the rowan were edged in deep red as they prepared for autumn.

"I will wait on the other side." Sinead gestured to the garden room on the other side of the yew. A seat was nestled under a climbing rose, and their guide retreated to the quiet spot.

Sera marched towards the tree and the dryad living inside. When she stood close to the trunk, she held up the wooden container. "Elowen? I spoke to Queen Deryn about Ebonfyre. She gave me this box."

Bark shifted and creaked as the dryad's form emerged from the tree and stepped onto the grass, where tendrils of green laced around her ankles. Today she retained her form made of nature and didn't change into a human figure.

"Are you able to open it?" Elowen tilted her head and her leafy hair draped over her shoulder like tumbling ivy.

"I don't know. I haven't tried yet. Queen Deryn couldn't tell me what is inside it, and I am somewhat reluctant to be the one to find out." Sera set the box on the grass and then knelt before it.

Elowen placed a hand on her shoulder, her fingers like twigs and each fingernail a small leaf. "It will not harm you."

"How can you be sure?" Sera looked from object to

dryad. If no one knew what the box contained, no one could make such a statement.

"What is in there will free Ebonfyre. It is specific to them, but it needs a particular type of mage to access and use it." She sat opposite Sera and leaned against the tree. The dryad's body half merged with the rowan and with her legs out before her, she looked like wandering roots, stretching away from the main trunk.

"I'll not let any harm come to you while you are channelling your gift." Hugh sat not far from her and within reach if needed.

The three of them formed a triangle with the box in the middle. She had told Kitty she would try, and time passed at an alarming rate in the human world. Sera drew a deep breath and steeled herself.

"Let us solve a centuries-old riddle," she murmured, and placed her hands on either side of the warm wood.

Sera drew shadows to her, pulling them from every shady nook and crevice in the gardens. Then she wrapped each gossamer-thin wisp around the box in layers as though it were a present. Slowly, one on top of the other, she obscured the wood with darkness. All the while, she kept her senses alert for anything that resembled a lock.

The world around her dimmed, as she called the night to blanket this corner of the garden. The midday sun faded, as darkness dropped over them like spilt ink and spread premature night. The box became a dark void that called to Sera. The taint in her blood thrummed, and power burst from her hands to envelop the carved wood covered in runes. Magic whirled around the container, and it disappeared from view. Only her palms told her she still touched it. The night swallowed the garden, the tall rowan, Elowen, and even Hugh.

Within the pitch black, the runes on the box shimmered silver. Each one lit up in turn as though mercury ran over them. Then a faint silver dot appeared near the edge of the lid. It pulsed, and the dot thickened and elongated.

"A keyhole," she whispered when she recognised the shape.

Sera had always enjoyed locks. While maintaining the inky night around them, she created a thin sliver of magic with one hand and guided it into the star-shaped keyhole. Pressing her tongue to her teeth, Sera caressed the hidden lock with velvety darkness, altering the shape of the shadow to exactly fit what she found within. She teased the mechanism into surrendering its hold.

A click reverberated along her connection, and a seam appeared around the edge of the lid.

"I have you!" Sliding her hands over the warm surface, she pressed her thumbs into the wood and paused.

Before Sera flung open the lid, she gathered the darkness to her and formed it into a dense shield. Daylight returned to the meadow as the shadows pooled all around Sera. Hugh's worried features peered at her through the twilight, where she had created an additional layer to shield him and Elowen.

"Ready?" she asked him.

His brow wrinkled deeper, but he climbed to his feet and nodded. His body was tense, ready to throw himself at her should poison creep from under the lid. Or drag her backwards if a mythical cephalopod sprang out.

Sera flexed her hands and opened the lid an inch while stretching out her arms as far as possible to keep her body away from the container. When no toxic mist wafted through the gap, nor did a suckered tentacle thrust its way free, she lifted the lid higher.

Nothing exploded or jumped out to latch onto her face. So she dared a peek inside.

"Huh." She let the shadows drop, and they scurried back into the hedges and depths of foliage in the garden. Somewhat disappointed, she opened the lid fully.

Within, nestled on black velvet, was a black sphere that resembled a highly polished billiard ball.

"A ball? That's it?" Hugh peered over her shoulder.

"Perhaps it is a weapon, designed to blow up where Ebonfyre is trapped?" Sera cautiously picked up the ball and held it up to the light. At first, it seemed to be solid black, but as she stared at it, it was like gazing at a darkened sky. Tiny dots like stars swirled within its depths. The black mingled with charcoal grey. In other places, it lightened to deep indigo. Fascinated, she ran a fingertip over the surface. It felt like smooth glass but radiated warmth.

"It is no weapon. It is an orb of essence. I have heard of such things, but never have I beheld one," Elowen said, leaning forward.

"How does it work?" Sera resisted an urge to shake it and see if anything appeared within the sphere.

"It contains the essence, or life force, of Ebonfyre. If you break the orb near them, the life force will return to their form, and they will be able to free themselves." Elowen held her hands near the orb. Vines spiralled down her arms and around her wrists to reach for it, but they stopped short before making contact.

"What do you know of Ebonfyre? Queen Deryn said they are an ancient Fae guardian. Is it safe to free this creature, whatever they might be?" Sera turned the ball in her hand, half expecting to see an eye wink from within its depths.

"And how did this guardian wind up with their essence contained in a ball?" Hugh leaned closer to peer at it. He tapped it with one fingertip, and it made a dull thud as though it were entirely solid.

"Their essence was ripped from Ebonfyre when they were caught in the rupture. Ebonfyre is honourable and serves Gaia. Do not be concerned that you are releasing a monster upon this land." Elowen dropped one hand to her side. Sweet peas clambered up her leg and then used her arm as a support to continue upwards to twine around her neck. They burst into flower, with deep pink blooms and a sweet fragrance.

Questions kept cramming themselves into Sera's mind. She wanted to know everything—what Ebonfyre was—how the Nereus had trapped the Fae guardian. But she was aware of the sand running through her hourglass, and there simply wasn't time to learn all Elowen could tell her. Even if the dryad had been more talkative.

She would have to trust that Lord Branvale's wife wasn't leading her into a trap. Or working with Queen Deryn to put an end to any possibility of another Nereus by killing Sera. A shaky sigh blew over her lips. Trust. A small word with heavy expectations upon it. Abigail had known her for years and betrayed her in the end. How could she trust people she'd known for only a few days?

Hugh took her free hand and laced his fingers through hers. "We have to go, Sera. Sometimes you just have to believe that everything will work out for the best and push forward."

If events went horribly wrong, there was a long list of people she intended to haunt.

She placed the orb back in its bed of velvet but left the lid open. Hugh took the box from her and tucked it under his arm.

"Keep Gaia in your mind as you navigate Bumble-foot Forest to the rupture. She will guide you," Elowen said before she spread her arms and stepped backwards to become one with the rowan tree once more.

"Bumblefoot Forest? Is that where we are going? It doesn't sound so bad," Hugh said as they walked back through the hedge to where Sinead waited.

Sera recalled the landscape on the wall in the queen's study. The dense forest with the gaping void in the middle, and the procession of Fae through the trees towards it. A shiver ran down her spine at odds with the harmless-sounding name of the place. "From the name, I would assume the biggest danger in Bumblefoot Forest is from tripping."

Sinead paced on the other side of the hedge and halted as they approached. Her eyes widened as she stared at the open wooden box and the midnight orb it held. "You will free Ebonfyre?"

Sera kept repeating her goal over and over in her mind so that she didn't waver. Free Ebonfyre. Defeat Lord Rowan. "Yes. Queen Deryn said that she would know when the box was opened. I don't want to lose any more time. We leave for wherever Ebonfyre is trapped as soon as our escort is ready."

"Our warriors will accompany you there. Appropriate attire has already been laid out in your room." Sinead set a brisk pace back through the gardens. Yet again, they took a different route and Sera wished for time to linger and enjoy each space.

In the palace, heads turned as they passed and whispers followed them. Whatever method the queen had used to learn about what Sera had done, the news had already spread among her court. Or her courtiers might have been alerted when night had cloaked one corner of the garden for several minutes.

When they reached their room, Sera set the box on the bed. Her favourite outfit appeared to have been cleaned and was draped over a chair. Another set of clothing was laid out for Hugh. She wasted no time, wanting to get the task done and get back to Kitty as soon as possible.

Once she'd done up the silver buttons on her double-breasted jacket, she spun. The circular wool skirt flared out around her legs.

"Perfect," she murmured. It seemed a fitting outfit in which to navigate her way through the mysterious forest that held the Fae guardian.

Hugh looked more warrior than surgeon in the leather trousers, boots, and leather coat. All he needed was a double-headed axe slung over his back.

Sera scanned the room and collected everything that belonged in the satchel. Using the ensorcelled paper, she dashed off a quick note to Kitty to say she had been successful and was about to head out on the next part of her mission. Then she tucked the folded paper safely away under her shirt and against her skin.

Hugh had his field kit laid out, and he reviewed his tools before rolling it up and tying the strip of leather that held it shut. Then he dropped it into a deep pocket inside his coat.

"Ready?" Sera stood before him, nerves skittering under her skin.

Hugh placed a hand on the side of her face and

placed a gentle kiss on her lips. "Wherever you go, I will be at your side." Then he tapped the pocket low on his chest. "With my field kit. But I hope we don't need it."

"So do I. You know I am horrendous at needlework. I am ordering you not to get hurt by anything larger than a thorn." She waggled her finger at him.

"Yes, Lady Winyard." He saluted her, then grabbed her hand.

Sinead waited at the door and once they passed the banqueting hall, they turned along a different route. This time they walked along a wide hall that could easily have allowed two carriages to pass one another. Twenty-foot-tall double doors opened out to a cobbled courtyard, surrounded by a smooth stone wall. A few courtiers watched from benches set between citrus trees in pots, which scented the air with the tang of orange blossom.

In the middle of the courtyard, six Fae warriors sat astride horses. A groom held the reins to two more. The men wore armour of the lightest chain mail made of metals unknown to Sera in shades of silver, ice blue, and butter yellow.

The horses' coats gleamed as though they, too, were made of metal—burnished copper and bronze that flashed with fire under the sun's caress. Their hooves were polished to a glossy shine and their long, thick tails would have been the envy of Rapunzel.

Sera approached a chestnut mare whose coat had a bright, rosy sheen. She took the reins and put one boot in the stirrup to swing herself up into the saddle. The equine gave a snort and pranced a step sideways. Nervous thing, she thought, and scratched the mare's neck and murmured under her breath.

When they were all ready, the Fae in the front wearing ice-blue armour kicked his horse and they surged forward. Sera's mare jumped straight into a canter, and she bit back her cry of surprise. Luckily, the equines had a comfortable gait, and she soon became accustomed to the rhythm. Hugh's bronze mount cantered alongside her so closely that if she reached out, she could have stroked the gelding's ebony mane.

Out through the palace grounds they cantered, across open meadows in the last bloom of autumn. Golden seed heads ripened, ready to spill seed that would winter in the soil.

"We'll meet again soon." Sera made the promise to her friend, and her enemy as they cantered on.

TWENTY-ONE

THEY RODE HARD ALL AFTERNOON, stopping only to water the horses and stretch their legs. The Fae didn't talk to Sera or Hugh. Any questions were answered by their leader in a perfunctory way with an arched eyebrow that silently said he thought they were beneath him.

Twilight brushed the horizon by the time a densely wooded area loomed ahead of them. The leader halted and rested his hands over the pommel of his saddle, while his mount took the opportunity to snatch a few mouthfuls of grass.

When neither Sera nor Hugh moved, he gestured to the tightly packed trees. "This is Bumblefoot Forest. We leave you here."

The queen had ordered her warriors to guide them only to the entrance of the forest? Then she and Hugh were on their own. Apparently, these Fae warriors didn't plan to emulate their painted ancestors. Sera held back her opinion of their usefulness as she dismounted.

Oh, look, a spooky oak tree... Honestly, how spooky could a forest be?

Two of the Fae leaned over to take the reins of their horses.

"We will need horses to return." Sera placed her hands on her hips as she glared up at their leader. The setting sun ringed his light blue hair with a halo.

He huffed in laughter. "If you are successful, you will not need horses. If you fail... you will need them even less."

The others chuckled at a joke they refused to share.

"Oh, very witty." Sera curled her hands into fists and wondered if it would spark a diplomatic incident if she turned the lot of them into toads. They would make ever so attractive and colourful toads, too.

Hugh took her hand and squeezed. "Just smile and wave. Then we'll find a place to camp before it gets too dark."

Letting out a huff, Sera raised her other hand and waved at the achingly attractive men. Well, she made a gesture at their retreating backs that *she* considered a farewell.

Hand in hand, she and Hugh walked towards the trees, whose foliage was a deep green smudged with black as though they were covered in soot. Their trunks were the colour of strong coffee. As she stood at the edge of the meadow and peered in, Sera couldn't tell the difference between the trees and shadows. The two blended together.

And yet... she didn't sense any danger. As though something in there waited for her and had not yet decided whether she was friend or foe. Tugging on Hugh's hand, she led the way between towering sentinels.

They walked a few steps into the forest, and the meadow disappeared. The fading light of twilight was deeper under the shelter of the foliage and Sera squinted to pick a direction. Behind her, Hugh tripped on a tree root that jutted over the faint path and fell.

"I think I know why it's called Bumblefoot now," he muttered as he brushed leaves from his trousers.

"Probably because tree roots trip everyone." Sera cast a light and sent it to hover above them.

"We should make camp for the night," Hugh said as he stepped over another root.

Sera shook her head. "That would lose us hours. We need to push on."

Hugh reached out and took her hand, pulling her to a halt. "We can't spot every danger lurking in here, even with a light. Far better to lose a few hours and have the advantage of what sunlight filters through the dense canopy, than stumble into something worse than spreading tree roots."

She wanted to argue, but then a pair of pale yellow eyes blinked from within the shadows and sent a warning ripple down her spine. "Very well. Let's find a small clearing or glade, and gather wood." She would use her magic to start a fire, but having fuel to throw on it would conserve her resources for any problems they might encounter, and erect shields to guard their sleep.

It didn't take long to find an area beneath a beech that would be sufficient for their camp, and far less exposed than the open meadow, and they settled in for the night.

THEY WOKE EARLY, with the first rustle of movement from whatever had roosted in the branches above. It didn't sound like birds, but Sera preferred not to know what had been keeping her company overnight. Watery light struggled to filter through the trees and light the undergrowth. Before they set out, Sera pulled the crinkled and worn half-sheet of paper from within her stays and wrote a quick note to Kitty.

> We start our journey to find Ebonfyre.
> The next note will report our success.

THERE WAS no need to say what she would write if they failed. For Kitty's sheet of paper would be forever blank, its silence shouting that their bodies resided for eternity somewhere in this forbidding place.

Sera tucked the paper into place. Then she checked her satchel to ensure the orb was still in the corner, wrapped in a piece of wool. The dangerous bracelet that could compel anyone to do the wearer's commands was the sphere's neighbour for the journey. She still hadn't decided what to do with it.

The trees crowded around them, their trunks towering overhead. Gnarled branches intertwined to block out most of the sun, leaving the wood in a state of perpetual twilight. An eerie silence permeated the air. Not a single bird sang or insect buzzed.

Hugh drew her to his chest and tipped up her chin with a fingertip. "We do this together."

"Always," she murmured, and reached up for a kiss —a gentle thing that strengthened her resolve to succeed. "This will be the first of many such adventures we will have together."

"Which way?" Hugh asked as he gestured to the woods. "Every direction looks the same."

Sera looped the strap of her satchel over her head and settled it at her side. Using a tingle of magic to orient herself, she pointed off to Hugh's left. "That way is opposite to where we came in. We need to go deeper. From the painting I saw in the queen's study, the rupture that trapped Ebonfyre is at the centre of the forest."

As they walked, glowing wisps of pinkish light darted between the trees. But they winked out when Sera turned her head to glance at them. Shadows seemed to flicker at the corners of her vision as though something unseen moved from tree to tree to follow them. While there was no birdsong, an odd melody echoed through the wood, its source impossible to pinpoint.

The very air seemed alive, watching, waiting. Like a predator that stalked its prey.

They talked a little at the start, but after an hour or two their conversation dwindled to murmured warnings to watch out for a root, or a low-hanging branch.

The path they followed was one worn by unseen animals trekking between a water source and wherever they ate or slept. The track twisted and turned, and at times was overgrown with thorns that grasped at their clothes as they passed. More than once, they had to stop to untangle themselves. Almost as though, Sera thought, the trees were aware of their presence.

Yet another branch snagged on the wool of her coat and as Sera worked the fabric free, movement made her glance up. A knothole eye watched her with an eerie intelligence shining through the gnarled branches.

Dryads? Elowen's kind might lurk here.

Then trunks groaned and creaked as trees shifted into unnatural positions, reaching out with long branches that twisted like fingers. The beech and oak tugged their roots free of the earth and then advanced upon them. Their roots writhed and wriggled like the many legs of a centipede, to carry the ancient sentinels towards them.

Sera gasped in surprise and jumped back to Hugh's

side, narrowly avoiding a twig that tried to snap around her wrist.

"Well, that's unexpected," Hugh said as he unsheathed his sword and stood in front of Sera. He brandished the weapon before the wooden enemy.

"Perhaps they are the bumblefooted ones the forest is named after." Sera whispered to her power and let it pool inside her, ready to be unleashed.

The trees began to close in around them, slowly moving closer with an unnatural grace that was both mesmerising and terrifying. Soon their trunks formed living bars that encircled the pair.

Sera tried to swallow, but her throat was too dry, her mouth filled with the salty tang of fear. She gritted her teeth, determined to stand her ground, even though every instinct screamed for her to flee. If they ran, they would lose sight of the path and could become hopelessly lost in the forest.

Hugh lunged forward and thrust his sword at one of the trees. The blade sparked against its bark and a loud *crack!* resonated through the forest as a branch snapped and fell to the ground.

The other trees stopped in their tracks and for a few moments there was silence. Trunks creaked and leaves rustled as the trees turned to one another as though deciding what to do.

"Didn't like that, did you?" Sera leapt on the creature's hesitation and raised her hands. With a quick swipe, she severed another low-hanging branch.

The tree emitted a high-pitched shriek and shuffled

backwards. Like all bullies, the trees didn't like it when their target fought back. A bold beech lashed out, whipping a solid branch towards them. Sera threw up a shield moments before it smacked Hugh on the head. Instead, the wood struck the invisible shield and then rolled off it.

Hugh lunged with the sword and lobbed off the attacking branch. The beech emitted a sharp cry that made Sera wince. She hadn't known trees could scream —it was a sound that would haunt her nightmares.

The cry tapered off to an angry groan before the beech retreated, shrinking back into its previous position among its peers. The other trees watched warily but stayed put, seemingly content to wait and see what the couple would do next.

Taking advantage of the reprieve, Hugh grabbed her hand and tugged her through a gap between two oaks. They found the path on the other side and ran as fast as they dared, only stopping to catch their breath once clear of any danger from strange wooden creatures.

"They weren't dryads like Elowen," Hugh said as he offered Sera the waterskin he carried.

She gulped down a mouthful of cool water, then handed back the skin. "Not unless dryads can become trapped inside the tree they inhabit and command it to move. Now I understand why those Fae warriors laughed when I asked them to leave our horses. They don't think we will make it out." Sera would make them eat their haughty words. Between Hugh's strength and her magic, they would find Ebonfyre, free them, and demand that Queen Deryn honour their agreement.

Hugh offered her a determined grin. "Let's prove them wrong."

With every step, Sera and Hugh learned that Bumblefoot Forest held a plethora of traps and pitfalls for the unwary. For all that it had an amusing name, those unfortunate enough to stumble under the sway of the sinister place seldom found their way out again. Around each turn lurked a new danger.

At one point their path turned into a murky pool of quicksand-like mud. Sera had trodden on the insubstantial surface before she realised what it was, thinking the reflective surface was merely a shallow puddle. She sank up to her knees in one quick swallow.

Hugh pulled her free before it sucked off her boots. They still had the energy to laugh about that near miss.

"I wouldn't want to be barefoot in here." Sera kissed him soundly in thanks.

The next curve of the path revealed a small mossy glade and a reprieve from the constant gloom. Here, warm shafts of sunlight created a circle of golden light that faded at the edges.

Brightly coloured mushrooms grew in clusters at the base of the trees. The fungi were a riot of reds and oranges, yellows and purples. Some bore tiny white spots, others green or purple caps. Some were so big that they would provide a satisfying meal for two people. They smelled of earth and of wet grass, like the forest floor after a rainfall.

"Do you think they are edible?" Hugh asked as he reached towards one.

"I don't think so. We should keep going." Sera pulled him back, her heightened awareness picking up a strange energy emanating from the mushrooms.

As they turned away, Hugh paused and pointed at one of the mushrooms, utterly different from its companions. It had a faint purple glow that seemed to pulse in time with some unknown rhythm.

"That one is a beauty. I've never seen the likes of it before." He reached out and tapped the dome.

At the gentle touch, the mushroom emitted a soft lilac mist into the air that slowly spread around them. As the cloud wafted over Sera's skin, an icy chill coursed through her veins.

"How odd. The air is nippy as though it blew off a frozen lake." Hugh held out his hands and turned them over. His fingertips were already turning blue as his blood circulation slowed. "My exposed skin is exhibiting signs of hypothermia."

Sera felt the same chill in her bones as the mist grew thicker around them, but when she tried to move, her legs wouldn't obey the command. The air changed, becoming so cold it stole their breath away. Every inhalation was a struggle against the suffocating frigidity.

The mushroom continued to pulse with its eerie purple light, growing brighter with each passing second. Sera could feel its malevolent presence like an icy finger caressing her spine. Would the fungi freeze them in place, or kill them with its frigid breath?

Her mind raced. "Why would a mushroom need to incapacitate people? They aren't carnivores."

A screech echoed around the glade, and undergrowth cracked as something bore down on them. The mushroom might not be a carnivore, but she guessed that whatever the fungi had summoned was.

"It must be a symbiotic relationship. The mushroom freezes prey for a larger predator." Hugh's words frosted on the air and shivers wracked his body. "In return, after it's eaten us, the mushroom gets to feast on our remains as we compost around it."

"I am not turning into compost." Sera's teeth chattered, and her feet turned numb and unable to move. She had to find a way to break the spell, but what could she do?

The obvious answer came to her. She reached inside herself and pulled forth the heat of a brilliant summer's day. She focused it outward into a swirling ball of flame and thrust it into the centre of the pale mist.

The flames convulsed and twisted as if angry, before plunging into the billowing fog. When they collided with the mushroom's breath, it ignited in a deep purple ball. It shot upwards with a boom, scorching leaves as it went. The trees shook with the sound, their needles scattering to the wind. The bright green of the foliage darkened to a dead brown.

The fireball exploded into shards of translucent

purple, iridescent like a peacock's feather. The glittering motes drifted to the ground as heated air rose upwards, warming their lungs and limbs.

Hugh shook his hands loose of the last vestiges of the cold. He grinned at Sera. "I won't touch any more mushrooms."

"Let's get out of here in case whatever thought to find us a frozen snack is still lurking." Sera didn't want to meet the creature that worked with the pretty mushroom, to strike at weary travellers who thought to warm themselves in the sun of the glade.

They found the narrow path again and continued on their way. The forest blocked most of the sunlight and Sera couldn't follow the passage of time. Had they walked for hours or minutes? Traversing a short distance in the forest seemed to take forever, as they had to be careful about every footfall.

As they moved deeper, the odd melody returned and echoed through the wood. Its source was impossible to pinpoint. The mournful keening stirred feelings of anguish and pulled at Sera's mind, urging her to step off the path.

"What is it? It's no musical instrument I'm familiar with," Hugh said. His head swung as he tried to find what direction the sound came from.

Hugh and Sera kept walking, trying to ignore the eerie melody. But with every step, its pull grew stronger, and it seemed harder to resist the urge to go astray.

"It makes me think of the siren's song that lured

sailors to their deaths." Was there an earthly equivalent? A type of dryad whose tree habitat was littered with the bones of those she killed? Even though Sera knew the forest was dangerous, still, the melody tried to compel her to follow its call through the twisted trees.

They put their hands over their ears, but it made no difference. The eerie tune reverberated through their bones and drilled into their heads. Sera muttered a spell to cast it off and shook herself to try and clear her mind. The melody continued. Now it came from all directions, wafting through the trees like smoke. Hugh stumbled on in front of Sera.

"Can you make it stop?" he called to her.

"I'm trying." A shield didn't work. The sound wormed through. Then she remembered the silence spell she had cast on the home of a banshee. That stopped their cry from getting *out*. It didn't make it quieter within the confines of the spell.

Even as she tried to cast a solution, the music muddled her thoughts, and the spell failed. Each note pulled them through a maze of intertwined trunks and branches. Then the trees thinned to create a clearing no larger than Sera's little parlour in Soho.

In the middle of the glade stood a tree unlike any she had seen before. Its gnarled trunk was a pale silver bark that peeled in long strips. Veins ran through it that pulsed a bright white. The tree didn't possess many leaves, but its branches held knotted masses of twigs.

Against the trunk, and cloaked by the draped branches, was a figure struggling against their bonds.

"There's someone tied there." Hugh took a step towards the person.

Sera flung out a hand. "Don't, Hugh—it might be another trap."

"Sera? Is that you?" a familiar voice called. "This blasted tree has lashed me to its trunk with a vine."

Sera sucked in a breath. "Kitty?"

Twenty-Two

"Yes, it's me. I used a spell to find you and now I'm stuck. Stop dawdling and get me out!" Kitty's voice wavered as she struggled against the vine.

Sera used a swipe of magic to brush the dangling limbs out of the way. All Sera's feet wanted to do was rush to her friend. Kitty must have paid handsomely for a locator spell to drop her near where they were, but she had then fallen prey to the many traps in the forest.

She trod another step closer. "How did the tree trap you?"

"I don't know. There was a melody, and I thought it might have been you. When I neared the tree, the vine grabbed me." An exasperated tone coloured Kitty's words.

Sera sent a wave of magic brushing over the ground before her, to trigger any lurking traps. The branches of the tree shook as the wave rippled over its roots, and Kitty yelped.

"What are you doing? It's pulling tighter. I can't breathe. Help me, Sera!" Panic entered the other woman's voice.

Sera took another step and ducked her head to look under the hanging boughs. The restrained woman had her head bowed. Tangled hair in russet tones hung over her face, obscuring her features. But the voice, hair, and shape all belonged to someone she knew as well as herself.

"Wait," Hugh cautioned, his hand catching hold of Sera's upper arm. "Miss Napier, do you remember when we fetched the Fae bracelet to free Sera? You made such a joke out of the poor chap's name that was carved on his tomb."

Miss Napier? Sera paused. After their adventures together, Hugh had started calling her friend Kitty. Why did she not reprimand him for reverting to such a formal address?

"Of course... I remember." The voice was weaker. Each breath was audible as her lungs were compressed.

"We need to save her first. We can discuss amusing anecdotes later." Sera tried to advance, but Hugh slipped his arms around her waist and spun her away from the tree.

"What was it again?" Hugh's eyes pleaded with Sera to give him just a few more seconds.

If Kitty's ribs were crushed, she would never forgive him.

"Richard... Cranium." The words were strained and each syllable spat out with a pause between.

Hugh held a finger to his lips, then he whispered into her ear, "It's not Kitty, quite apart from the fact she would berate me for calling her Miss Napier after our adventure, the name inscribed on the tomb was N. E. Body. It's a trap, pulling the image of the person you care about most from your mind."

N.E. Body? Anybody. A sob welled up in Sera's chest. The person sounded just like Kitty. Digging her nails into her palms to stop herself from flying to the imposter's rescue, she forced herself to stay by Hugh's side.

"You're not Kitty. Reveal yourself." Sera sent a swirl of magic around the figure, whispering a spell to reveal its true face.

A raspy scream tore across the glade. It raised its head, and the creature grinned, empty sockets where eyes should have been and the lower jaw missing. All colour bled from the shape's clothing, then it fluttered to the ground like snowflakes. Stripped bare, it revealed a skeleton dancing in the clutches of the vine. Its bones moved like a marionette, held by the black tendrils growing from the tree.

The branches of the tree moved and stretched. Buds formed and burst open to reveal tiny suckers that opened and closed like kissing lips.

"It's all part of the tree, like the light of an angler-fish. Luring its prey close," Hugh said, pulling Sera with him as he walked backwards.

The tree roared and twisted. The opposite side of the trunk split open to reveal long, jagged teeth. A tongue like a strip of turf unfurled and whipped back and forth.

"What tortured mind created these plants?" Sera yelled as they scrambled through the dense growth to find the path once more.

Wailing replaced the haunting song. Sera's eyes burned with tears. This was too hard. Every trap they stumbled into might be the last. Even her magic couldn't save them if the forest could dig into her mind to conjure those she loved to use against her.

"I can't do this," she whispered in a tiny voice.

Hugh stopped and grabbed her upper arms, giving her a gentle shake. "Yes, you can. We will do this together. I will stop you from rushing to rescue fake friends, and you will save me from eating toxic mushrooms."

A small laugh worked its way free of her chest, and she placed one hand on the side of his face. "That is a deal."

How she wished she had a charm or something to protect them. Then she recalled Elowen's parting words. "Before we left, Elowen said to me, *Keep Gaia in your heart*. That's it! Everything we have encountered so far is crafted from nature. The walking trees, the quicksand, the mushrooms and whatever... that... was. Gaia is protecting Ebonfyre. I need only make it clear that we are on her side."

"This is the source of your magic, the dark side of Gaia?" Hugh's eyes widened.

"I don't know." The idea saddened her. Did the

shadows that tainted her magic mean that she was the sort of mage to create perversions of nature? But she had never seen such creatures anywhere else. Sera chose to believe that what Gaia did here, was because of what she protected.

Sera tapped the side of her head, the repetitive motion aiding the flow of ideas. "I've got it."

Hunting around the ground, she found a fallen branch that was as thick as her wrist and about as long as a femur. Then she laid both hands on it and whispered. With Gaia in her heart, she sent her magic spiralling deep beneath their feet as far as she could send it. Then it twisted back up through earth and her body to the branch.

A shadow swept over the lump of wood. As it faded, luminescent green leaves sprouted along the length. Tendrils erupted and laced around the wood, forming an intricate pattern. The very end swelled and grew until it was larger than Hugh's fist. Its outer layer strained and thinned, then it burst open to reveal a pale pink and yellow bloom like a lotus. A gentle pink light emanated from the flower.

When Sera waved her staff, shadows skittered away from the rosy glow that announced to everything around them that she was a daughter of Gaia. "Now, let's find Ebonfyre."

They pushed on, continuing along the track. Twilight dimmed, quickly followed by full night. The lotus light was soon the only way they could see where they placed their feet.

"We should stop for the night. This is too dangerous," Hugh said from behind her.

"No. We can't afford to lose the time. We're close now. I can feel it." Like a boat trailing an anchor, Sera still had a tendril of magic below her. Gaia tugged on it, pulling her in the right direction. With every step, the vibration grew stronger.

Sera and Hugh trudged along in the gloom, the light bobbing ahead of them from the end of the staff. The trees around them reached out, but drew their limbs back when they entered the arc of pink light thrown by the flower.

They walked cautiously through the deepening night, not sure what would fall in behind them. Wisps of fog swirled around them, further obscuring their vision.

"This is madness! I cannot see my hand in front of my face," Hugh exclaimed.

Sera reached behind her and took his hand. "Trust me. Gaia will guide us."

Holding tight to Hugh, she closed her eyes and wrapped her senses around the tendril that connected her with the earth goddess. Drawing a breath laden with trust, she placed each foot on the soil and carried on. Step by step, the ground beneath their feet began to rise.

Sera could feel Gaia's presence around her, comforting her even as she was urged on. When she cracked one eye open, the fog and darkness had receded. The light of the lotus staff opened a path ahead of them, illuminating an occasional tree or bush here and there as they wound their way through the trees. They were guided by a soft whisper that navigated their way over fallen logs and around gnarled trunks until, finally, they emerged into a clearing.

Sera let out a soft gasp at what the moonlight illuminated before them. A small glade filled with verdant grasses was surrounded by ancient trees that reached up towards the stars like an amphitheatre for a celestial show. There was a stillness to the air that seemed sacred, and she felt both welcomed and watched by unseen eyes deep in the shadows.

At the centre of the glade was a black, bottomless scar on the landscape, from which no light or sound could escape. The fracture had ripped through the forest millennia ago. Over the centuries, nature had healed most of the wound, leaving the gaping mouth open. They had found the prison that held Ebonfyre, looking just as it did in the queen's painting. Even from across the glade, it possessed an oppressive presence.

Hugh pulled her closer to him as if he were afraid she'd be drawn into its depths.

Sera paused in his embrace and drew strength from him before she moved to the edge of the pit. She could feel Gaia's power reaching out to her from somewhere down below.

Hugh kept his fingers laced with hers and together they stood at the lip of the abyss. She looked down but could see nothing but darkness below—it felt like staring into an eternity of night-time shadows and secrets waiting to be revealed. The darkness loomed up at them like a void that swallowed any light that entered its depths.

The air around them felt thick and oppressive as if a hundred unseen eyes stared back at them from the dark. From what she could see with the lotus staff, the walls of the well were slick black stone. Bands of heavy iron circled the edges of the pit like a cage, securing whatever lay within. Sera could sense movement in its depths, as something strained against its confines.

Cold air flowed upward from the well. Her mind couldn't make sense of what she saw. Did she look down into a pitch-black well, or up into a starless sky? With her body unable to decide whether up was down, a moment of vertigo made her sway on her feet.

"Careful!" Hugh grabbed her arm and pulled her backwards as she tipped towards the void.

"It draws you in and makes you think you are looking up." She rubbed both hands on her arms to dispel the chill raised by the draft coming from the hole.

"We've come this far, Sera. Finish what needs to be done in this realm, so we can return to ours." Hugh wrapped his arm around her waist and pulled her close to kiss the top of her head before he let her go again.

Sera reached into her satchel and pulled out the orb. It vibrated softly in her hands, containing the essence of the Fae guardian. Its surface swirled with dark mist and flecks of light. Power and magic within the orb pulsed against her fingers.

Steeling herself, she stepped forward, raising the orb high. It felt light, yet thrummed with energy as if the glassy surface barely held back the magic within.

"Ebonfyre, hear my words!" she called in a clear tone. "I have come to set you free. I pledge my magic to you for this purpose alone."

A rumble vibrated through the ground and rippled up her calves. Her offer had been accepted.

With a push of magic, Sera set the orb spinning over the void. When it hung suspended in the centre, she clapped her hands together. The orb shattered with a crack like a bolt of lightning. Every fragment seemed to sparkle in the darkness, like stars twinkling in a night sky. A dark mist coalesced where the orb had once been. Flecks of obsidian mingled with purple and silver sparks. When the cloud was larger than a horse, it split in two. One part reached for Sera and wrapped around her like a cloak. The other half plunged into the well.

Sera gasped as energy surged through her and fuelled her magic like never before. Power bloomed in her bones and buzzed in her ears. She was a vessel that overflowed and couldn't be contained. Magic gushed from her, and she channelled it downwards—into the gaping mouth that greedily consumed all the magic she poured into it.

Seconds expanded into years and then time snapped back again with each breath from whatever dwelt beneath the earth. She tipped forward as the last drops of her gift trickled free. But still the creature far beneath her feet demanded more as it struggled to break free of its prison.

"It didn't work. I wasn't enough." Sera cast a wild look at Hugh.

"Embrace the shadows. It's a part of who you are and what you needed to channel to open the box," he called.

Yes. Nyx would throw all the magic of a night sky into the bottomless abyss. Closing her eyes, Sera reached into all her dark corners. The shadowy spheres where secrets dwelt. When the night answered and wreathed her hands in black fire, she threw it into the well. A bolt of inky black spiralled downwards. Dark shapes flew from the surrounding trees and augmented the cascade as it tumbled into the void.

Sweat dribbled down Sera's face and ran between her shoulder blades. Not stopping, she summoned more, pulling it from every space inside her and from the forest, to cast it to Ebonfyre. Yet still it demanded more. Sera had nothing left to give... except herself.

She swayed towards the hole.

"Enough!" Hugh tackled her and flung her to the ground.

As the inky flow was severed and snapped back into her body, the other end tumbled into the fracture. A series of booms shook the forest and winged creatures took flight in panic, squawking and calling out as they shot upwards and away from the disturbance. The earth undulated around them.

Hugh rolled Sera away from the well and didn't

stop until they reached the treeline. She lay on her back, panting, sucking the chilled night air into her heated lungs.

Hugh kept his body wrapped around her and worry crinkled his eyes. "I think you triggered an earthquake."

"No. It's Ebonfyre." Sera squirmed in his grasp as an ear-splitting roar came from the well. The narrow sides amplified and echoed the noise, and it blasted out like a physical thing. Ebonfyre raged and clawed at whatever held it prisoner in the earth.

Ruptures appeared in the soil and raced back towards the trees, as the old scar opened anew.

"Time to move!" Sera struggled to her feet and, hand in hand, they raced into the cover of the forest.

The moon cast a silvery glow on the scene below. The well seemed to collapse as its prisoner burst forth, clouded in obsidian mist, shaking off clods of earth and splintered iron, like a snake shedding its skin. Ebonfyre's scales shone like volcanic glass. The creature's wingspan was three times its body length, and its eyes glowed in the night like two black stars. They shook their head and bellowed.

The roar shook Sera's bones, but she couldn't stop grinning. Her heart pounded from the display of raw power and the last remnants of shadow magic tingled across her body.

Wings the length of a house beat a downward stroke, and the mist was swept into the forest. Free at last, Ebonfyre shook off centuries of imprisonment.

Then they flew up into the sky, trailing dark tendrils of power. A few filaments still ran from creature to Sera, but as they flew higher, the strands pulled taut and then snapped.

Sera slumped back to the ground and lay there in awe at what she had unleashed from beneath the ground. *"Dragon,"* she whispered with reverence.

Her obsidian dragon had come to life.

The ancient creature became smaller as they climbed. Once high among the clouds, they performed loops and circles, scattering birds trying to return to the trees. Scales glinted brightly in the moonlight. Coming out of a loop, the dragon dived towards the earth.

With a thump that rattled Sera's teeth, Ebonfyre landed on the ruptured ground. They stomped their feet, and the mounds shook themselves level.

Sera stared up at the enormous obsidian dragon. Their shimmering black scales appeared to continuously change colour from midnight blue to deep black, with hints of magenta and purple in the depths. Its wings were webbed with veins of silver. They stretched out and cupped the sky, like a hand reaching into a chest of dreams. Its tail was a long, winding road, smooth and seamless, like an onyx river. The creature appeared to be made of living stone, a being whose beauty and strength evoked both awe and fear in Sera's heart.

Ebonfyre's head slowly lowered. Their silver eyes gleamed with ancient intelligence and curiosity. Black smoke curled from their nostrils—a mixture of sulphur and campfire smoke as if they had swallowed a star from the night sky. The powerful aroma combined with their deep and rumbling growl created a sense of comfort at the same time as it inspired wonder. Their body thrummed with energy.

They had been fully restored.

"How did all that dragon get squashed into an orb that fit in my hand?" Hugh stretched out his hand and turned it over in wonder.

"Magic," Sera murmured.

"You freed us," Ebonfyre's voice rumbled like distant thunder.

"Yes. Only I could unlock the prison that held you. We are both crafted from shadows and darkness." The mighty dragon before her would dwarf the one Sera had cast in the banquet hall at the palace. Had some part of her known when she conjured a reptile carved from black stone?

"We are obsidian. We protect and are sharp and enduring." Ebonfyre lowered their head to peer closely at Sera. Then they sniffed. A tongue the size of Hugh snaked out and the very tip nudged her cheek.

She only hoped it wasn't a taste test. The dragon must be hungry after hundreds of years trapped in the well, but what would it consume to appease its appetite... apart from all the magic Sera could summon?

Twenty-Three

"That's why you are the Fae guardian!" Sera recalled what she'd read about different gems and stones and their uses. Obsidian was a protective stone. Because of its sharpness, some said the stone could pierce darkness to reveal the truth hidden within.

Once, she had tried to reject the dark song that flowed in her blood. Now, she realised it made her a fierce guardian of the people of England. Just like Ebonfyre.

"Look at their claws. You could perform the quickest and cleanest amputation in history if you used one of those." Hugh pointed to the sharp talons the length of a sword, but with the gleam of the black stone.

Ebonfyre's front leg extended forward, like a bridge made of stone, offering Sera safe passage onto its back. Though a part of her wanted to resist, another part of her longed to feel the creature's power underneath her.

Besides, the Fae warriors had ridden off with their horses. How else were they to return to the palace?

With a glance backwards at Hugh to ensure he would follow, Sera took a deep breath and slid her hand along the dragon's front limb with tentative fingers. Her mind relished the feel of its ridged scales against her palms. As she climbed, their muscles shifted beneath her weight, writhing as if they were eager to show off their strength. Sera felt a thrill course through her veins as she reached the highest point on their back.

She settled onto the dragon's hide, surprised at the warmth of it. Hugh tucked himself behind her and reached for the spines in front of them. His solid presence anchored her in the moment. Closing her eyes, she inhaled the sensation of power that emanated from Ebonfyre. It was as if all of nature had paused in anticipation of their flight as though it had been waiting just for them, for millennia.

"Ready?" she asked Hugh.

"Yes," he answered in a firm tone, but she detected a faint trace of worry in his voice. A dragon would fly much higher and faster than a gargoyle.

The dragon shifted beneath them as if sensing their anticipation. With a mighty roar that shook the earth, they launched into the sky. Sera felt the thrill of flight like nothing she had ever experienced before. The air whistled around them as they flew higher and higher, until they were above the clouds and flying among stars. Below them, the world seemed to shrink until it was only a speck in their wake.

As the dragon's wings grazed the clouds, an idea came to her. "Wait!"

Ebonfyre banked left and made lazy circles above the glade. A question shot through her mind. Good. She could communicate with the dragon the same way she did with birds.

I need to hide something far away from the grasp of men. If I drop it into the fracture, could you close it?

Ebonfyre turned their head and regarded Sera. A silver eye blinked once. *Yes. But we have a better solution. Drop it, please.*

Though unsure of what the dragon planned, Sera trusted its protective nature. Fumbling in the satchel, Sera pulled free the cloth-wrapped bracelet.

"Ebonfyre is going to make sure no one ever uses this again," she said to Hugh, raising her voice to be heard over the wind rushing past them.

Leaning as far to one side as she dared, while Hugh had her anchored with one arm, she dropped the bundle. Ebonfyre chased the object and caught it between their massive jaws. They gulped, and the magical piece of jewellery disappeared down their gullet.

That will work, Sera thought. Who would climb inside Ebonfyre to retrieve it?

"Won't they excrete it?" Hugh asked.

She hadn't thought of that and politely asked the same of the dragon.

No. It will become part of us. No man or Fae will touch it again.

She relayed the message to Hugh, and she watched a thousand questions flash across his face. Her beloved surgeon would need several lifetimes to satisfy his curiosity about all they had encountered.

Where would you like to go?

"Home," she whispered. She longed to see Kitty and reassure herself that her friend hadn't fallen foul of some devious trick. But …

The Fae palace, please.

All thought left Sera's mind as she became one with Ebonfyre and experienced freedom like never before. Her worries and fears melted away as they soared through the air, Ebonfyre's powerful wings beating a steady rhythm. The stars sparkled around them, and the moon hung heavy in the night sky, casting an eerie glow over the land below.

The air was cool against Sera's skin, and she marvelled at how quickly they travelled across the land with just a few powerful flaps of their wings. From the back of a dragon, infinite possibilities opened up before her as they flew higher and higher. They soared through clouds made of glittering ice crystals, past mountains capped with snow, and valleys filled with lush green vegetation.

Part of her was glad the Fae warriors had taken the spare horses. By Dragon was a far superior way to travel.

Onward they flew until eventually, Ebonfyre began to descend towards the Fae palace. Below them was laid out a mosaic of different coloured stones, arranged in intricate patterns and shapes. The pale lanterns made of crystal glimmered in the night, casting a soft light over the palace grounds. From the courtyard, the majestic spires of the palace loomed above, their silver roofs reflecting the starlight like mirrors. They soared in a circle over the cobbled courtyard. The dragon bellowed and courtiers streamed from the colonnades at the sound.

When Ebonfyre settled on the ground with a gentle thud, an excited group of Fae gathered around them. They had come to marvel at the majestic beast, the ancient guardian of their realm that they had only ever heard about in legends and stories. The dragon seemed to sense their awe and admiration. Ebonfyre extended their wings, scales glittering in the moonlight.

Sera and Hugh slid down the dragon's forelimb. Only when her feet touched the ground did Sera's body protest its time spent hunched over the dragon's neck. Her clothing was dirty and covered in bits of twig and leaves despite the wind of their going. A feral tree had torn a hole at her side that would need to be repaired. When her magic had recovered.

"I'd love a bath," she said, and Hugh's eyebrows shot up.

Conversation fell in a hush as the crowd parted to make way for a regal figure. Queen Deryn was dressed in a gown of bright blue silk embroidered with silver thread and adorned with ornate jewellery.

Her face shone with happiness as she stepped forward to greet them. "Well done, Lady Winyard, in freeing Ebonfyre. You have shown great courage and strength, and for that, we offer our blessings. Should you wish to stay in this realm, we would offer you a place at our court."

She reached out her hands towards them, her smile warm and genuine as she embraced them both.

The crowd roared their approval, showering Sera and Hugh with cheers of joy and admiration. From somewhere high above, rose petals in sparkling hues rained down upon them, scattered by a magical hand.

Before Sera could scan the crowd for the Fae mage responsible for the shower of blooms, Ebonfyre arched their neck and trumpeted to the night sky.

Once they settled down and the last notes of their call drifted away, the queen approached. She raised one hand to the dragon, their protector, who had been trapped for so long.

The mighty creature bowed their head and gently rubbed their nose against the queen's outstretched palm. A look of wonder crossed the monarch's face as she silently communed with the dragon. She scratched their muzzle and Ebonfyre closed their eyes and hummed deep in their throat.

"Will you stay with us?" Queen Deryn said after several quiet moments, her question directed at Sera.

Sera squeezed Hugh's hand. Temptation lured her to stay. Whispered that she could put down roots as deep as the dryad's. Said that she could stand beside a queen who valued her for what she could do.

But there was another queen she had chosen to

serve. One who needed her help. Besides, she could never leave Kitty.

"No, but I thank you for the honour. We have dwelt too long in this realm. We struck a bargain, Your Majesty. I have freed Ebonfyre. Now I ask for safe passage home and a way to summon Ebonfyre when my need is greatest." Sera kept hold of Hugh's hand, and he squeezed her fingers.

Queen Deryn held her gaze for a long breath and a sharp pang of fear shot through Sera. What if the queen reneged on their deal? Had she overlooked some tiny loophole the Fae would exploit?

With a smile, the monarch turned to the obsidian dragon. "Might I have a scale, please, ancient one?"

Ebonfyre lowered their head to present their glossy black muzzle to the Fae queen. She reached out and appeared to stroke the top of the dragon's head. When she pulled back her hand, she had a single scale between her fingers. No more than two inches in diameter, it glimmered with an otherworldly beauty.

Queen Deryn turned to Sera and took her hand. She placed the scale on Sera's palm. "This will allow you to summon Ebonfyre. It can be used only once."

Sera held the object up to the moon. It absorbed the light but gave off a faint shadow. A small hole lay close to the edge. Removing her necklace, Sera threaded the scale onto the chain so that it lay next to the silver disc from Hugh, and the autumnal leaf from Elowen. She seemed to be collecting important charms.

"Thank you. Now we will return to our realm if

you could direct us to a portal." Entering the Fae realm had been easy. They had crossed the magical meadow called Shadowvane. Were they to return the same way? Sera didn't think so, as the portal had deposited them in the Fae court, not at the other side of the field.

"With the help of our mage and Ebonfyre, we can return you," the queen said. She gestured to someone, and a figure detached itself from the crowd of courtiers.

Sinead.

"You're a mage?" Sera gasped. She didn't want to believe it. All the time that the Fae woman had acted as their guide, Sera had thought her some type of attendant. Had she known Sinead was a mage, the questions she could have asked!

Sinead bowed, a suppressed smile on her lips. "No. I am a conduit. I serve a master who can no longer leave his chambers."

Disappointment weighed down Sera's shoulders. For a brief, wonderful moment, she thought she had discovered a Fae version of herself.

Raising one hand, Sinead traced a series of Fae runes in the air. Then she began to chant softly. Her words were old and powerful, like an ancient song that had been lost in time until now. The air shimmered and electricity arced between them and their surroundings. Sera's hair prickled along her arms and the back of her neck as the power of Fae magic filled the space around them.

A swirling vortex appeared in front of the dragon.

It picked up leaves and dirt from between the cobbles, creating a mini tornado around them.

Sinead waved her hands through the air as she continued chanting. The air in the middle of the vortex solidified into what looked like two door panels joined together by intricate Fae runes.

Hugh took Sera's hand, and together they stepped into the portal. As before, the wind walled them in and the wail of air battered their ears. Sera huddled closer to Hugh's bulk and gritted her teeth. There was an almost imperceptible shift in pressure when the portal closed behind them as if a door had been firmly shut.

In an instant, the vortex jerked to one side and pulled their feet out from under them, and the night became even darker.

The chill brought Sera back to her senses as damp grass soaked through her wool coat. The sweet fragrance of night-blooming plants tickled her nose. Sitting up in the moonlight, she found Hugh within reach. He ran his hands through his dishevelled hair.

"Why don't the Fae just use doors?" he muttered.

"There are doorways, but they open in different areas of the Fae realm. Some open upon Unseelie territory." Sera stood and brushed twigs and dirt from her clothing.

They were close to the edge of the enchanted meadow. Moonlight caressed the squat stone cottage tucked under the spreading oak. A golden light spilt from the large window that faced Shadowvane.

Taking Hugh's hand, Sera tugged him through the

lush flowers before the traces of magic lured them back to the other side.

The temperature dropped as they walked. By the time they stepped onto the shorn grass that edged the meadow, winter had reasserted itself.

"Let's get warm, and I will send a message to Kitty." Sera marched towards the squat cottage, rubbing the mage silver ring on her little finger as she thought of her friend. She hoped Kitty was awake and would fetch her ensorcelled sheet of paper.

Raising Ebonfyre had almost entirely drained Sera and exhaustion weighed down her limbs. She needed to sleep and give her magic time to heal. The door of the cottage swung open to greet them. Within, a mage light glowed, suspended from the ceiling in an orb crafted of willow boughs.

Sera used a spark of magic to start the fire, and its flames added to the cosiness of the cottage. Then she tugged off her boots and curled up in one of the armchairs. While Hugh looked in the cupboards for something to feed them and set water to boil for tea, she pulled the crinkled piece of paper from her stays. In a pocket, she found a stub of pencil.

We are safe. Our task done. We are at the watcher's cottage. Please come.

Then she waited and stared at the paper, willing Kitty to reply. She ate and drank what Hugh urged on her, but her eyelids grew heavier with each passing moment.

"You need to sleep," Hugh said as he tossed another scoop of coal onto the fire.

"I will. But I need to know Kitty has seen my message." Standing, Sera shrugged out of her damp coat and draped it over the back of the armchair to dry.

When she glanced down at the page, words marched across it. Three simple words, but that was all she needed.

On my way

Relief heaved through her. Kitty and Elliot would ride to them with spare horses. There was much to tell one another, once reunited.

"Where do we go next?" Hugh asked as he guided Sera to one of the narrow cots.

Lying down still in her clothes, she let Hugh fuss with removing her boots, and tucking a woollen blanket around her.

There was one place Sera knew that would offer them safe harbour while they plotted their next move, and she regained her full power. Before she let sleep gather her to itself, she murmured, "The Crow's Nest."

SERA's adventure will conclude in MAGE'S END GAME

If a pawn makes it across the board...it becomes a queen...

Sera has had enough of others trying to control her life. She intends to send a message so loud, no one will ever try to assert dominion over her again. There's just a few problems to clear out of the way first...like the fact she in on the run, Lord Rowan has labelled her a dangerous traitor, he has set magical traps throughout the country, and there's even a bounty on her capture.

Sera joins forces with her loyal comrades as they plot to overthrow the tyrant and release King George from the grip of a horrifying curse—one that harkens back to long veiled secrets, and threatens both king and country.

As the stakes escalate, Sera and her companions

must navigate a treacherous path with their every move shadowed by Lord Rowan's malevolent forces. Will they triumph over the darkness about to engulf the throne and all they love, or will they succumb to a fate worse than they could ever imagine?

History. Magic. Found family.

I DO HOPE you enjoyed Seraphina's adventure. If you would like to dive deeper into the world, or learn more about the odd assortment of characters that populate it, you can join the community by signing up at:

https://www.tillywallace.com/newsletter

About the Author

Tilly drinks entirely too much coffee and is obsessed with hats. When not scouring vintage stores for her next chapeau purchase, she writes whimsical historical fantasy novels, set in a bygone time where magic is real. With a quirky and loveable cast, her books combine vintage magic and gentle humour.

If you love found family and comfort reads, then come and escape reality with me.

Email: tilly@tillywallace.com
Web: https://www.tillywallace.com
STORE: https://www.tillywallacebooks.com

facebook.com/tillywallaceauthor
bookbub.com/authors/tilly-wallace
goodreads.com/tillywallace
instagram.com/tillywallaceauthor